Why she had noticed him she could not imagine.

He had neither wealth nor style. The only attributes she looked for in a man. The first thought in her mind had been *charming rogue*. The worst kind of man for a woman like her.

Was it the sheer male beauty of him, then, that had held her attention a fraction too long? The long, lean frame, the shoulders wide but not brutally so, the narrow waist tapering to hard, firm flanks in tight buckskins that had seen better days? While his form was lovely, she'd seen others equally fine.

She closed her eyes briefly to break the spell that seemed to see all the way through her with a blinding purity.

Unsettling thought. Horrifying when she inspected her own darkly stained soul. A dark, twisted creature from a gothic novel, drawn to his light like the proverbial moth to a flame and the inevitable burning of wings.

One more such singeing and she'd float away as ashes.

AUTHOR NOTE

This is my third book about the Gilvrys of Dunross. In 1820 the visit of King George IV to Edinburgh was a momentous occasion. I have been able to give you only a small taste of the impact this event had on the city. He was the first monarch to visit Scotland since before Bonnie Prince Charlie made his unsuccessful attempt to regain the throne for the Stuarts.

King George—who was previously Prince Regent, as I am sure you know—was a great admirer of the Stuarts and enjoyed his visit and the enthusiastic welcome immensely. One local gentleman actually wrote a book detailing almost every minute of every day of the visit and I have tried to be faithful to his record. I only took deliberate artistic licence on one occasion: the description of the King's pink tights. In truth, he wore this particular outfit to the Levee, but since only men were invited it did not fit well into my story of Logan and Charity. On the other hand it was just too deliciously funny to leave out altogether, so I reclothed him in his kilt for the Drawing Room, where he was introduced to the ladies. I hope you will forgive me.

I hope you enjoy Logan and Charity's story. If you want to learn more about me or my books please visit me at http://www.annlethbridge.com

FALLING FOR THE
HIGHLAND ROGUE

Ann Lethbridge

First published in Great Britain 2013
by Mills & Boon, an imprint of Harlequin (UK) Limited.
Harlequin (UK) Limited, Eton House, 18-24 Paradise Road,
Richmond, Surrey TW9 1SR

© Michéle Ann Young 2013

ISBN: 978 0 263 89869 9

Harlequin (UK) policy is to use papers that are natural, renewable
and recyclable products and made from wood grown in sustainable
forests. The logging and manufacturing process conform to the
legal environmental regulations of the country of origin.

Printed and bound in Spain
by Blackprint CPI, Barcelona

Ann Lethbridge has been reading Regency novels for as long as she can remember. She always imagined herself as Lizzie Bennet, or one of Georgette Heyer's heroines, and would often recreate the stories in her head with different outcomes or scenes. When she sat down to write her own novel it was no wonder that she returned to her first love: the Regency.

Ann grew up roaming Britain with her military father. Her family lived in many towns and villages across the country, from the Outer Hebrides to Hampshire. She spent memorable family holidays in the West Country and in Dover, where her father was born. She now lives in Canada, with her husband, two beautiful daughters, and a Maltese terrier named Teaser, who spends his days on a chair beside the computer, making sure she doesn't slack off.

Ann visits Britain every year, to undertake research and also to visit family members who are very understanding about her need to poke around old buildings and visit every antiquity within a hundred miles. If you would like to know more about Ann and her research, or to contact her, visit her website at www.annlethbridge.com. She loves to hear from readers.

Previous novels by this author:

THE RAKE'S INHERITED COURTESAN†
WICKED RAKE, DEFIANT MISTRESS
CAPTURED FOR THE CAPTAIN'S PLEASURE
THE GOVERNESS AND THE EARL
  (part of *Mills & Boon New Voices…* anthology)
THE GAMEKEEPER'S LADY*
MORE THAN A MISTRESS*
LADY ROSABELLA'S RUSE†
THE LAIRD'S FORBIDDEN LADY
HAUNTED BY THE EARL'S TOUCH
HER HIGHLAND PROTECTOR **

And in Mills & Boon® Historical *Undone!* eBooks:

THE RAKE'S INTIMATE ENCOUNTER
THE LAIRD AND THE WANTON WIDOW
ONE NIGHT AS A COURTESAN
UNMASKING LADY INNOCENT
DELICIOUSLY DEBAUCHED BY THE RAKE
A RAKE FOR CHRISTMAS
IN BED WITH THE HIGHLANDER
ONE NIGHT WITH THE HIGHLANDER **

And in Mills & Boon® Historical eBooks:

PRINCESS CHARLOTTE'S CHOICE
  (part of *Royal Weddings Through the Ages* anthology)

And in M&B:

LADY OF SHAME
(part of *Castonbury Park* Regency mini-series)

*linked by character
†linked by character
**The Gilvrys of Dunross*

Did you know that some of these novels are also available as eBooks? Visit www.millsandboon.co.uk

I would like to dedicate this book to my husband,
who chauffeured me all around the Scottish Highlands
to help make the settings for this
and the other Gilvry stories come alive.

Chapter One

Edinburgh—August 1822

'Ye're late!' the voice on the other side of the door grumbled to the sound of a grating metal bolt being withdrawn from its socket.

There's gratitude, Logan thought, glancing back down the line of ponies filling the dank and dark alley behind him. 'Aye, well, let us in quick, man, or your whisky'll be filling the revenue man's cellar come morning. Either that or McKenzie will have it off ye.' Above him, the darkness in the narrow slit between the tenement buildings gave way to the grey of morning. At any moment they could be seen. 'Hurry, man. McKenzie's men are up and down the Royal Mile from Holyrood to the gates of the castle.' He wouldn't help the man out again in a hurry if this was his welcome.

Finally, the door swung back.

A hugely fat man, with a day's growth of beard on his heavy jowls and a sagging belly covered in a stained white apron, peered out. 'Good heavens. Is Gilvry so desperate for men he must needs take them from their mother's teat?'

Logan ground his teeth. All right, so he was younger than most in the trade, but at twenty-two, he'd been at it for years and he was tired of people commenting on his youth. 'You are Archie, right? Do you want the whisky or no?'

'Aye, bring it in.' The man stood back.

At a quick gesture, Logan's men leapt into familiar action, pulling barrels from their racks on the ponies, passing them down the line with one or two of them running them down the cellar steps. The innkeeper, his eyes as shrewd as a stoat, counted each barrel as it passed. 'Twenty?' he said as the last of the wooden casks passed him. 'Is that all you can spare me?'

Logan signalled to his men to depart for the stabling he'd arranged at the edge of the city. He grinned at Archie. 'It is lucky you are to get that. We've been dodging McKenzie's men half the night and the excise officers the other. Not that we had to worry about them.'

Archie grimaced. 'McKenzie's men no' saw you, I hope. He'll be round breaking staves if he gets even a hint I bought elsewhere.'

Logan chuckled. 'He couldna' catch a pig in a passage.'

Archie grunted, closed the cellar door in the floor and covered it with wooden boards. 'Aye, weel, I was beginning to think you were no comin' an' me with a house full of cursed *Sassenachs* all demanding *uisge beatha*.'

Englishmen all wanting what the Scots called the water of life for some reason. Scottish whisky. And the Gilvrys made the best there was. Logan doubted the *Sassenachs* appreciated the finer points seeing as they also drank Geneva by the bucket full. Still, the imminent arrival of fat auld King Georgie was a gift from the gods, with McKenzie making it nigh impossible to sell their whisky in Edinburgh under usual circumstances. What they really needed was a buyer in London. Another reason he was here.

Noise battered at the door leading into the lower level of the tavern. Archie was also making hay from the Royal visit. Like everyone else in the city, Dunross included. 'Aye. Well, here I am the now. And I'll be having my due.'

Archie bolted the door to the street. 'You'll

have a drink on the house while I get your gold, I hope.'

'Aye. But I'll be having ale, if you dinna mind. Tonight has been thirsty work. And you'll not be giving me any of that swill you keep for yon visiting *Sassenachs*.'

The innkeeper grinned and went to the other door, pausing to look back. 'Ye'll excuse the company, I am thinkin'. I heared as how these London *gentlemen*,' his voice held a sneer as he said that last word, 'like to gamble away their fortunes. So I thought I would give them the chance.'

Logan arched an admiring brow. 'You've opened a hell?'

'Why the hell not?' He chuckled at his own joke. 'Wi' King George bringing all and sundry from London, and all the Scots comin' in too, there's a good few with a wee bitty extra gold burning a hole in their pockets.'

'Ye're a right cunning auld bugger,' Logan said, and followed the waddling innkeeper into one of the upper cellars filled with tables instead of barrels. The noise—men and dice and raucous laughter—filled his ears. Smoke from pipes and cigars set his eyes to water and his throat stinging. He set his elbow on the bar and took the foaming mug the innkeeper drew off for him. He raised the tankard in a salute and downed half of it in what felt like one swallow.

'Wait here,' Archie said and lumbered off to fetch Logan his purse.

Logan turned and leaned back, both elbows on the bar. A mass of men of all shapes and sizes and walks of life, rich and poor, filled the place. One old gentleman, with a nose like a cherry and too drunk to stand upright, leaned on his lanky friend. They stood like two books leaning inwards for support. One tap of an elbow and they'd fall to the floor. A young man wiped beads of sweat from his brow as he glowered at his cards. Another, laughing, shook the dice box as if his life depended on a good throw. The place reeked of sweat, liquor and smoke.

There were women too. Doxies, not ladies, hanging over their mark for the night. A barmaid fought off the clutching hand of the patron with a laugh and a slap as she passed by with her tray held high.

And then he saw her. On the other side of the room beside the hearth. At a table with four richly dressed fops. Everything else in the room receded. The noise. The smells. The men. It was as if she was sitting on an island surrounded by dark empty water.

An oval face, skin pale as milk, dark eyes, wide-set, long lashed, tilting slightly upwards at the corners. High arrogant cheekbones lightly rouged. Lips full and lush hinted at a pout. A proud face for all its stunning beauty, a head held high on a long neck, softly sloping shoulders and an expanse of creamy flesh where a necklace of gold and diamonds dipped into the valley between her bounteous breasts.

He swallowed hard, forced his gaze back up to her face. Their gazes met. Clashed like finely honed swords, giving off sparks as they met thrust for thrust in some deadly encounter.

A finely arched brow lifted slightly. The pout changed to a faint smile of derision and she looked down her small nose, taking in the rough home-spun of his coat and no doubt the streaks of sweat and dirt on his unshaven face.

A slight turn of her head brought her lips close to the ear of the man beside him, her lips moved slightly and, as if weighted by the words she was breathing, her eyelids lowered a fraction, the long dark lashes casting shadows on those magnificent cheekbones.

Logan felt the breath that carried her words in his own ear. Heard the darkness reflected in her expression as if he heard her low voice. His blood heated. To his disgust, his body hardened.

The man beside her turned his head to her, muttered something. His companions roared with laughter. Logan narrowed his eyes. Wealthy gentlemen from their dress. The woman helped the man to his feet with her shoulder beneath his arm. He staggered, grabbing her for support, his fingers digging into her delicate flesh.

Logan started forwards at the slight grimace that tightened those beautiful lips. She glanced up as if she sensed his movement and in those dark cold eyes he saw a warning. He hesitated.

The man leaned down and scooped a pile of winnings from the table. He handed the woman one of the coins and put the rest in a pocket. A faint wash of colour stained high on her cheeks, but the coldness in her expression, the hardness in her eyes, gave the blush the lie as she tucked the coin inside her glove.

Then they were turning away, the heavy-set man leaning heavily on her slender frame. Too heavily, even for a woman he could now see was almost as tall as her companion. Again he took a step towards her.

'Here,' Archie said, 'come awa', lad, out of sight of prying eyes.'

He could hardly leave without his pay. Ian would tear a strip off him. And his men would have no coin to pay for a bed for the night for themselves or their animals. And besides, from her glare, help was not something the woman wanted.

He turned and followed Archie into a dark corner beside the bar.

'Can ye give a little on the price?' Archie asked, his beady little eyes glimmering in the dark.

'You're an auld skinflint,' Logan said mechanically, flashing a smile, his mind still on the woman, at how beautiful he had thought her eyes until he saw the hardness in their depths. And the cold calculation on her face as she pocketed, or rather gloved, that golden coin.

Archie sighed. 'You can't blame a man for tryin' seein' as how your mind wasna' on business the noo.'

Logan dragged his mind back to the business at hand. 'Aye, well, that is where you are wrong.' Ian would flay him alive if he did not get the agreed-upon price.

'I'll need more next week, mind,' Archie said.

Logan's mind was fully focused now and he narrowed his eyes. 'Why? I thought McKenzie had only a temporary shortage. This was a favour, man. That was what you said.'

Archie shifted his feet. 'When McKenzie saw how well I was doing he wanted some of the profit.'

'Did he now?'

'Aye,' Archie said morosely. 'The man's a bully. Thinks he owns Old Town.' He gri-

maced. 'I ha' to be honest with you, Logan, lad.
Ye got awa' wi' it the night, but McKenzie's
bent on locking the town up tighter than ever.
His whisky or no one's. It's no just cudgels any
more. He's arming his bully boys with pistols.'

The restlessness that hummed in Logan's
veins rose to a clanging of bells. There was
nothing he liked better than a challenge and
the damned excisement were so predictable he
rarely broke a sweat. 'Next week, you say? I
am sure something can be arranged. Leave it
to me.' He patted Archie on the shoulder and
pushed his way through the crowds and ran up
the stairs to the front door.

Outside, in the grey of a smoky dawn, there
was no sign of the woman and her escort in the
street winding downhill.

And glad of it he was. While he thoroughly
enjoyed the sight of a beautiful woman, that was
as far as it ever went for him. No female would
lead him around by his nose or that other part
of his anatomy that was painfully hopeful.

Then why the hell had he been so eager to
catch another glimpse?

The sovereign burned in Charity's palm. A
hot chestnut drawn from the embers and tossed
to the unwary. A cruel flash of scalding pain
inside her glove. Impossible, of course. She let

her body rock to the motion of the carriage, let the grind of the wheels over rough cobbles drown out the sounds of the city around her and the drunken snores of her companion. Soon they would be back at their hotel and he would awaken, but until then she was alone with her thoughts.

With tentative fingers, she touched the hard round shape beneath the York tan leather of her glove. A sovereign. More than her usual take. Jack could be generous when the cards went his way. The coin was the same heat as her hand, of course, and nestled like a bird in the curve of her palm. A treasure to be guarded. Along with her thoughts.

No, the heat was not about the coin.

She'd noticed him the moment he had walked in from somewhere in the back. A swagger to his long stride. A cocky set to his handsome head. A quirk of humour to his mouth. A blond Adonis. A green-eyed panther, so sure of his world. There wasn't a woman in the tavern not looking at him. Some openly. Some from beneath their lashes. Like her.

Not that he'd seemed to notice them as he glanced around the room, a spark of devilment in eyes the clear green of spring grass.

Then the fool had actually dared to catch her gaze. To stare at her boldly. With admiration.

And speculation. He was lucky Jack hadn't noticed and called him out. No. She shook her head at the thought. Jack wouldn't call out a man so clearly below him. He'd set Growler and his bully boys on to teach him a lesson.

She sighed. Idiot indeed, if he could not see she was taken.

Why she had noticed him, she could not imagine. He had neither wealth nor style, the only attributes she looked for in a man. The first thought into her mind had been *charming rogue*. The worst kind of man for a woman like her. And so young. Far younger than she, if not in years, then in experience.

Was it the sheer male beauty of him, then, that had held her attention a fraction too long? The long lean frame, the shoulders wide but not brutally so, the narrow waist tapering to hard firm flanks in tight buckskins that had seen better days. While his form was lovely, she'd seen others equally fine.

She closed her eyes briefly to break the spell of a gaze that seemed to see all the way through her with a blinding purity.

Unsettling thought. Horrifying, when she inspected her own darkly stained soul. A dark twisted creature from a Gothic novel, drawn to his light like the proverbial moth to a flame and the inevitable burning of wings.

One more such singeing and she'd float away as ashes.

Purity? Even as she mulled over the word, she dismissed it out of hand. No male of the species deserved the adjective. No matter how handsome. For all their talk of honour, beneath their coats of superfine and bright white linen, their hearts were black as night.

The coach halted at the front door of their hotel and she shook Jack awake. His eyes were shadowed, but his lips curved cruelly as he focused. She cursed her cowardice. If she'd not made him leave so early, he would not be nearly so wide awake.

'Let us have champagne, shall we?' she murmured in sultry tones. 'To celebrate your winnings.'

His gaze dropped to her breasts. 'Aye. Champagne first.' He grabbed her and hauled her towards him so she landed hard on his chest, his hand pressing her fingers against his arousal. Winded, she stared up into his square face with its cruel thin lips, hawkish nose and cold blue eyes. 'And then you can play me a tune with that pretty mouth of yours.'

A shudder rippled down her spine. It was a jest, but like all Jack's jibes it carried the edge of a threat. Something he couldn't help. A habit.

Swallowing the bile of revulsion, she retreated behind her wall of ice, presenting a false smile that masked her inner turmoil. A drunk Jack was a dangerous man. And if she couldn't avoid him…she'd do what she had to do. This was business. And the path to freedom to live life the way she wanted.

Only a fool let a pair of pretty green eyes and a jaunty open face melt a hole in hard-won defences. To remind herself where she stood, she gazed up at the man who held her future in his hands and smiled. 'Not before I offer you a toast.'

She freed herself from his grip with a light laugh and descended the steps to the path.

Arm in arm they walked inside, his grip possessive as if he sensed her fear. It would not be wise for Jack to sense fear. It always brought out the worst and winning had stirred his appetites, something she usually managed to avoid. Their relationship was all about business. Nothing else. But it did not mean she could relax her guard. A couple more drinks beside the fire and he would fall asleep. If she was lucky.

She closed her eyes and once again saw those clear green eyes gazing at her with awe. It was as if he somehow saw her how she had been, not how she was.

Damn him.

* * *

The next evening, to his surprise, Logan found himself in very different surroundings and company.

'Well, brat,' Sanford said, squinting at him through eyes already fogged with the effects of wine at dinner followed by several bumpers of whisky. Such a dandy, this Sanford. Blue-eyed, pale, delicately built, his fair hair carefully ordered, his linen white and crisp. Logan wouldn't be surprised if the young lordling spent as many hours at his *toilette* as did most women.

'If this is the best entertainment Auld Reekie has to offer,' Sandford continued, 'I can see I am in for a great deal of dullness over the next week or two.'

Sanford was an acquaintance of Lady Selina, his brother's wife. The *Sassenach* lord was part of a contingent of gentlemen preparing for the King's upcoming visit to Scotland. He had invited Logan to dine at The New Club in Princes Street, Scotland's finest gentleman's club. From here there was an excellent view of the castle. For some reason, Logan had been intrigued by the idea of seeing the inside of the place. So much so, he'd borrowed an evening coat from his brother Niall.

Sanford was right. It was as stuffy inside as it was imposing outside.

He shrugged. 'Edinburgh has it all. High or low. Drinking. Gambling. Women.' Perhaps he could leave the lordling at the nearest brothel.

'Definitely low,' Sanford said with a sardonic twist to his mouth. He brushed at the sleeve of his immaculate black coat. 'A little drinking and gambling wouldn't go amiss, if the stakes are right.'

As far as Logan could see, Sanford had too much of the former and was ripe for the plucking at the latter. But he wasn't the man's keeper. He'd run into Sanford by chance and been swept into the young dandy's orbit like a stray asteroid. He rather wished he'd been rude and ignored the man when he'd heard himself hailed on the Royal Mile earlier in the day. He'd intended to unload the *Sassenach* right after dinner.

Apparently not. He swallowed a sigh. 'I've an appointment at the Reiver in Old Town just off The Lawn Market. There's gambling to be had there.' And women. A particular dark-eyed beauty. A high flyer to whom he'd responded on a visceral level. And was still responding to, damn it all. He shifted in his chair.

Sanford lifted his quizzing glass and observing the men seated around the baize tables playing whist and faro. 'As long as it's for more than a few pennies a point.'

'I'm no a gambler myself.' Logan got more than enough excitement pitting wits against excisemen, 'but from what I saw, the play looked deep enough. And if you are looking for low, you canna do better than the wynds of Old Town Edinburgh.'

Jamie arched one fair brow, his lips curving in a cynical smile. 'It sounds like my kind of place.'

They left the club, Logan leading the way through the tenements and closes of the streets crowding at the foot of the castle. The evening was warm, which meant the usually dense air of Auld Reekie was breathable, though, of course, fires were always needed for kitchens so the air was never completely fresh. He dove into Ridell's Court where Archie's tavern hunkered at the end, the light from its windows gleaming off the muck in the runnels. He ushered his guest inside.

Sanford lifted his quizzing glass at the occupants of the taproom, some engaged in dominoes or a rubber of whist with tankards of ale in their hands. 'Hardly a hive of vice,' he said mildly.

'This way,' Logan said and took the stairs down to the cellars, into the noise and the smoke.

As he left the bottom step, his gaze went straight to the table beside the hearth. Not there.

He should be glad. But he was not. He was disappointed.

He shook his head at himself. At the strange longing to see her again. He was not in the petticoat line, he had enough excitement in his life, and nor could he afford such a high flyer, even if he wanted her.

But want her he did. In the worst way. Not something he needed to be thinking about now or at any other time. Wanting was one thing, having was quite another.

With a judicious shove here and an elbow in a rib there, he secured them a place at the bar.

Archie grinned at him. 'Back already, is it then? Do you have word for me?' His gaze slid to Sanford, who was idly looking around him.

Logan shook his head in warning. 'Just visitin'. An ale for me and a whisky for my friend.' He gave Archie a hard stare. 'The good stuff, mind.'

Archie served up the drinks. After a quick look at Sanford, he leaned over the counter to speak in a low voice. 'There's a man asking after you. A gent from London.'

'Is that so?'

'Aye. He's against the back wall behind the pillar. Ye noticed his woman yesterday.' Archie leered.

Logan's heart stilled in his chest. He forced himself not to look. 'Did I now?'

'You did.'

Casually, he glanced past Sanford and over the heads of the men standing at the bar. He saw them now. The table squeezed into a corner far from the hearth. And there she was. In a gown the colour of blood, her lips painted to match. The colour made her skin look like snow. Against his will, his body tightened. He forced himself to look past her, to the man at her side, the big brawny fellow with a cheroot clenched in his teeth and a pile of gold coins at his elbow. The man she'd helped to his feet the previous evening. And behind them a ruffian with a face flattened by more than a few fists.

'Who is he?'

'O'Banyon,' Archie said. 'And that's his doxy.'

Logan bristled at the word even as he acknowledged the truth of it. He nudged Sanford in the ribs. 'If you are looking for high stakes, I would say that's your man.'

Sanford's seemingly bleary blue eyes sharpened for a moment, taking in the Irishman and the play. He shook his head. 'Not me. I'm no green boy, my friend. I have no desire to fatten the pockets of a Captain Sharp.'

'You know him?' Logan asked as Archie moved away to serve another customer.

'Runs Le Chien Rouge in town. Where the play is deep and the women deeper. A place where a man can indulge in every kind of vice imaginable.' His smile was self-mocking.

'And the woman?' Hell, why had he asked?

Sanford raised his quizzing glass and took his time perusing the lass. Logan kept his gaze focused on Sanford, aware he was holding his breath, but unable to do anything about it. 'Quite the piece, ain't she. And as hard as nails, I'd wager.' He dropped the glass and looked at Logan. He raised a brow.

Logan shrugged.

'Ah,' Sanford said, amusement pulling at his mouth. 'I see a couple of gentlemen over there who will give me a chair at their table.' He nodded to the middle of the room where a dandy was waving. 'You are welcome to tag along.'

Logan shook his head, astonished at the thunder of his heart in his ears that blocked out the noise around him and the sudden unexpected dryness in his throat. He hadn't felt like this since the first night he'd taken to the trade. 'I'll take my chances, yonder.'

'You are a fool if you do,' Sanford said with an indifferent lift of one shoulder.

Aye. Perhaps he was. But his idiocy had nothing to do with the depth of the play and everything to do with the lady in red. But then what could he do?

O'Banyon was the man Ian had sent him to Edinburgh to meet.

Chapter Two

He was coming their way. The golden Adonis from the previous evening. Charity's heart pounded against her ribs. She wanted to disappear under the table. To flee the room. If she did anything of the sort, if she even flickered an eyelash, Jack would know. He had uncanny instincts that way. And he'd like discovering something had the power to disturb her. That someone did. He would use it to his advantage.

Ignoring disaster's approach, she picked up her wine and gazed from beneath lowered lashes at the young gentleman sitting on the other side of the table. A young Scot with bulging pockets and the face of a new-born babe. Jack's pawn. His mark. She curved her lips in a smile. The young man went red to his ears. Vermilion. Or scarlet. Maybe puce. She touched her tongue to her top lip, collecting the ruby drop of wine she had deliberately left there. Definitely puce, poor lad. She drew in a breath, lifting her bosom.

Gasping like a landed fish, he put down a card. Jack trumped it. The boy looked confused. Disoriented as he gazed at the cards he had left. Men and their lust. So stupid. It was the end of him, of course. The rest of the hand went Jack's way and with a shaking hand the boy wrote his vowel. So damned easy.

At her back, she could feel golden boy, standing there, watching. Waiting his turn to be fleeced. A shudder went through her bones. An urgent need to tell him to leave. She glanced at Jack, wondering if she could excuse herself while he gathered his winnings. Use the moment to warn her green-eyed panther away from danger.

Hers. Hardly. Men, handsome or not, left her cold. Even young handsome ones.

Why would she even consider taking such a risk for a fool of a man who was little more than a boy. What was it to her, if he lost his coin? It would put more money in her pocket. Money she needed. Thank goodness Jack had recognised her worth at his tables after her utter failure in the brothel. While she might look the part, while she could drive a man to losing a fortune for the sake of a smile, men didn't like a cold woman in their beds.

Which was why she didn't understand why the man at her back heated her blood with no more than a glance.

The boy pushed his vowel at Jack and stood up, his face ghostly, his hands shaking. 'I'll send the money round tomorrow morning.'

Jack smiled coldly, a quick baring of crooked teeth. 'You will find me at the White Horse Inn. Gold only. No paper.'

The boy swallowed and stumbled away with one last longing glance at her face. She cut him dead. He no longer existed. The next mark was waiting his turn. Him. The handsome rogue. Tonight he would lose his swagger and, like all the others, she'd consign him to the flames of unrequited lust.

It was as inevitable as day following night. It had to be.

Jack handed off the winnings to Growler standing behind him and raised his gaze, looking up at the man standing behind her right shoulder out of her line of vision, though she could see him in her mind's eye, see the arrogant set of his head, the confident expression on his handsome face.

Damn you! Can't you see what we are? Go away.

Jack gestured to the empty chair. 'Faro?' he asked around his cigar.

The other two men at the table looked up expectantly, saying nothing. They each had some winnings. Money they would return to Jack at the end of the night. His boyos, Jack called them in the private sanctum of his office at the back of Le Chien Rouge. It was the only place he ever acknowledged he knew them. They took their orders from Growler.

Lean and lithe, her panther sat down. He glanced at her face, his eyes blazing heat for a brief betraying moment, a heat that burned in her belly. She swallowed an indrawn gasp and picked up her glass, sipping slowly, retaining her mask of indifference.

Jack didn't notice anything amiss. He was used to the hot looks young men cast her way. It was what he paid for. He assessed the young man with a knowing eye. He wore clothes quite different from last night. A dark coat of superfine slightly worn at the cuffs, the linen good, but not expensive. A man of few means, but a great deal of pride. And a fool.

She set her glass down with more force than she intended. Jack glanced her way, a quick sideways glance and a faint trace of a frown. A shiver slid down her back. It did not do to make Jack angry. To ruin his play. She touched a finger to her smiling lips. 'Oops.'

'A shilling a point to begin,' Jack said, with

his friendliest grin. He looked around the table. 'All right with you, gentlemen?'

They murmured their assent on cue and Jack raised his brow in the direction of the young man. 'Jack O'Banyon at your service.' He nodded at the other two men in turn. 'Mr Smith and Mr Brown.'

Not their real names of course. Only Growler knew those.

'Gilvry,' the young man said, his Scottish burr a startling velvet caress in her ear. 'You were asking after me.'

Clearly surprised, Jack leaned back in his chair. 'You'll be excusing me, Mr Gilvry. I was expecting someone older.' He glanced from him to her and his eyes gleamed with cunning, deciding how to use that first hot look to advantage. She tapped a fingernail on the wooden table. 'My glass is empty, Growler.' She spoke in the husky murmur men loved to hear in bed.

Not that they ever heard it in her bed. She preferred to sleep alone.

While the bruiser went in search of a waiter, Gilvry's gaze focused on Jack. There was a wealth of understanding in that look. 'My brother asked that I meet with you.' His voice didn't carry beyond the confines of their group.

'Why don't we play while we talk?' Jack

puffed smoke in Gilvry's direction. 'We'll attract less attention.'

Gilvry's eyes narrowed to slits. 'Do that again, man, and I'll stuff that wee cheroot down your throat.' Then he grinned, an open devil-may-care smile that was both charming and dangerous.

Charity shivered as if she, too, had been caught in his predatory gaze. But it wasn't quite that. It was the razor edge to his voice, the sense of a blade with a silky sheath. Her breathing shallowed, her chest rising and falling, the edge of her satin gown pressing against her skin like a touch. She wanted to scream. Anything to break this tension.

Brown's hand went beneath the table, to the pistol she knew he had tucked in his waistband.

Jack threw back his head and laughed. He mashed the hot end of the cigar between his stubby fingers, his gaze fixed on Gilvry's smiling expression. A battle of strength fought in silence.

Jack's other two men relaxed, watchful, but at ease.

A breath left her body. Relief. Glad Gilvry wasn't about to die. She caught herself. She did not care. Not at all.

Growler plonked the fresh glass in front of her and took the empty one away.

'I've no interest in cards,' Gilvry said softly. 'Or drink. If it is business you want to discuss, we'll do it in private. Or we'll no' do it at all.'

Not once did he look at her. Not once, since that first look the moment he sat down, yet her skin shivered with the knowledge of his strength of will. His blind courage. Fool man. She lifted her glass and drained it in one draught. A dangerous thing to do, to let the wine cloud her judgement around Jack, but the tension was too great, too impossible to let her resist the warm slide down her gullet, steadying her nerves, calming the frantic beat of her heart.

'We'll be going back to my rooms at the White Horse then, is it, Gilvry?'

'Aye, that will do.'

'Ride with us?'

Say no, she willed, the thought of being confined in a small space with him a suddenly terrifying prospect.

'No,' he said, once more flashing the smile with its edge of wickedness.

She almost sagged back in her chair with relief. Almost.

'Give me a little credit, O'Banyon,' Gilvry said. 'I'm no' advertising our business to all and various. I'll meet you there in half an hour.' He cocked a brow at the men at the table. 'Am I needing to bring my own gang of ruffians?'

Jack barked a short laugh. 'You'll find no one with me but Growler, here.'

He nodded. 'Half an hour, then.' He rose gracefully to his feet, so tall and almost as broad as Jack, but not nearly so heavy set. There was an elegance, a manly grace, about him as he prowled away.

Deliberately, she kept her gaze on Jack, waiting for her cue.

He looked at his men. 'I'll not be needing you any more tonight,' he said curtly. 'Growler will bring you my orders in the morning.'

He rose to his feet with a sour look at Charity. 'It seems you are losing your touch.'

The lad had caught him left-footed. He didn't like it. She smiled slowly. 'It seems to me, Jack, you are rising from this table with a pretty good profit.'

His gaze flicked to Gilvry where he was speaking to a blond man, who glanced in their direction and nodded. So, the young panther had the sense to let someone know where he was going, but he was still a fool, wandering into an old lion's lair. It wasn't her concern. She cared for nothing and no one. As long as Jack paid what he promised.

And he would, as long as she did exactly what he wanted. If not, he wouldn't hesitate to take it out of her hide, even if it meant he had to find another cat's paw.

She arched a brow at him.

'Growler,' he muttered, like a curse.

The pugilist handed her a couple of coins. Her percentage of the take. Her lust money. She slipped them inside her glove. It had been a good night. Two guineas in two hours. Not bad for one evening. If only the night ended here. Her heart gave a strange little jolt. Her job was done. Jack would not need her presence to conclude his business. Would he?

Outside, he helped her into the carriage. Growler took his seat on the box and the coach rocked into motion. She was looking forward to a warm bath. A chance to get the stink of smoke from her skin. Her maid always hung her clothes at the window to air them to no avail. Even the lavender she sprinkled between their folds when she put them away never quite rid them of the stale odour of beer and smoke, or the taint of her soul.

Sitting on the seat opposite, Jack was watching her face. From beneath her lowered lashes, she could see the intensity of his stare in the street lanterns' regular flash into the depths of the compartment. She held herself still, relaxed. Waiting.

'What did ye think of him?' Jack asked, his rough voice cutting through the dark.

Careful now. The question was not an idle one. 'The mark? I doubt we will be able to lure him in again. Not when his head clears in the morning. My guess is, his trustees have him pretty well under control.'

A hand moved impatiently. 'Not him. Gilvry.'

As she'd supposed. Jack was no fool, in or out of his cups. To hesitate too long would give too much away. 'A boy sent to do a man's job,' she said musingly, speaking the truth, somewhat. 'He seems more adventurer than negotiator. Ian Gilvry should have come himself.' Perhaps Jack would send him home to his brother and insist on dealing with the man himself. A pleasing thought. Or it should be.

Silence prevailed as Jack mulled over her words. 'He's got ballocks of steel,' he said finally, 'behind that baby face.'

The note of admiration did not entirely surprise her. Few men had the courage to face Jack down and this one had done it with a bold smile.

'I was that way myself as a lad.' He shook his head and sighed regretfully. 'Still, an' all, business is business. I'd be wise to take him down a peg or two, I'm thinking.'

Hurt him? Her insides cringed. 'Likely,' she

murmured, keeping her voice indifferent and her hands still in her lap. Business was business.

'He wants you.'

Anger flared. And fear? She dammed it up with a smile. 'What's it to be then, Jack? I'm to lure him into some dark alley so Growler and his boys can make him sorry he was ever born? Teach him a lesson in humility?' More taint for her black soul.

Jack laughed. 'Lordy, what a cold bitch you really are, Charity.'

She shrugged, but the laugh and the words grated. It was all right for him to be merciless, but it made her a bitch. She was cold, though. Inside. Mark had seen to that. And she had no plans to change because of a face designed to break hearts. She didn't have a heart. Not any more. She let her eyes drift closed. 'Tell me what you would have me do, Jack.'

'I'm thinking you should spend some time with him,' Jack said.

Her eyes flew open. 'What sort of time?' She sat up. 'You know I don't like—'

'You will do as you're told.' A flash of light caught crooked white teeth bared in a grin, but it was the clenched fist that caught her attention.

'You will spend whatever kind of time is needed to keep him out of my way for a day or so while I see what McKenzie has on offer.'

'You don't think Gilvry can deliver?'

'When they send a boy to do a man's job?'

Damn Jack. Sometimes he listened too well. Spend time with young Gilvry? Torture. But her heart raced in a way it hadn't for a very long time. An odd sort of anticipation. Her insides trembling as if she was a filly at the starting gate. Her breathing far too shallow for comfort.

'I'm sure I can find a way to keep him busy.'

Jack grunted and his fist relaxed.

Distract Gilvry. It was what she did best. So why did she have a sinking feeling in the pit of her stomach? What? Did she pity the wretch who had eyed her with heat like so many others? He was no different to any of them. None of them deserved consideration. 'It will be my pleasure.'

Pleasure. He was a pleasure to look at, certainly.

She stared out of the window and for the first time in a very long time she wrestled with regret for what had brought her to this life. The youthful folly that had made her think she could rely on a man's honour.

With Tammy Gare standing at his shoulder, Logan knocked on the door to O'Banyon's chambers. The bruiser, Growler they called him, stared when he saw Tammy, but he said nothing, just ushered them into the foyer like a butler, taking his hat and his gloves and opening the door to the parlour.

'Gilvry.' O'Banyon came forwards at once to meet him, hand outstretched, his smile warm and his pale blue eyes dancing. 'I see you brought reinforcements.'

Logan shook a hand that was warm and dry and just firm enough to be a warning. 'Edinburgh's streets can be just as dangerous as those in London, I imagine.'

'To be sure.' He shifted, giving Logan more of a view of the room and the woman seated on the sofa by the hearth behind a tea tray set with three cups and a pot already steaming.

The deep red of her gown was shocking against the pale fabric of the cushions. His heartbeat thundered in his ears. He had not expected her presence or he would have steeled himself.

'You must be forgiving me my manners,' O'Banyon was saying. 'I did not introduce you earlier. Charity, this is Mr Gilvry with whom I have some business. Gilvry, Mrs Charity West.'

Married, then. Disappointment gripped him.

Heather-purple eyes gazed at him coolly. They were not as dark in colour as he'd thought at the Reiver, but they held dark knowledge. A small smile played at the corners of her lush red lips. Blood on snow. The thought made him vaguely light-headed as he bowed over her outstretched gloved hand. Not the York tan she had worn in the alehouse, but lacy gloves through which he could feel the warmth of her skin. Searing warmth. As he bowed he was afforded a close view of the rise of her bountiful bosom and the shadow of the valley between. 'I am pleased to meet you, Mrs West.'

Her lips tilted upwards as if he had said something humorous. 'Oh, no, Mr Gilvry. The pleasure is all mine.' He voice was low and husky and hinted at all things carnal.

The hairs on the back of his neck prickled. And he felt a throb of lust in his groin. It wasn't the first time a woman had played the siren to his face, but it was the first time in years that his control had been this elusive.

What could not be cured, could be ignored. Something he'd taught himself well in the years since he'd run afoul of Maggie.

Pleasure was not why he was here.

He turned back to O'Banyon, who was watching him with a hard expression. Damn it all, he hoped the man didn't notice…or think… he had any more interest in the woman than that of any male faced with a stunningly beautiful woman who had her assets on display. As instructed, Tammy now stood on one side of the parlour door and O'Banyon's man on the other.

'Will you be taking tea?' O'Banyon asked. 'Or can I pour you a dram of whisky?'

'Perhaps you would like to try a drop of what Dunross has to offer.' He snapped his fingers. Tammy stepped forward smartly as they had practised and handed Logan a bottle of the whisky put down in his father's time. O'Banyon looked surprised and pleased.

Tammy returned to his place. Growler eyed him, measuring and weighing. Tammy returned the favour.

Noticing the direction of Logan's gaze, O'Banyon chuckled. 'Shall we dispense with their services?'

It was what he had hoped when he had given Tammy his instructions. 'Certainly.'

'Take Mr Gilvry's man down to the servants' hall,' O'Banyon instructed. 'Offer him some re-freshments.'

Whatever he was offered, Tammy would stand by his word and only take tea. He would not let O'Banyon's man out of his sight until he and Logan were reunited. Logan took the chair opposite Mrs West. Charity. Now there was a name for a woman who looked like sin personified.

'I will take tea,' he said, surprising himself.

'With a dash of whisky in it?' O'Banyon asked, pouring himself a glass at the table near the window and holding out the bottle to Logan.

'No, thank you. It is your gift from my brother.'

'Charity, my dear?'

'No, thank you, Jack,' she murmured in a voice that made Logan think of skin sliding against skin.

Glass in hand, O'Banyon wandered back to sit at the other end of the sofa, facing Logan, while Mrs West poured tea in the style of a well-born lady. Come to think of it, her voice was also that of a lady, not the rough accents of the street or the drawl of the country. She spoke much like his brother's wife, Lady Selina. But accents could be learned.

She smiled at him and once more his body tightened. 'Your tea, Mr Gilvry.' She held out a cup and saucer and he rose to take it from her hand. Somehow their fingers touched, though he was sure he had been careful enough not to do anything so clumsy. The heat of that brief touch made his hand tremble and he had to catch the cup with his other hand to prevent a spill.

Not that she seemed to notice. She was pouring another cup for herself and he could see only the crown of artfully arranged curls the colour of toffee as she bent to the task.

O'Banyon was busy gazing at the whisky in his glass.

Logan sat down and, getting command of himself, took a sip from his cup. Tea. He'd far rather have ale any day of the week.

The Irishman took a slow sip, swirled the liquid around his mouth and then swallowed. His eyelids lowered as he slowly nodded approval. 'Fine. Very fine. And expensive, I am thinking.'

'Naturally. It is the best we have. Old. But we have grades to suit all tastes and purses.' He waited for O'Banyon to rise to the bait. There was a reason Ian had sent Logan to woo this man from London. Over and over again they had proved that one look at his face and men trusted him to speak the truth. And he did. But trust was hard-won in this necessarily illegal business of theirs. The English Parliament continued to keep a boot on the neck of Scotland.

'I could see serving this to some of my special customers,' O'Banyon said, his gaze direct, chilly, fixed on Logan's face. 'But I'd need to taste the other stuff, too. The Chien serves gentlemen who might not want to be paying for the very best, but it has to be decent.'

Despite the hard gaze of the man he was facing, he could feel the woman's eyes upon him, too. She was looking him over, as if waiting for him to fail to impress. Why he had that impression or why he was even aware of her, when this deal with O'Banyon was so important to the clan, he could not fathom.

He took another sip of his tea, let the pause grow just enough to make O'Banyon's shoulders fractionally stiffen. He loved the twists and turns of this game. The risks, whether it was in the taverns where the deals were done, or on the heather-clad hills where gaugers lurked behind every bush.

He put down his cup. 'You were drinking it tonight. Archie served you this year's distilling.'

O'Banyon's eyes widened. 'Did he now?'

Got you. 'I delivered it yesterday.'

The Irish man's eyes narrowed to slits. 'I heard it was only McKenzie whisky in Edinburgh.'

'It appears you heard wrong.' Logan shrugged. He glanced at Mrs West. There was a look on her face he could not quite interpret, her lips were parted and he could have sworn a smile lurked in her misty gaze, but she had already turned that gaze on O'Banyon as if waiting for his reply.

'And what makes you think you can do business with me?' O'Banyon asked.

'The Laird looked into the Chien Rouge through his contacts before he answered your enquiry.'

Her gaze dropped down to her teacup as if to

hide her thoughts, but then she looked back up at Logan. 'Your brother is a clever man, Mr Gilvry.' Her voice held a trace of amusement, but whether at his expense, or his brother's, or even O'Banyon's, he had no way of knowing, because her expression was quickly one of indifference. The woman kept her secrets well in hand.

But he was not one to avoid a challenge.

'He would not remain in business long if he was not, Mrs West.'

O'Banyon grinned. 'It seems we may be able to do business, Gilvry.'

Logan did not like the word 'may'. With Edinburgh mostly shut off to them by McKenzie's ruffians, they needed to get an outlet in London as soon as possible. But smuggling held risks not to be taken lightly. 'What more is required?'

'Naturally, I will want to see your terms.'

'I can bring the documents around in the morning.'

'I will also need to consult my partner in London.'

Not what he wanted to hear. He had not planned to linger. Other customers were waiting. 'I understood you had carte blanche, Mr O'Banyon. Perhaps it is your partner to whom I should be speaking.'

O'Banyon ignored the jab. 'A letter giving my positive opinion is all that is required. And of course the transfer of funds. A payment sent on account for the first shipment. Unless you wish to dispense with such formality.'

This was the problem doing business outside of Scotland. He acknowledged the other man's hit with a slight nod. 'Certainly not.' Knowing his propensity to work on nothing but a handshake, Ian had warned him to agree to nothing without money up front. Such trust was all well and good between Scotsmen, Ian had said, but *Sassenachs,* other than his wife of course, were not to be trusted.

'And besides,' O'Banyon said, 'Mrs West is anxious to catch a glimpse of Edinburgh's welcome of the King.'

'His ship arrives the day after tomorrow, I understand,' she said, becoming animated. 'The first visit of a reigning monarch to Scotland since Charles the Second. There are several grand spectacles planned. Cavalry, Highland regiments in their kilts, the newspapers are saying…'

For the first time, her eyes were sparkling. No longer did they remind him of heather at dusk, instead they were as bright as amethysts in sunlight, her lips curved in a smile so lovely it stole his breath.

'Mr McKenzie has offered us a place at his window overlooking the Golden Mile from where we can watch a procession later in the week,' she said, looking pleased.

O'Banyon shot her a silencing look. She dropped her gaze and caught her lip with white teeth. 'It was kind of Mr McKenzie to offer, but I expect it will be nothing of consequence.'

The heat of anger at that small gesture of submission flared in Logan's chest. His fists wanted to smash O'Banyon in the face, which made no sense at all. 'McKenzie, is it?' he said, not bothering to hide his disgust. 'If you are so deep in bed with him, then I doubt we can do business.'

O'Banyon looked at the glass in his hand. 'McKenzie has nothing to match what I have tasted from Dunross.'

But that didn't mean he would buy it if the price wasna right. Ian had warned him to tread carefully. To turn the man up sweet. He reined in his anger and forced himself to think.

'If Mrs West is so keen to see the King, I can drive you both out to Leith the day after tomorrow to see his official welcome.' At least he hoped he could. Surely Sanford could get him a pass.

The smile he had thought lovely before became utterly enchanting. And yet, it seemed a little too practised. She turned from him to O'Banyon. 'Can we, Jack?'

Jack grimaced. 'All you'll see is a fat old man

waving, but if it pleases you to go, then we will do so.' He got to his feet and offered his hand to Logan. 'I will look forward to seeing you in the morning with the documents, then, Gilvry. Let us hope we can conclude our business satisfactorily in a few days.'

'I am sure we can.'

He took Mrs West's hand in his and was once more aware of the feel of her warmth and the fine bones of that elegant hand in his palm and the shadows deep in her eyes. Shadows he wanted to pierce. 'I will come for you and Mr O'Banyon at nine in the morning on Tuesday, Mrs West, if that will suit you?'

'Jack and I will be ready,' she said, giving him a sultry smile that sent heat careening straight to his groin.

An effect she'd intended. The knowledge showed in her eyes as plain as day. He found it irksome to say the least. She was not the kind of woman he imagined ever finding attractive, though he doubted there were many men in whom she did not engender lustful thoughts. He had thought himself more in control. Forearmed, as it were, with the knowledge of the damage a woman could do to a man not on his guard.

'The day after tomorrow, then,' he said, and

did not fail to catch her glance at O'Banyon. A glance seeking his approval. But for what?

The back of his neck tightened.

The well-being of his family hung on the success of this deal with O'Banyon. One wrong move and it could all go to hell.

Without doubt O'Banyon's woman was temptation incarnate. A move in her direction and he would see his negotiations fall to ruin. Still, he wasna likely to make such a stupid mistake with a woman of her ilk. He had years of practise controlling the urges that got most men into trouble.

Chapter Three

Mr Gilvry had been just as easy to manipulate as any other man. He had done just as she wanted and Jack had been pleased. She still didn't understand her own sense of disappointment. Since when had she cared what sort of man she put her hooks into? Usually she felt nothing but the satisfaction of a job well done. Satisfaction that she had made a little more money to add to her hoard, which was growing, but nowhere near as much as she needed.

The leer on Fergus McKenzie's red-bearded face brought her wandering thoughts back to the present with a lurch. She let a small smile play across her mouth and separated the grapes on her plate with the scissors. Thank goodness they had finally reached the dessert course.

Dinner in their private parlour with a lout

like McKenzie had been as pleasant as watching a pig at the trough. Thoughts well hidden, she delicately popped the plump red globe into her mouth and cast him a come-hither glance from beneath her lashes. The crude Scot licked already too-moist lips surrounded by all that untrimmed wiry red hair.

A small secret shudder ran down her spine at what she knew he was thinking. It shocked her, that sudden flash of fear. If Jack ordered her to his bed, she would do it. If she didn't, she would face his wrath. A swift incapacitating punch which would keep her from the table for a week or more and no money coming in. Or a return to the brothel as a reminder of what her life would be without his support. She preferred the former. As Jack knew only too well.

'Shall we get down to business?' Jack said, drawing the man's attention back to him with the signal she should go.

She breathed a silent sigh of relief. 'If you gentlemen will excuse me,' she said, smiling at McKenzie, 'I will leave you to your port and your discussions.'

Jack rose with her. Clearly startled by the courtesy, the lowland Scot followed suit.

'It has been a pleasure to meet you, Mr McKenzie,' she said with a graceful inclination of her head he didn't notice, so busy was he eyeing her barely covered breasts. Men. They were just so predictable.

Most of them.

Knock his eyes out, Jack had requested. So she'd chosen a gown even more revealing that the one she had worn the previous evening. A celestial blue that skimmed her nipples.

McKenzie inhaled a rasping breath as he stared at what he hoped was on offer. 'Goo' night, then, Mrs—er—Mrs...'

'West,' Jack supplied. 'I'll see you later, darlin',' Jack said with a leer of his own. Staking his prior claim, though he was not beyond serving her up to any man for the sake of business.

He'd served her up to Logan Gilvry. In a manner of speaking.

The difference, the small difference, was that Mr Gilvry was a gentleman. The squat man now lusting for her favours was as far away from a gentleman as the pig he resembled. She gave him her warmest, most seductive smile and batted her lashes. 'I hope we meet again soon.'

She swept out.

'Now,' Jack said as she closed the door. 'Tell me about this trouble you are having with the Gilvry brothers and what you intend to do about it.'

'Logan is the worst. He's a thorn in my side.'

'Is he, now?' Jack replied musingly.

She would have lingered to hear more, but the maid, a little mousy thing assigned to her by the hotel, trundled in from the bedroom next door. 'Is there anything I can be getting you, Mrs West?'

She wouldn't put it past Jack to have the girl in his pay. Watching her. 'Brandy, please, Muira.' She needed something to take the edge off the revulsion she'd been feeling all night.

Logan Gilvry's innocent smile with a touch of wickedness floated across her mind. A smile she would be resisting tomorrow. Or not. She inhaled a quick breath. She'd have no difficulty keeping him at a distance, lovely as he was. Giving in to passion had served her ill in the past. A mistake she had never made again. Compared to some of the men she had dealt with, handling this young Scot should be a simple matter.

Muira handed her the brandy and she took a sip, let the warmth slide down her throat. It did nothing for the coldness inside her. A good thing, too. It was a coldness she had cultivated and now carefully nurtured. 'That will be all, thank you.'

The girl bobbed a curtsy and left.

She took another sip. And if she refused to drive out with Jack and Gilvry on the morrow? If she sent her regrets? She leaned her head back against the chair cushions, plush and soft against her head. Jack paid her because she was useful. The world was a cold hard place for women alone without family support. Unless she had money.

She drained her glass. As usual, she would do what must be done. And to hell with green-eyed panthers.

An hour or so later, Jack entered without knocking, rubbing his hands together, his eyes glinting with pleasure.

'What did you think?' he asked, crossing to the console to pour a drink.

A chance to nudge things in the direction she preferred? Perhaps. She put her book aside. 'A man who gets the job done.'

'Aye.' Jack brought his drink and stood with one foot on the hearth. 'But I wouldn't trust him with a farthing.'

True. 'You don't have to trust a man, if you understand him.'

He cast her a sharp glance. 'Throwing your weight in his direction, are ye?'

She shrugged non-committally. 'He's a known quantity. He can deliver. He holds Edinburgh in his palm.'

Jack narrowed his eyes at her. 'Almost. We drank Gilvry's whisky at the alehouse, don't forget.'

Daring. Jack was always drawn by anyone who beat the odds. His one weakness. The reason he had taken her on. She let her opposition fill the silence.

'For all that McKenzie brags, the Gilvrys have him worried.' He drained his glass in one swift swallow. 'I don't understand what makes them such a threat to a man like McKenzie.'

Intelligence. 'Ask Gilvry. He'll probably tell you.'

'Aye.' He kicked at the grate. 'But does he have the courage to take what he wants, no matter the cost?'

Her, did he mean? She raised a brow. 'He's a boy. Really, Jack. You want me to waste my talents. For what? Assurance that he's as reckless as you?'

He was across the room in a trice, pulling her up from her seat. A quick ruthless twist and her arm was pressed high between her shoulder blades. Her eyes blurred from the pain.

'Are you questioning me?' His voice low and menacing in her ear.

'No,' she gasped. 'I am just trying to understand what you want me to get from him.'

He released her with a push that made her stumble. She rubbed at her reddened wrist. Likely she'd have a bruise there tomorrow.

'I'll do whatever you want, Jack. No questions asked.'

'I thought you might, colleen.' He sipped at his drink.

'So what will you tell them?' Sanford asked.

Logan eyed the languid figure on the other side of the carriage. The young lord had kindly offered him the loan of his carriage, once he'd been dropped off at Holyroodhouse where he had been called on some official business. 'I'll tell them the truth. That King is no' landing today because of the rain and offer to take them tomorrow.' He looked out of the window at the torrential rain, at the bunting and soggy flags draped across the buildings to welcome King George. 'Unless they have some other idea. Perhaps they'll want to go stare through the mist at his ship out in the harbour.'

'You could take them shopping.'

He turned back to look at Sanford's mocking face. 'Why would I do that?'

The smile broadened. 'Since you asked me for the loan of my carriage today, I've been thinking. If you really want to impress this O'Banyon fellow and his lady friend, there are several events you could take them to besides the public processions. There's a levee. A draw-

ing room, and a couple of balls. None of which
will depend on the weather.'

Logan glowered at the smirking fop. 'None
of which I've been invited to.'

'Ah, but you see, I happen to be friends with
Sir Walter Scott, the man in charge.'

'Oh, aye. And you think we wouldna' stick
out like sore thumbs at the King's Drawing
Room? You are daft in the head.'

'As long as you wear your kilt, my dear boy,
you will fit right in. But as for the lady, well,
she would need something a little more…well,
something different from what she was wearing at the Reiver the other night.'

He frowned. 'I liked what she wore.'

'So did every other man in the place. She
needs a proper court dress. With ostrich plumes.
And a ball gown for the Peers' Ball. That is, if
you really do want to take her and her friend.'

'I would like to see O'Banyon wearing a kilt.'

'The Irish wear kilts, I'm told.'

They did, but somehow he couldn't quite picture one on this particular Irishman.

'Have you ever had the pleasure of clothing
a woman?' Sanford asked idly, but there was a
sharpness in the look he shot Logan's way.

The man was making it sound as if it was the
sort of thing a man of his age should have done

hundreds of times. 'Any woman worth her salt knows what to wear.'

Sanford grinned.

The young lord was having altogether too much fun with this new idea of his. And yet if O'Banyon liked the idea of mingling with the cream of Edinburgh's society, it might help him decide in Dunross's favour. 'I'll ask if they have any interest.'

'Let me know by tonight.'

Would they want to be introduced to the King at a drawing room and go to a ball? It was hard to imagine, but Mrs West had been pretty keen to see him from a distance, so it stood to reason this would be even better. 'All right.'

The carriage pulled to a halt. Sanford reached for the door handle. 'You can drop the carriage back at my lodgings. I'll get a ride back.' He waited for one of the grooms to arrive with an umbrella before descending into the street. Afraid he might melt in a wee bit o' rain. Or perhaps ruin his carefully ordered fair locks.

As the coach moved off, Logan peered out of the window to watch Sanford head into the Palace. He couldn't imagine why he liked the languid dandy. But he did.

It was only a few moments before the carriage was stopping in Abbey Hill. He hopped out and gestured for the coachman to wait. The man nodded and a torrent of water rushed off his hat and landed in his lap.

Hell, it was raining harder than ever.

He found O'Banyon and Mrs West waiting in the lobby.

She offered him that practised sultry smile, when all of yesterday he had remembered the one that had lit her face when he had talked about taking her to see the King. He'd labelled it her real smile, though he had no way of knowing for sure.

O'Banyon shook his hand. 'Gilvry. Not exactly the best of days to view a parade, is it? I am glad you arrived on time. I have an appointment with a banker in a few minutes and cannot join you as planned.'

Logan masked his surprise. 'It doesna' matter. The King's disembarkation has been postposed until the weather improves.'

Mrs West rose to her feet and once more he was surprised at her height and elegance. Today she was wearing a dark greenish-blue spencer over a yellow gown. A flower-decorated straw bonnet covered all but a few curls artfully arranged about her angular face. A perfect frame for a work of art. Her smile was calmly accepting. 'Thank you for coming to tell us.'

Her manners were faultless. Dressed as she was, it would be easy to mistake her for a gently-bred lady. It would have fooled him. And anyone else.

'I'm sorry,' he said. 'But perhaps I can offer something better. The King is to hold a Drawing Room at Holyroodhouse Tuesday next and a ball at the Assembly Rooms on Friday. You are invited to both.'

Her rosy lips parted in a gasp of surprise. Then her expression turned icy. 'You are joking, naturally.'

He looked at O'Banyon.

'Is this a jest, Gilvry?' the Irishman asked.

He didn't look at Mrs West. 'No, indeed it is not, sir. I am invited to represent my family and you would go as my guests.' It was stretching the truth a bit, but Ian was a Laird and no doubt he would have been invited, had he been in Edinburgh. Though it was more likely that Niall, as the next eldest brother, would have been sent as his representative.

O'Banyon raised his brows at Mrs West.

She shook her head. 'No. It wouldn't be right.'

The Irishman frowned. 'What is not right about it? Gilvry here has invited you.'

'Us, Jack,' she said with almost a note of desperation. 'You invited both of us, did you not, Mr Gilvry?'

'You are correct, Mrs West. Both of you.'

'Pshaw,' O'Banyon said. He made a sweeping gesture with one arm. 'If you think I want to lick the boots of the fat flawn who calls himself King of Ireland, you can think again. You Scots can bow and scrape before him if you like.'

Some heads turned in their direction.

'Jack,' she said. 'Hush.'

He grinned. 'You go. And tell me all about it after.'

She stiffened slightly. 'Jack, you know I can't.'

'I know nothing of the sort.'

Well, here was the part he'd really been dreading. 'Mrs West will need the appropriate attire, of course, if she is to be introduced to the King. And a ball gown.'

'So this invitation of yours is going to cost me a pretty penny, is it, Gilvry?'

Colour touched those high elegant cheekbones. Chill filled her gaze. 'Jack. I do not wish to put you to such an expense.'

It was a rare bird of paradise who cared how much she cost her keeper. 'Please, allow me to take care of it,' Logan said. And wished he'd bitten off his tongue when she looked startled and none too pleased. 'It would be my pleasure.'

O'Banyon jabbed him in the ribs. 'I'm sure you'll find the colleen here suitably grateful.'

The words made him feel like a lecher. And was it a flash of anger in her eyes he saw, or a flash of some other emotion? Since she was now smiling calmly, he could only guess that she was pleased with the idea. 'It seems the matter is settled,' she said briskly. 'Do you happen to know of a seamstress who can meet my needs at such short notice, Mr Gilvry?'

'As it happens, I do.' There was the mantua maker his sister-in-law used. He'd occasionally picked things up there for Selina when she hadn't been able to come to town.

'Naturally, you do,' she said with a look that he did not comprehend. 'Shall we go now?'

He looked at O'Banyon. 'If you have no objection.'

The other man grinned widely. 'None at all. Just don't let her completely empty your pockets.' He chucked her under the chin. 'Eh, puss?'

She arched a quizzical brow.

Logan wanted to swallow the dryness in his mouth. He hadn't felt this nervous since the gaugers had almost trapped the clan in Balnaen Cove with a shipload of brandy. God help him if after all this expense the Irishman did not come through with a large order.

He'd be up to his ears in debt to Ian. But the compensation of squiring Mrs West around might just be worth it. Enough. He was her escort and nothing else. He wasn't a fool. He had no illusions about the sort of traps a woman could lay for an unwary man.

* * *

While rain streamed down the outside of the windows and drummed on the roof, drowning out the noise from the streets, Charity observed her escort discreetly. He was far too handsome for a male of the species. Chiselled perfection, that face of his. A temptation for most women, But more attractive to her was his pleasant smile, his gentlemanly demeanour and his aura of innocent pleasure in the day.

Innocent? He was no better than Jack. A smuggler. A man wanted by the law. Yet so confident in his ability to charm, he sat opposite her in the carriage, his long legs stretched out before him as if he had not a care in the world.

She, who had thought she was dead to all emotion, fairly seethed with irritation.

Did he have no idea the danger she presented? The knot of guilt in her stomach pulled tighter. Guilt. She had no reason in the world to feel guilty. He knew she was Jack's creature. His tool. If he did not, then he was a fool and he deserved all he got. She clenched her hands in her lap and cast him a look from beneath her lashes that hinted at erotic desires.

It gave her some satisfaction to see his gaze drop to her mouth, to see the movement of his strong throat as he swallowed, to know she had not lost her touch. Even as it galled her to know he was no different to the rest of them.

Though why that should be, she did not understand. And not understanding increased her anger.

It would cost him dear to parade her about like a prize. To a ball, no less. And worse yet, a Drawing Room. Something five years ago she would have taken as her due. Would have revelled in. Now she could only think of it with dread. But that wasn't the reason for the knot in her stomach. It was the knowledge of the price he would expect her to pay for his generosity. He would expect to take her into his bed.

Her stomach gave an odd little flutter of excitement.

Horrified, she pressed a hand to her waist.

'Are you nae well?' he asked in that soft burr of his that she felt rather than heard. It was as intimate as a caress across her breasts. She felt them tighten and grow heavy against her will.

She prevented her fingers from curling into claws and raking across his pretty face, or from sinking into his shoulders to test the strength of him, to feel muscle and bone. Either response would not help her cause of remaining detached.

But he would pay for causing that little jolt of lust.

She smiled calmly. 'Perfectly fine, Mr Gilvry. Your Edinburgh roads are less well made than London's.'

He grinned, his eyes lighting with a flash of humour. 'Please accept my apology. We Scots are a rough lot, so we do not mind a bit of bouncing around.'

A *double entendre?* Likely. She pretended not to understand. 'And is it like this in Dunross also?' She frowned. 'Where exactly is Dunross? I do not believe I have heard of it.'

His smile broadened. 'Oh, aye. Not too many people have heard of it, even in Scotland.'

'I assume it is not a large place, then?'

'Not large at all.'

He was hardly being forthcoming. Did he suspect her of an ulterior motive in her questions? If he didn't, he should.

'And you have brothers, I understand. Do they also live in Dunross?'

'My older brother, only. And his wife. My other brother Niall lives here in Edinburgh.'

Not someone she would be meeting, no doubt, but she could not help sharpening her claws on his conscience.

'Oh, how nice for you. Are you staying with them?' Her expectant look said she hoped he would take her for a visit.

His mouth tightened a fraction and his gaze slid away from hers. 'I have lodgings elsewhere.'

The man had quick wits, clearly. 'So you live and work in Dunross. It must be hard, living so far from civilised society. From town. From all this activity.'

He shook his head with a rueful smile. 'I am thinking I get activity enough in my line of work.'

'Smuggler.'

'Aye. Not that I'd be admitting it to just anyone, you understand.'

'Naturally.'

He leaned back against the squabs with an expression of curiosity. 'What about your family, Mrs West?'

'I have no family.' None that would admit to a relationship, anyway.

'Then no Mr West, waiting for you in London.'

Checking out the pitfalls. He was a smart lad. A husband might be one way to keep him at a distance. But, no, Jack would not countenance such a move on her part. 'Sadly, no.' She gave him a mocking smile and saw faint colour stain his cheekbones. 'I am quite alone, now.' Except for Jack and his damned schemes.

'I am sorry for your loss.

He looked sorry. And her heart gave a stupid little hop.

'You find living in London to your taste?' he asked.

She hated London and its dirt and corruption. 'There is no finer city in the world.'

He glanced out of the window with a grimace. 'I might have argued, but this weather does not help my cause. Hopefully you will see Edinburgh on a better day.'

'It is certainly full of people.'

'Aye. All the folk have come to see the King. It is not usually quite sae full as this. O'Banyon was lucky to find rooms so close to the heart of it all.'

The carriage slowed, then halted. He leaned forwards to peer out at the street. 'We are here.' He opened the door.

Rain splattered his hair and face and shoulders. He reached up, grabbed an umbrella from the footman perched on the box, opened it and let down the steps. He held the umbrella up, ready for her to alight. Held it so it covered her completely and left him in the rain. She did not hurry. Let him catch a cold from a damp coat, or soaking wet feet. Not that he seemed to care about the rain as it trickled down his face and disappeared into his collar.

She took his hand and stepped lightly on to the pavement. 'Thank you.'

He nodded. 'Come back for us in an hour,' he

called up to the coachman and she trod daintily across the flagstone and under the portico of the shop. Petty. Very petty. It was almost as if she had to remind herself to despise him. How could that be? She wasn't one to play favourites. She despised them all equally.

He opened the door and she stepped into the dry of a well-appointed dressmaker's shop.

The seamstress came forwards with a smile of greeting when she saw him. Her smile turned to a slight crease in her brow as she realised Charity was not someone she recognised.

'Good day, Mr Gilvry,' she said. 'I was not expecting you, was I? I don't think I have any items for Lady Selina.'

Lady Selina, was it? Not just a common smuggler, then. Well, he would be, wouldn't he, if he could command an invite to a ball attended by the King. Oh, he really deserved to be punished for that piece of folly. Even if it did fall in with Jack's plans.

'What a lovely shop you have, Mrs...' She arched a brow.

'Donaldson,' Gilvry supplied. 'This is Mrs West. She needs gowns for the King's Drawing Room and the Peers' Ball.' He flashed the woman a charming smile. 'I told her that you are the best mantua-maker in Edinburgh.'

The seamstress preened at his flattery, then

caught herself with a frown. 'I am no' sure I can do anything so grand at such short notice, Mr Gilvry. I don't mean to be disobliging, you understand.'

Charity trilled a little laugh. 'Oh, come now, ma'am, any dressmaker of note in London would not disoblige a customer of Mr Gilvry's standing.' She unbuttoned her spencer. 'I swear I am damp to the bone after braving the rain. A cup of tea would not come amiss.'

Mr Gilvry helped her out of her coat. His eyes widened when he took in the gown beneath it. A sheer lemon-muslin creation that had a bodice more suited to the drawing room of a bordello than an afternoon of shopping. She smiled up at him. 'Do you like it?'

One look at the dress had the seamstress as stiff as a board. 'Mr Gilvry. I really do not appreciate you bringing your—'

For the first time since she had met him, his jaw hardened as if carved from granite and Charity felt a flash not of the pleasure she had expected from making him pay for his lustful thoughts, but of anxiety for the seamstress.

'My what?' he asked in what to Charity sounded like a very dangerous tone.

Apparently it had the same sound to Mrs Donaldson. 'Your friend,' the seamstress gasped.

'This is a respectable establishment. Please, Mr Gilvry. I have my reputation to consider.'

'And how many other ladies are you dressing for the King's Drawing Room?' he asked. This was the man who challenged revenue men and criminals like Jack. She should have guessed that the youthfully innocent demeanour was a front.

She should have known better than to throw down such a challenge. And yet his anger thrilled her in the oddest of ways. It touched a place in her chest that seemed to warm with a feeling of tenderness. Because he was acting as if she was a lady. It had been years since anyone even hinted she had a shred of honour worth defending.

She hardened her heart against such nonsense. Such weakness. He was a man. He wanted what he wanted and would do anything to get it.

Still, she felt sorry for the seamstress's quandary. She put a hand on his sleeve. 'Really, Mr Gilvry. We can go elsewhere. It does not matter.'

'It will matter to Lady Selina,' he said grimly.

Mrs Donaldson sank inwards on herself. 'Well, if the young lady is a friend of Lady Selina's,' she said, weakly grasping at a very fragile straw, 'I am sure I will do everything in my power to…please.' Desperation shone in her gaze. 'I have a private room in the back...' she swallowed '...where you can view...fabrics. Fashion plates. Take tea. I will have whisky brought on a tray...'

The green eyes were chips of ice as he sent an enquiry Charity's way.

'That would be lovely,' she said, not wanting him to cause the woman embarrassment. 'Thank you.'

The woman whirled around. 'This way please, madam, Mr Gilvry.'

He put his hand on the small of her back and urged her to follow. The pressure of his hand seared through her gown and came to rest low in her belly. Heaven help her, what was she going to do about him?

Nothing. She could not afford to be weak. To care how low she brought him would be a mistake that would cost her dearly. Sentiment had ruined her life once. She could not let it happen again. Even so she would let him dress her respectably. She had no reason to want to shame him before his peers and his King.

She owed him that much for his defence of her today.

That much and no more.

Chapter Four

The pleasure of clothing a woman. Sanford's words drifted through Logan's mind as he sat tucked away in a back room of Mrs Donaldson's establishment. He gazed openly at the beautiful woman standing without shame in naught but shift and stays on a pedestal. Surrounded by mirrors on three sides, there wasn't an inch of her he could not see. Sanford had been right with his use of the word pleasure. It was the sort of pleasure reserved for a husband. Or a man with a mistress. Which was likely what the seamstress thought and the reason for her hiding them away at the back of her shop.

In times not so distant, according to his mother, it hadn't been at all unusual for a married woman to entertain her particular male court in her boudoir. Allowing them to choose her garments for the day while they gossiped and flirted. All perfectly respectable in the presence of a maid.

This didn't feel in the least bit respectable, despite the presence of the seamstress's assistant busy taking her measurements with pieces of string.

Stretching out his legs to one side of the low table in front of him, he admired her lovely form. The curve of her bountiful milky-white breasts above the lace edge of her transparent chemise, pushed higher by her close-fitting stays, beckoned his touch. The deep valley between begged for exploration. The crescent of areola, darker smudges of rosy brown, located her nipples and hinted at decadent delights. The dip of her waist was so tiny as to be unbelievable. He could span it with his hands and the view of the triangular shadow at the apex of her long slender legs, not dark, but not blonde, left him dry-mouthed.

She was Venus come to life. And for the second time in as many days, he struggled to maintain his detachment. She was not easily ignored, despite years of practise.

He glanced up to find her gaze fixed on his face. Pride tinged with wariness.

Her expression challenged, even as her lips curved in her carnal pouting smile. Her eyelids drooped, acknowledging his thoughts, his lust, and threw down the gauntlet. I'm ready for you, those eyes said. Do your worst. You can't touch me.

The thought shocked him. Angered him. Did she think he was an animal? That he would ravish her where she stood? Press her up against the wall and have his way with her? Lust hit him unexpectedly hard.

Ruefully, he acknowledged that he'd been aching with it on and off since the moment he saw her. But that didn't mean he had lost control. He meant he needed to be more on his guard.

He wasn't a fool, he knew she was Jack's creature, that they would try anything to gain the advantage. Normally, he wouldn't care. For some reason, it infuriated him that such an outstandingly lovely woman should be so debased.

And so he would not play the game.

He withdrew his hands from his pockets and sat straighter in the chair, trying not to break his granite-hard shaft in two as he crossed his legs at the ankles. He picked up a magazine from the table beside him. Flipped through its pages. Ignoring his body's demands was second nature.

His eyes finally focused on the page before him. Damn it all, he was looking at corsets for the male figure and swallowed a laugh. At himself.

'Do you need one?' Amusement flickered in those cat-like eyes as if she had shared in the joke. A brief exchange of mutual understanding.

He laughed out loud and looked at her face. He had no need to ogle her body, her face was so very lovely. 'Not for a while, I'm thinking.' He nodded at the tea tray one of the assistants had brought while the seamstress had fussed around with her measurements. 'Can I pour you a cup?'

Something else flashed in her eyes. Surprise? 'Yes, please.'

Her voice was low and husky. It grazed his skin like a caress. Two simple words and he wanted to purr like a cat. Rub himself up against her skin. Feel the weight of those luscious breasts in his palm.

No. He was her escort. Not her lover. He pushed to his feet and poured the tea. 'Sugar?' he asked, the tongs hovering over the bowl.

'Lots,' she said.

After he dropped in three lumps, he raised a brow.

'More,' she said. 'Please.'

And he almost dropped the damned things in the tea at the vision of what more might mean when said in that precise tone of voice in a different location. But he knew it to be artifice and added two more lumps and carried the cup and saucer to her outstretched hand.

She took a sip and smiled her pleasure. A sweet smile that softened her sharp edges to the point of vulnerability.

A shocking transformation. And one he wanted to explore. He nodded at the sugar bowl. 'You've a sweet tooth.'

'I do.' Her eyes became distant. 'My father was the same. He carried bulls' eyes around in his pocket and would pop one in my mouth when my mother wasn't looking.'

'Your mother didn't approve.'

A twinkle gleamed in her eye. 'They made me very sticky.'

The vision made him chuckle.

'I have found just the thing, madam,' the seamstress said, marching in with a froth of gowns over her arm.

The smile disappeared and the mask dropped again, hard and impenetrable. Disappointment tightened his gut. The icicle had returned. More frosty than before, judging from the chill wafting in his direction as she imperiously held out her cup to him. And yet he found himself more drawn to a sticky little girl, than the siren who now appeared before him.

He returned the cup to the tray, feeling very much in the way as they pondered fabrics and styles. Wandering the room, he gazed at fashion plates artfully framed and placed on the walls like fine works of art. Drawings of women in various poses, ridiculous hats perched on starchy curls. He hoped she didn't turn out looking like that!

The sounds behind him dwindled. Curious, he turned and caught her critical gaze as she took in her reflection. The seamstress gave a final twitch to the pale-peach skirts falling from beneath that magnificent bosom rising above a teasing edge of spangled lace.

'Mr Gilvry?' the seamstress asked. 'Will it do for the ball?'

The effect was stunning. She'd gone from ladybird to lady in a few beats of his heart. She looked elegant. Graceful. And more than the sum of her parts. She looked as if she belonged to the upper echelons of society.

The slight stiffening of her body brought his gaze to her face. 'You don't approve,' she said.

Approve? 'It looks eminently suitable.'

'Indeed,' Mrs Macdonald said. 'It was made for a young lady's trousseau. Her mother was most particular.'

'But she did not take it?'

The dressmaker's face drooped. 'Her betrothed died shortly before the wedding. She wanted none of the gowns.'

'How sad,' Charity said, sounding grim. She

gave the woman a sharp look. 'Then you have received some payment for these gowns?'

Was she trying to save his money? That he had not expected.

'A deposit only,' the seamstress was saying. 'I will deduct it from the price, of course.'

She would now, Logan thought. He glanced at Mrs West, but she was focusing on the image in the mirror. 'The hem must be lengthened,' she pronounced.

Indeed it must. A good three inches of her lower legs were visible, exposing beautifully turned ankles. Fine boned like the rest of her. And long and slender feet.

'I'm not entirely sure about the colour,' she said.

He caught her unguarded expression in the mirror. Not coquettishness. Not looking for a fulsome compliment. She was uncertain.

'The gown is perfect,' he said soothingly.

Faint colour stained her cheekbones as if she had forgotten his presence. 'An expert in fashion, Mr Gilvry?' she said haughtily, hiding her misgivings, no doubt.

'I have eyes in my head, Mrs West. This one will do. A court dress now, if you please, Mrs Donaldson,' he said firmly. A man could only stand so much of this, pleasure or not.

The seamstress gestured to a white gown

draped over the *chaise*. 'This one is all I have, Mr Gilvry.'

'Then we will take it. You have the measurements you need.' He recalled Sanford's earlier words of advice. 'Mrs West will need ostrich feathers for the Drawing Room. And whatever else you deem is required.'

Mrs West looked startled, then gave him the smile of a cat who had trapped a bird against a window. 'Why, how very generous, Mr Gilvry.' She turned to the seamstress. 'I'll have five pairs of stockings.' Her almond-shaped eyes scanned the room. 'And the painted fan I saw in the case as I came in. The one with views of the city.' She raised a questioning brow in Logan's direction. 'If that is all right with you, Mr Gilvry?'

It wasn't really a question. He bowed. What else could he do? He just hoped the bargain he made with O'Banyon would make it worth the cost.

'Then it seems we are done.' She stepped down from the pedestal.

'If you would care to disrobe behind the screen, Mrs West?' the seamstress asked.

Charity gave her the most charming of smiles and disappeared behind the screen with the assistant trailing behind her.

More sounds of undressing. He forced himself not to imagine the scene.

'This way if you please, sir,' Mrs Donaldson said. 'You can give me Mrs West's direction and so forth while Aggie helps her dress.'

Trembling with shame, Charity could barely hold still while the maid fastened the buttons down the back of her gown.

Never before had a man chosen her clothes. Not even Jack. All these years, she had managed to keep her pride, and then he came along and made her see what she had become. And what on earth was she doing talking about her father, when she hadn't thought of him in years?

And she'd thought him angelic? The man was the devil incarnate to make her feel so...so... She didn't know how she felt. What was more, the rogue must have dressed a string of courtesans in his time to sit there with so much aplomb while she stood before him in her shift.

Fury beat a drum at her temple. Anger that she'd not seen right through him, along with the disappointment that she had let her guard down. She didn't care that he wasn't the man she'd thought, just that he'd fooled her. It had to be the reason for the unpleasant sensation in her stomach.

She put her hands on her hips and received

a tut from the seamstress's little assistant. She dropped her hands back to her sides. To think she'd felt sorry he found himself pitting his wits against the likes of Jack.

'All done, ma'am,' the girl said.

Charity gave her a sweet smile, though her teeth was gritted so hard they hurt. 'Thank you.'

Smoothing her gloves, she strolled into the front of the shop. Mr Gilvry had a small bundle wrapped in brown paper and string hanging by a loop from a finger.

'My purchases?' she asked.

'Mrs Donaldson thought you would want to take them with you.'

The older woman gave a brisk nod. 'I will have the gowns ready for the day after tomorrow.'

'You will find me at the White Horse.'

Mrs Donaldson looked down her thin pointy noise. 'Aye. Mr Gilvry told me.'

Mr Gilvry put a hand in the small of her back to usher her out. A light possessive touch. And far too intimate for a gentleman with a lady. She leaned a little too close and felt the hitch in his breath with a smile as the doorbell tinkled overhead.

'Very successful, I'm thinking,' he said, shielding her with the umbrella and his body from the wind and the rain.

'Mmm,' she murmured giving him an arch sideways glance. 'Is there a cobbler nearby?'

She could not help the little kick of triumph at the brief flash of dismay on his face. It restored her confidence no end.

Jack poured himself another coffee.

'Where were you last night?' Charity asked idly, trying not to look worried.

He leered at her across the congealing remains of his breakfast. 'Sampling the local fare.'

From the look on his face he was not talking about food. So he'd not gone to the tables without her as she had suspected. She hated missing a chance to augment her funds, but she was glad he'd fed his other appetites. It made him less unpredictable.

'You?' he asked mildly, but his eyes were sharp and watchful.

'Here. He dropped me off after I emptied his purse. He'd a dinner engagement with friends.' Not surprisingly, she wasn't invited. Nor had she asked him to come to her later. She could hardly tell Jack she hadn't been sure he'd accept.

Jack gave her a speculative look. 'Losing your touch, dear heart? Perhaps you'll have better luck with McKenzie.'

Repressing the urge to shudder, she looked

down her nose at him. 'I know what I am doing. I hope to see him today.'

'Did he say anything of interest?'

'Interest in what regard?' she asked cautiously.

He pinched his lower lip between thumb and forefinger as he considered his reply. 'About his business. About him. Anything of use in negotiations.'

Things he could use to beat down the price. 'He's not flush with coin, yet he spends freely to impress. So this deal must be important.' She took a breath, remembering how generous he'd been, with his coin and his protection. 'He's a man of his word. Not to mention stiff-necked. He has a brother here in town. A lawyer. That might be cause for concern.'

He put down his cup and sat back with narrowed eyes. 'You think they are desperate?'

Trust Jack to focus on weakness. 'Desperate? I'm not sure, I would go that far, but he seemed keen. He dropped a lot of blunt on me yesterday without a murmur.' Or not much of one.

Jack looked pleased and she felt the stiffness go out of her shoulders.

'Did he talk about his business at all?'

A trickle of something cold ran down her back. 'No. I spent most of the afternoon with my clothes off. It wasn't conducive to that kind of conversation.'

'Conducive, is it? I suppose you had your hands full.' He leered. 'Or your mouth.'

She restrained the urge to slap his smiling face. He liked to torment her with her failings as a harlot, yet make her feel like one. Bringing her down a peg or two, he called it. 'We had tea, Jack.'

'And you will see him later today?'

She glanced out of the window. The rain had stopped, but the sky remained overcast. 'If it stops raining.'

Jack's neck darkened with the blood of sudden anger. 'Then you had better hope it does.'

'Why so anxious? It is you who sounds desperate now.'

'If it is any of your business, I want to be sure of where he is for an hour or two. McKenzie is introducing me to someone today. I don't want the Gilvrys to know.'

She opened her mouth to ask who, but Growler swaggered into the room with a note in his hand.

Jack reached out to take it, but the ruffian avoided the blunt fingers and gave it to Charity.

She shot Jack a look of triumph and broke the seal with her fruit knife. She hadn't been sure, even after he paid for all those clothes, that she hadn't pushed him too hard, hadn't forced his eyes open just a little too much.

He wasn't the sort of man she usually toyed with. There was too much intelligence behind that pretty face.

She scanned the note.

'What does he say?' Jack asked.

She tossed the note across the table. It fell in the egg, the ink blurring. 'He will pick us up here in one hour and take us to the docks at Leith. To see the King land.'

Jack grinned. 'I knew I could rely on you.'

She narrowed her eyes. 'Remember that, Jack. I gather you don't come with us?'

He shook his head and stood up.

'Will we go to the tables tonight?' The tables was where she earned more than her keep.

'Greedy wench.'

'Jack?' she warned.

'No. I have other plans. I may go out of town for a day or so.'

'Days?'

'I'll leave Growler here, in case you need anything.'

'To keep an eye on me, you mean.' She couldn't quite keep the bitterness from her tone.

'You and him, too.'

Gilvry, he meant. Jack trusted no one. Sometimes she wondered if he would even let her go when it was time, knowing what she did. Indeed, she feared he would not. Hence her contingency plan. Her secret bank account in a false name. It was nowhere near enough for her to live on yet.

'He's no threat to me, as far as I can see.' She certainly didn't want Growler and his bullies hurting him. Not unless he got out of hand.

Jack pulled out his watch and glanced at it. 'If you've only an hour, you best stir your stumps.'

An hour. She put a hand to her hair still in its night-time plait. 'You are right. I will want to look my best.' She gave him her stock-in-trade smile and he nodded slowly.

'Aye, colleen. That you do.'

His hard-eyed smile said he'd make her pay, if Gilvry so much as strayed an inch from her side. Oddly enough, though, she was looking forward to spending more time in his company. He made her feel like a lady.

The moment Logan saw her, he wanted to graze his fingertips across the delicious flesh rising above her gown and then taste it with his tongue. First however, he wanted to cover her from anyone else's view.

He took her hand and forced himself to keep his gaze on her face, but even then her sultry smile of greeting sent hot blood pounding in his groin. He raised a brow. 'Where is O'Banyon?'

'He has business elsewhere,' she said in a low husky voice. 'Would you prefer we did not go?'

He'd like a bath full of cold water. 'Not at all. I am sure he is a busy man.' Busy avoiding Logan for some reason.

Her head tipped on one side, her mysterious eyes gleamed like a cat's about to pounce. 'Didn't you know? He expects me to exert my charm. To lure you into giving him a good bargain.'

Honesty. Now that was a surprise. 'I hadn't guessed,' he said drily.

'Is it working?'

There was such sly innocence in her face he couldn't help it. He laughed. 'Let us find out, shall we?'

He was pleased to see that his answer turned her smile from sultry to genuine amusement. 'I shall look forward to the discovery.'

Heaven help him, he liked her when she smiled that way. And it wasn't just lust. Lust he could handle, though he'd be hard pressed to keep his head if she kept up that smile. No, lust wasn't the whole of what gripped him. It was the fear he saw behind the smile that made his hackles rise and fed the urge to keep her safe. Heaven help him. The last time he'd felt the need, a woman's lies had almost ruined his life by trapping him in marriage. Seeing the kind of marriages his brothers had, had caused him to make very sure he wasn't caught out again.

He let his gaze drift down to that daring neckline. 'Perhaps you would like to bring a shawl. The carriage is open and the wind is cool by the shore.'

'I am prepared,' she replied, lifting her arm to display a frothy parasol dangling from a ribbon at her wrist. 'It is a lovely day.'

Say more and she'd be insulted. Or pretend she was. She was playing him. Testing to see if he was man or mouse.

To hell with it. The day was fine and she was a beautiful woman. Let her display herself, if she'd a mind. He could defend any insult with his fists and a good brawl would get rid of the energy burning in his veins.

He held out his arm and escorted her out to the hotel yard where a groom was holding his team's heads. After consulting with Sanford, he'd hired a landau and a fine pair of black horses. There would have been plenty of room for three. But he couldn't deny, he liked it better with two.

He helped her in and gave the driver the signal to be off.

She opened her parasol and positioned it to shade her face from the morning sun. 'You will point out the sights as we go, Mr Gilvry?'

'If I can be bothered to look at them, when the finest thing in Edinburgh is sitting beside me.'

Her eyes widened a fraction. She placed a hand on his sleeve below his elbow. A casual searing touch of gloved finger tips. 'Prettily said. I hadn't taken you for a courtier.'

He covered her hand with his palm. She'd challenged, he fully intended to see the game through. 'I speak naught but the truth. 'Tis a bad habit.'

Faint colour stained her high cheekbones beneath the rouge she'd applied. If he hadn't been watching closely, he would never have seen the evidence of having reached his mark. Hah. He might not be a courtier, but he wasn't without eyes or ears around his brothers and their wives. He knew where to place the point of his verbal arrow.

'I will keep that at the forefront of my mind, Mr Gilvry,' she said in that come-hither voice of hers.

'Shall we stand on ceremony, Mrs West? Call me Logan, if it pleases you.'

She smiled and her eyelids lowered a fraction. 'Logan, then. And you may call me Charity.'

'An unusual name.'

'For such as me?'

'For anyone.'

'It is Jack's joke.'

He looked at her, waiting for her to explain, but she shook her head. 'Perhaps when we get to know each other better.'

A cruel joke. He sensed it. Viscerally. Perhaps it was the flash of vulnerability he saw in those heather-coloured eyes. The echo of pain quickly quelled. Or in the quick scornful smile. Whatever it was, he wasn't sure he wanted to delve so deep. She was Jack O'Banyon's woman and it was better he keep a little distance. They drove along Abbey Hill, skirting the Palace.

'It is surprising to see a mountain so close to the city,' she said.

'Oh, aye. Arthur's Seat, but I have no idea if he sat there or no'. It lies in the Palace grounds. There is a grand view of the city from the top. They had an enormous bonfire up there last night to welcome the King. Not that he could be seeing it through the rain.'

He turned on to Regent Road.

'And what is that?' she asked pointing at the enormous pale stone edifice on the left.

'Bridewell Prison.'

She stared up at the high walls and gave a small shiver. 'You know the city well.'

'Well enough. I visited a few times as a lad

and now my brother Niall and his wife live here.'

He waited, half-expecting her to share some titbit about her family. A tit-for-tat exchange of information. She twirled her parasol. 'Let us hope the weather holds today.'

Not giving away anything today, then. Disappointment surprised him, when there was no reason for him to know anything about her.

On Kirkgate, the broad busy street leading into Leith, the traffic became congested. Logan stood to see ahead. 'The soldiers are directing the traffic.'

She sighed. 'Does that mean we must walk?'

He grinned at her obvious disgruntlement. 'No' wearing the right kind of shoes for a hike through the streets, I'm thinking.'

She lifted her chin and afforded him a view of her lovely profile. Quite deliberately enchanting and very haughty. What a strange mixture she was of earthy woman and high-and-mighty miss. Intriguing. Mysterious. Not his concern. His only concern was to get O'Banyon to make a bargain with Dunross. Getting tangled up with his mistress would only get in the way. Though at least one part of him thought it would be a worthwhile risk.

Knowing the sort of trouble it could lead to, he had that part well under control.

Play with fire, expect to get burned. Ian's harsh words from long ago. The scars of that burning had remained with him for years and an echo of them still tightened his skin whenever he thought of Maggie. He'd been lucky her father was an honest man or he'd be married by now, tied down as a husband and father to a child that was not his own.

Not that this lass was anything like as deceitful as Maggie. This one was honest about her devious intentions. Still, if he toyed with this particular ember and O'Banyon objected, the whole of the Gilvry clan, not just him, would suffer the consequences.

Like ruin and starvation.

Nothing was worth that.

After a good half-hour, they reached the barricade formed by a troop of soldiers. A sergeant stepped up smartly and Logan handed him his pass. The man peered at it closely, then waved them through.

There were a great many pedestrians on the road now. Narrow streets cut off on either side, but he headed straight for the docks and there they found crowds lining the east and west piers. People were flocking to find places on both sides of the harbour. A lucky few had obtained a window overlooking the scene, and a few hardy souls risked life and limb clinging to ridge poles. The mood was one of a grand holiday. A fête. He directed their driver to cross the drawbridge to the North Shore

On that side, soldiers directed the carriage to the customs-house yard. He tried not to chuckle at being a guest of the excisemen as they walked the short distance to a scaffold that had been constructed with seats for local dignitaries and their ladies. It provided a perfect view of the procession lined up on Bernard Street and the platform where the King would land. He couldn't help his 'I-told-you-so' grin as she looked around. 'I hope this suits you, my lady?'

A rigidity seized her body. She sent him a black look from beneath her lashes.

'What is wrong?'

She looked at him, then averted her gaze, staring down at the milling scene below them. 'Nothing. It is nothing. And indeed, Logan, this is a very good spot. The view is perfect.'

Not true. He had said something that struck a nerve. Mentally he shrugged. If she wouldna' tell him, then how could he fix it? He reached inside his jacket and pulled out the telescope he'd begged from Niall. 'You will see more through this.'

Her expression relaxed. It wasn't quite a

smile, but it was no longer arctic. 'You do think of everything, don't you?'

'I aim to please.'

She gave him an arch look. 'Is that what you are doing?'

The courtesan was back. His body tightened in response, but his heart seemed to swoop down and away, an unpleasant sensation. He brushed the sensation aside. It was part of who she was and he could either accept it, or leave. He leaned back against the seat and watched her face as she peered through the telescope. She handled it easily, adjusting the eyepiece, staring out to sea with parted lips. Now she looked more like a girl on an adventure. No artifice. No icy-hot stares. 'My word, there are a lot of boats out on the water. Oh, listen. Is that bagpipes I hear?'

She looked and sounded like the sort of girl one might meet at a local assembly. The sort of girl a man might marry. If he was the marrying sort. Except that she was not at all the kind of woman a man would introduce to his mother. 'Aye. Bagpipes.'

What game was she playing today, then? He did not trust her an inch.

His gaze drifted downwards to the neckline of her gown and he gave his head a shake. How could he think sensibly, when she wore such revealing clothes?

They settled down to await the arrival of the King. They watched the welcoming party get themselves ordered and laughed at the myriad little boats in the harbour sailing up and down sporting flags and pipers. And on the larger ships at anchor, men and women waved and cheered atop the masts and among the rigging. And all before the King was in sight.

Opposite their position, across the narrow harbour, were two platforms at the water's edge, one floating, where the King would step off his barge, and an upper one, on dockside, where the magistrates of Leith, important merchants, in blue and white, and the royal company of archers massed on three sides to greet the royal visitor.

A gun roared, fired by one of the ships standing out in the Firth. 'The signal that King is departing the *Royal George*,' Charity said. 'I read of it in the newspaper.'

A deafening shout went up from all around them. More guns fired, from the shore battery this time.

'There's the barge now,' Charity said. 'Heading between the piers.' She turned to him with a smile. 'Would you care to see?'

He was seeing everything he wanted right

now. He took the telescope. Their hands brushed and, even through their gloves, he felt the tingle of awareness. Of her. Another deliberate ploy to set him off kilter? 'Thank you.' He peered through the glass.

It was not difficult to focus in on the royal barge and its royal occupant. The King wore the uniform of an admiral and an expression on his round face of intense satisfaction as he stared at the waiting crowds. By Jove, the man was fat. They must have needed a dozen ropes on him to get him into that boat.

All around them people were waving hats and handkerchiefs, while bands and lone pipers did their best to outdo each other with music.

He could not understand the fascination with this Royal King who had been Regent for nine years. Surely folks were used to him by now? They were acting as if the King Across the Water had finally come home.

He handed her the telescope. 'I pity the sailors.'

The boat was close enough now to see without aid and she rested the instrument in her lap. 'He is enormous, isn't he?' she said, leaning close to his ear to make herself heard. 'He is very unpopular with the common people in London.'

'Well, he's getting a grand welcome here. I

must have heard a dozen songs all composed in honour of his visit.' His Majesty doffed his hat and bowed in all directions to the crowds surrounding him both at the water's edge and on the water.

'He is lucky to have sunshine, after yesterday's rain,' she observed.

Moments later, George was ascending to the upper dock to a cacophony of cheers and trumpets, surrounded by officials from the city in their robes and guarded by soldiers in their red coats and gold braid. While on the water, the sailors stood in their boats, oars in a vertical salute.

While they could hear nothing of what was being said from their vantage point, Logan was able to explain that this was the traditional ceremony welcoming the King to the capital, which went on for about fifteen minutes with much talking and bowing by the mayor and his minions.

The open carriage was brought up and the King climbed in.

'That's it, then,' Logan said. 'He'll be off to Edinburgh in a grand procession. I think perhaps we should wait a while before following. If we drive along the shore, we might get a better look at the royal yacht at anchor. I know a snug little inn where we can stop for refreshment.'

She gave him a considering glance as if weighing up his true intentions. Did she think he would ravish her at some lonely out-of-the-way place? Did she hope he would? Hot blood coursed in his veins. Anger. And, yes, damn it, the sharp edge of lust.

She clutched at his arm. 'Who is that?'

He looked over the heads of the milling people. A mounted man, in full Highland dress, was galloping along the dockside towards the royal carriage from which the King beamed and waved at the people lining the road.

None of the soldiers had seen him.

The King's equerry put a hand to his holster as the Scot pulled his horse up hard and swept off his bonnet with a courtly bow from the back of his horse. Logan laughed. 'It's Glengarry. Giving him a proper Highland welcome. I gather his nose is out of joint because his True Highlanders were nae invited to make part of the honour guard. Got a lot of pride, the Glengarry.'

The King bowed affably and his carriage moved on.

'So if true Highlanders weren't invited, who were?' Charity asked.

'The Celtic Society. A group invented by Scott.'

'He's a talented man. I loved *Waverly*,' she

said. 'It was one of the reasons I decided to come with Jack on this trip.'

Now how many lightskirts were avid readers? Och, now that was pure prejudice. She was clearly an educated woman who likely had more time for reading that he did.

He helped her down from the stands. 'So what is it to be, Charity? A drive up the Firth before we head back to Edinburgh, or a drive through the countryside to avoid the traffic on the roads?'

'We can't watch him receive the keys to the city?'

'We'd never get ahead of him. Not in these crowds.'

She arched a brow. 'I'll take your word for it.'

They strolled through the crowds milling around the docks back to the carriage. Her hand on his sleeve barely registered, she touched him so lightly. Yet he was aware of it as he would have been of the heat of a branding iron. Aware, too, of the sway of her hips that caused her skirts to brush against his leg at ever other step and the graceful carriage of her head beneath its flower-decorated hat brim. And the occasional whiff of her floral scent over the tang of the sea and the more earthy scent of the people around them. Not that he would ever let her see his awareness.

A gentleman didn't.

He handed her up and ascended on his side. 'What did you decide?' he asked.

'The coast road.'

No hesitation there. She'd made up her mind a long time ago. No doubt she'd been teasing him. Something women seemed to do as a matter of course. He gave the coachman the instructions.

'I haven't been to the seaside since…for ages,' she said. 'I love the wildness of the winds and the waves.'

So that was the reason for the longing he had seen on her face when she had looked out beyond the pier to the rough North Sea. Her expression softened to one of recollection and he was loath to break into her reverie, so he remained silent, watching her lovely face.

'We swam and we sailed, my brothers and I,' she murmured her voice low and achingly sweet as she gazed at the horizon. Slowly, she turned to look at him, looking younger and for once vulnerable. As if she had let down her guard in order to share this moment with him alone. 'Have you ever played cricket on the sand?'

'I can't say as I have.' He kept his voice low so as to preserve the rare sense of intimacy.

To no avail. Her eyes sharpened as if she had only just recalled his presence, her expression turning wary. The moment was gone and he grieved its loss.

'Which part of Britain's coast did you visit?' he asked, hoping to recapture her attention.

She made a dismissive gesture. 'The Southwest. Dorset. Cornwall.'

'Nowhere near as wild as here.'

'There are terrible storms there in the winter.'

'Is that where you lived, before—?'

She froze, her eyes chips of smoky glass, and her face cold and distant. She smiled a hard brittle smile. 'Before what?'

No sense in beating around the bush. She'd see it in a heartbeat. And she didn't deserve to be taken for a fool. 'Before you lived in London with Jack O'Banyon.'

She gave him a sugary-sweet smile. 'Before then I lived with someone else.'

'Dunross is near the sea, in what Glengarry would call the True Highlands.'

Her shoulders relaxed. Her easy smile returned. 'What a wild man Glengarry looked riding up to the King. I half-expected him to make use of his broadsword.'

'What a sight it would have been. Revenge of the Scots on the Hanovers at long last.'

'Would you like a Stuart back on the throne?'

He chuckled at the question. It was one often raised behind closed doors in Scotland even yet.

'What, commit treason? And besides, there are no real Stuarts left. It is better left as it is.'

And as they discussed Scotland's past, they were back on neutral ground. For now. But if he could, he was going to find a way to break down her walls and find out what lay behind the mystery in her eyes. To discover what had brought a woman of obviously gentle birth into the arms of a man like O'Banyon. Was she as willing an accomplice as she appeared?

For some reason, he did not believe it. And that gave him a bad taste in his mouth.

Chapter Five

She was enjoying herself far too much. The sea breezes off the widening Firth of Forth, the cry of the gulls overhead. The occasional bright warm flashes of sunlight sparkling on the choppy waves in the long narrow bay.

And his company.

As if it was he who made her feel happy. The thought of going back to Jack was a nagging ache in the back of her mind. Something she didn't want to think about at this moment.

Logan had been right about Scotland being wilder than Dorset, but she couldn't quite believe she had actually told him from whence she hailed. She made a point never to tell anyone anything about her past. For a moment, she had forgotten and had talked to him as if they were friends.

Too quickly, he had picked up on her careless words, proving again he was no slow-top. She would be wise to be wary. More on her guard than usual. For no matter how hard she tried not to, she kept finding herself liking him as a person and forgetting he was a man. It was a long time since she had engaged in anything so risky as friendship. Besides, she had no illusions. A man might profess friendship, or even love, but only in aid of getting what he wanted.

And once he had it, he lost interest.

She must take care when alone with him at this inn he had mentioned. She really did not want to go down that path, if it could be avoided. Flirtation was one thing, a challenge to her wits. Bedsport for money, on the other hand, left her cold. And men did not like a cold woman in their bed. No matter how she tried, she could never quite work up the required enthusiasm.

A pang of longing hit her hard. A longing to be herself. To have what should have been her rightful future. What she would have had, if she had not let a girlish desire to please overcome good sense.

Pushing such a lowering thought aside, she tied the ribbons on her bonnet tighter against the breeze and looked up at the sky. Some of the clouds lowered darkly. 'Do you think it will rain again?' A downpour while they were so far from her hotel would be a very bad thing if it forced them to seek shelter. A shiver ran down her back at the vision of them together alone.

She stilled. Inside. Caught without air to fill her lungs.

He shook his head. 'It won't dare, not while the King is travelling in an open carriage.' At her wry look, he shrugged. 'I really don't think so. But we can turn back if you wish.'

Did she wish?

And if she went back, what would there be for her at the hotel? Jack was off on business of his own. She would be left sitting in her parlour. Alone. Thinking. She did not want time to think. 'How far is it to this inn of yours?'

'A scant three miles, I would say. Just beyond the Seafield Toll. It has a good view of the Firth from its windows and we can walk along the sand if you wish.'

A walk along the sands sounded a little too intimate. And was likely to bring back memories of happier times. 'A cup of tea would be welcome before we head back.'

Because they were heading away from the King and his procession, traffic remained light. He pointed out several glassworks on the seaward side and a ropeworks on the other, and then they were clear of the town. The open fields with the hills in the distance made a pretty view on one side and the wide Firth a wild one on the other. The clouds seemed less black than they had earlier and the sun appeared for longer intervals. She carefully shaded her face from its rays. Milk-white skin was her stock in trade, one of her attractions, and it would be a fatal mistake to take it for granted.

When she had her own cottage, and a garden, well, then she wouldn't care if she got freckles, or a little colour, when she worked outside. When. Or, perhaps, if. It might be years before she had enough money. So right now, living as she did, it was vital that she keep every scrap of advantage.

'Are you warm enough?' he asked in that lovely, dark, lilting voice that made her toes curl in her shoes and her insides flutter.

How could she be attracted to him? To that false air of purity. The open face designed to send the most careful female to her knees. But not her. She knew all the pitfalls of letting the hot desires of her body rule a rational mind. Not even this angel sent to bedevil women everywhere could make her forget the lessons of the past.

'I am quite comfortable, thank you.'

'And what do you think of this part of Scotland?'

Polite conversation. What a gentleman he

was to treat her to such niceties. That was what made her like him more than she should. She looked about her at the rugged hills and the white-flecked waves racing towards land. 'It is a very fierce land, I think.'

He shot her a sideways glance. 'Like its people, you are thinking.'

'I wasn't thinking about its inhabitants at all.'

'Really,' he said in a low seductive murmur. 'And here I was believing you were thinking about me.'

He looked so very pleased with himself, she laughed. A real laugh that broke free from somewhere deep down. He was an unashamed rogue, for all her thoughts of angels and purity. And a charming one to boot. She relaxed against the seat back, closed her eyes and inhaled a breeze heavy with the tang of salt. Such a long time since she had breathed sea air.

Her old life seemed decades behind her. A life of privilege tossed away for the sake of a man who in the end hadn't cared. Was it really only four years since her father had cast her from her family home in disgust? And why think of that now? When she had sworn never to think of it, of her family, again.

The breeze turned cold as the sun faded behind another bank of black-lined clouds. Chilled to the bone as much by her thoughts as by the wind, she straightened. Perhaps it would rain and he would turn back. Perhaps she would prefer to be alone at the hotel, after all. He had her thinking things that hadn't crossed her mind in ages.

'Are you cold?' he asked, reaching under the seat. He pulled out a blanket. 'Use this.' He spread it across her lap. 'It is not far now. The tollgate is just ahead.'

'There isn't much here,' she said, looking about her.

'Mostly farms,' he agreed. The carriage halted beside the tollgate. The keeper shambled out and took money for both directions.

'We will be coming back this way in an hour or so,' Logan said. 'Be sure to have the gate open for us.'

The man touched his cap and opened the gate. 'Aye. I'll keep watch.'

They went through the gate at a smart clip and it wasn't long before they arrived at the inn. A snug little place indeed. It faced the sea and had an air of comfortable well-being.

An ostler appeared the moment they pulled into the yard and grabbed the horses' heads. Logan leaped clear and came around to lift her down. As he reached up to grasp her around the waist, he smiled and she found herself entranced by those direct green eyes all over again. They danced with mischief of the purest kind.

Whichever woman lost her heart to him would never get it back again.

A pang squeezed somewhere in her chest, a painful awareness, like numbed fingers coming to life. She gritted her teeth against the unwanted sensation and smiled her sultry smile, letting it play over her lips as she gazed down at his handsome face.

'I vow you are quite spoiling me, Logan. And so I shall tell Jack.'

The subtle shift in his expression was not lost to her. The slight withdrawal. The recollection of who and what she was. He lifted her down, keeping careful distance between their bodies, when hers craved the feel of his, like a harlot.

She picked up her skirts and tripped into the establishment with his hand light at the small of her back. Still possessive. But a little withdrawn. Good.

Then why did she suddenly feel so lonely?

A few words from Logan to the innkeeper bespoke a private parlour with a view of the sea. He seated her at the table by the window, took her gloves and saw to her comfort like a gentleman should, but not many would. Not knowing what she was. And if he hadn't been the man she knew him to be, an honourable man, she would never have risked letting him bring her here. She gazed out of the window at the rough sea and the waves rolling up the sand and felt an odd rush of gratitude. A feeling that life was not so bad after all.

It was both heartwarming and frightening.

He sat down kitty-corner, so they would both have a view out of the window. It brought him close enough that she could feel the warmth of his body washing up against her skin. See the strength of his features, in all their symmetrical beauty.

'Thank you,' she said, impulsively.

A brow shot up and he turned to look her full in the face. 'For what?'

'For taking me to see the King. For bringing me here.' She glanced out of the window. Off in the mist she could see the land on the other side of the great slash in the land named the Firth of Forth. She had seen it on maps. But she could never have imagined its stark beauty.

'I thought him disappointingly ordinary,' he said with a smile.

He could have said anything, but nothing else would have put her so much at ease. She laughed. 'You should not talk so about your King.'

'Aye, well, he is a man too. And a mite over-indulged, I'm thinking. But I'd no be him. All that pomp and ceremony. It would drive a man to drink. Talking of drink, would you like wine or tea?'

The maid who had entered stood waiting to hear her answer. Wine would be more in character, but with this man she needed all her wits. 'Tea, please.'

'And scones?' the girl asked, looking at Logan.

'Aye, scones, and cold meats and cheese.' he said. 'And I'll have ale, if you please.'

The girl bobbed her head and left.

'The fresh air has made you hungry,' she commented.

His smile was rueful. 'I don't deny I'm sharp set. But it is auld George there I blame. I was scarce outa my bed when I heard he was to disembark today. I had a fine job of it to find a carriage at such short notice and no time to break my fast.'

'Then the blame is mine. For if you had not promised to bring me, you would not have had to miss your breakfast.'

An angelic smile curved his lips and she felt her heart quake.

'The pleasure was mine, Charity.'

A foolish girl's blush heated her face. A blush! How could this be?

The maid saved her by entering with a tea tray, swiftly followed by a male servant with the food they had ordered. In the hustle and bustle of setting down the food and arranging the plates, she regained her composure.

But a blush. She was mortified.

The servants left and he helped her to a scone and butter. She refused the meats and the cheese. He filled his plate, eating heartily, but with perfect manners.

She sipped her tea and nibbled her scone.

After a draught of ale, he glanced at her plate. 'You should eat more.'

Food held no interest. She ate to live. Not the other way round. She took another bite just to please him, surprised to notice how well the little scone tasted.

He nodded as if pleased. As if he cared whether she ate or not. When in reality he had only one thing on his mind and it had been shimmering in the air since they walked in this room. He wanted her.

And she would say no. She was positive she would.

But there was no tension in her decision. No fear he would not accept her refusal with grace and honour. A strangely comforting thought. And that she could not like.

To restore her faith in herself, she would torment him a little, before he had her answer. Make him pay for her temptation. It was only fair.

She stroked his upper arm lightly, as if to get his attention, and was surprised by the tingles in her fingers. 'Tell me more about your family,' she said a little breathlessly. 'You said you have brothers, so more than one?'

'Aye. There were four of us growing up. My second oldest brother disappeared in America.'

'I'm sorry.'

He shrugged. 'It was years ago.'

Yet he still felt the loss. She could tell from the note in his voice. As much as she felt hers, though as far as she knew none of her family had met such a final end.

'But your other brothers are well and married, I think you said.'

'Aye.' His expression brightened. 'And very happy they are, too. My older brother is the Laird. He married an Englishwoman.' He grimaced a little.

'That does not please you?'

'Our families were enemies. But she's a good woman. Good for Ian. It is no' my place to be pleased or displeased.'

'And he runs the distillery?'

'Aye.'

'How do you manage to avoid the authorities?' She managed an admiring expression, the sort of simpering face men expected.

'We would do it under the law if we could.'

He grinned. 'Which would put an end to my adventures.'

'You like it,' she said. 'The danger.'

His eyes sparkled wickedly. 'It was all I ever wanted as a lad. To be allowed to go along with my brothers. Now I'm the only one in the trade.'

'How is that?'

'Ian and Niall have families. They are needed at home.'

'But surely it is just as dangerous making it as transporting it. There are revenue agents everywhere, Jack tells me.'

'Gaugers, aye. But as far as they are concerned our still is legal. And there isna' a man in Dunross to tell them otherwise.' He sounded proud. Of his brother. Of his family. Of his clan. A man who knew his place in the world.

Where she had none. Or rather what she had she hated. She quelled the dismal thought, focusing on his puzzling words instead. 'Are you saying there is some trick to it?'

His eyes narrowed a fraction as if she was pressing him too hard. 'All O'Banyon needs to know is that we can deliver what he wants.'

He assumed she was spying for Jack. Let him. It would obscure the truth. 'And you will get the whisky across the border.'

'Aye.'

'Your other brother, the lawyer, he approves?'

'Niall and I don't agree on much.'

Dissension in the family? Jack might find that of some interest.

She broke off another piece of scone and popped it in her mouth with a careless smile that said she'd held up her end of polite conversation and now it was his turn.

He gazed at her silently, as if trying to think of something to say.

'What brought you here?' he asked, his voice so gentle it raked at a raw place in her chest she hadn't known was there. She could barely remember the last time anyone had been interested in her as a person.

A shiver trembled in her bones. She stiffened. Froze. She angled her body and gazed at him from beneath lowered lashes, smiling at the concern in his face, the interest. 'Why, Logan, did you not just drive me here?'

Clearly dazzled, as he should be, he blinked. But he was not easily diverted. 'Not here. To this inn. To this life? To Jack O'Banyon. A woman of your sort deserves far more.'

'A woman of my sort?' she asked with dangerous quiet and a glittering smile. 'Do you judge what sort of woman I am?'

Answering a question with a question. Accompanied by a smile that promised everything a man could ever want from a woman. A confusing combination for any man, she'd learned.

Not this one. His gaze was sharp and clear and painfully direct. He put his hand over hers, a comforting touch, and she wished she had kept her gloves on for protection. The sensation tingled under her skin, trickled warmth through her veins, all the way to her belly. Her flesh yearned to be held, to be stroked, to be treasured. It was a lie. A trick.

She held still, as if she had not noticed the growing warmth in the room. The heat between them.

And then he lifted her hand in his, carefully, as if it could be broken by his greater strength. Eyes fixed on her face, he turned it over and, bending his head, touched his lips to her palm. A warm velvety brush of his mouth against sensitive skin. A whisper of hot breath. Sensual. Melting.

Her insides clenched. Her heart stopped, then picked up with a jolt and an uneven rhythm. She felt like a girl again, all hot and bothered and unsure. And full of such longings. Such desires.

But the woman inside her knew better. She craved all that kiss offered. The heat. The bliss. Carnal things, that shamed her. Things she had resolved never to want again. They left her vulnerable. A challenge she could not let go unanswered. To do so would be to admit he had touched her somehow.

'Charity,' he said softly, as he lifted his head to look at her, still cradling her hand in his large warm one, his thumb gently stroking. 'Never in my life have I met a woman like you.'

The words rang with truth. And they pleased her. She leaned closer and touched her lips to his, let them linger, cling softly, urging him to respond. And he did. Gently at first, with care, as if he thought she might take offence, or be frightened. Then more forcefully, his mouth moving against hers as he angled his head, his free hand coming up to cradle her nape while the other retained its hold. The feel of his gentle wooing of her mouth sent little thrills spiralling outward from low in her belly. On a gasp she opened her mouth and, with little licks and tastes and deep rumbling groans in his chest, he explored her mouth. The gentleness of it was her undoing.

The way he delved and plundered her mouth as if making the discovery for the very first time was incredibly alluring. If she didn't know better, she might have thought this was his first time. Passion hummed in her veins. Dizzied her mind. Sent her tumbling into a blaze of desire.

He drew back, his chest rising and falling as

if he too could not breathe, his gaze searching her face. And she melted in the heat in his eyes.

Horrified by such unbridled responses, she fought to hide her reactions. She managed a long slow smile before striking. 'I doubt this is the sort of partnership O'Banyon had in mind.'

She had the dubious pleasure of watching his lips thin and his jaw harden. Not quite so angelic now. She braced herself for rough words. Welcomed the proof he was no different from other men.

He put her hand down until it once more rested on the pristine white cloth beside her plate of crumbs. As he released her hand, she felt the loss deeply and smiled at her girlish foolishness. He gave a slight shake of his head. 'Let me help you.'

'Help me?' She let her lip curl in derision. 'If I did need help, which I do not, what help would I get from a smuggler?'

'You don't belong in this life. What you are doing to yourself is wrong.'

Doing to herself? Yes. Hers was the blame. The weakness. Hers the punishment, too. And deservedly so. Stupidity had its own reward.

Yet somehow he had sensed this was not what she wanted. Was he offering more? Afraid of what she might see in his face, she looked out of the window to the gulls wheeling free above the turbulent water. 'You are offering me a cottage beside the sea, no doubt. And occasional visits from a Highland gentleman.'

Silence confirmed her suspicion. 'I would die of boredom in a week.' She covered a yawn to hide her sadness. 'Indeed, I'm already bored.'

His face darkened as her knife struck home. 'Then it is time we returned to the city.'

She pouted. 'Do you think so?' She picked up her gloves and put them on, drawing the cool, buttery-soft leather over the still-searing brand of his touch on her hand. Yet still those unwelcome shivers chased over her skin. Longing. Desire. Along with the knowledge that the touch of this wild bold Scot drove her to want things she'd long ago decided to do without.

She'd spent too long hardening her armour against such longings. To let them in now, with him, would be the worst mistake of her life. She would never survive when he realised she had betrayed him. Because as much as she wanted him, she was bound to Jack. A hard lump formed in her chest. 'Then by all means, let us go.'

The coachman whipped the horses into a steady trot. Logan resisted the temptation to look at the woman who sat languidly, so unmoved beside him.

So she found him dull. Boring. Like hell she did. But for a man who lived by his wits he'd been remarkably obtuse. It was not his place to pry. Or to tease her with kisses. And especially not to seek out the vulnerable woman he'd glimpsed beneath her brittle shell, like a child digging out a winkle with a pin.

He should have left well alone and accepted her for who she was. She had gone from friendly and warm to distrustful in a single breath. And she should mistrust him, he thought bitterly. She meant nothing to him but his path to Jack's business for his family.

This other thing, the slow burn of heat left from delving deep into her mouth, was something neither of them should or would admit. Lust did not drive him. It was simply an inconvenience. Something he had no trouble ignoring. Usually.

Right now it was not easy.

Ahead the gatekeeper rushed to open the way for them. He tossed the man a sixpence as they bowled through.

The silence between them was something he could almost touch. A physical barrier. And he needed to break it down before it became insurmountable.

Other women were easy to charm—a smile, a compliment, a teasing remark and they melted to his flattery. But she was not like other women. This one did not fall for easy blandishments. She fended them off with a sharp-edged tongue. And he liked the challenge almost as much as he liked those rare real smiles of hers.

'I'm sorry,' he said. 'I overstepped my bound-aries.'

The tension left her body. He felt it in the air, though she said nothing, and breathed a sigh of relief. He kept his gaze fixed on the road ahead. No sense in saying more and losing the ground he'd gained.

They turned on to a road that would take them around Leith. Her wistful glance back over her shoulder at the sea revealed far more of her feelings than words ever would. More than she probably realised. He tucked the knowledge away.

She stared off to their left. 'Is that a golf links?'

'It is. A fine and famous one at that. Leith Links.'

She frowned. 'Don't tell me you are another man who spends his time hitting a little ball from one hole to another?'

He laughed at the indignation in her tone. 'It sounds as if you do not care for the game. Does Jack play?'

'Yes. When he can. For hours.'

More useful information. ''Tis said King

Charles was playing here when he heard about the Irish rebellion.'

'Really?'

'Aye.'

'Perhaps King George will follow suit.'

'I doubt he could walk sae far. They'd have to put him up on a horse.'

'Poor horse.'

They both laughed at the image. And suddenly things were comfortable again. As if they had never kissed.

'I am thinking the man is not so energetic as to play a round,' he said. Edinburgh lay before them in the distance. The castle on the mountain, the Palace at its foot and the tenements of old town between.

Once more cheerful crowds of pedestrians brought their progress to a crawl and for the rest of the drive they chatted like polite acquaintances as he pointed out the sights of the city. Logan felt redeemed in her eyes. Somewhat.

And there he would have to leave it. A wise man let a sleeping dog lie and this one had a bite that could damage his family's plans. But for that, he might have been tempted to chance his luck.

Which in and of itself was a surprise. Oh, he liked women well enough. Too much for his peace of mind. But he'd learned that the tricky wee things had their own ideas about right and wrong. He'd paid a heavy price to learn that lesson and wasn't about to forget it. Not even with a woman as beautiful as this one. Yet he had forgotten for a moment back at the inn. And he had the feeling he might be tempted again, if he wasn't very careful.

When they reached her hotel, he helped her down. 'Mrs Donaldson will bring your gowns tomorrow morning for a fitting.'

An expression of understanding crossed her face, the knowledge that Mrs Donaldson would sooner wait on her here, than have her in her shop. She made a small gesture with one hand. Acceptance.

It made his blood run hot. Anger on her behalf.

She gave him a rueful smile as if she sensed his annoyance, but her gaze was temptingly warm when it rested on his face. 'Would you care to come up to our parlour? Jack may have returned by now.'

And if he hadn't? The limit of his control had been reached during that kiss. More hours alone in her company, in a private apartment no less, would likely tip him over the edge of reason. And pleasant as the idea might be, and as much as he liked danger, he knew when discretion was the better part of valour.

He won against the temptation, barely, and took her hand in his. 'I am otherwise engaged, I am afraid.'

The disappointment on her face was a surprise. But was it real or was it feigned? How to be sure? And if O'Banyon was not there, as he suspected, he would return at some point. No, definitely not a good idea. Not at the moment.

He bowed. 'Perhaps you and Mr O'Banyon would like to join me for dinner this coming Saturday. Otherwise we are not scheduled to meet again until next week's Drawing Room.'

'I will speak to Jack about his plans.' She spoke calmly, but there was a slight crease of worry between her brows. Because she did not want to meet, or because she did? Or was it worry about O'Banyon?

He contained his curiosity and gave her an untroubled smile. 'I shall look forward to hearing your answer, then. Send word by way of my brother's office, in New Town. Niall Gilvry, Lord Aleyne.

Her eyes widened a fraction at the title. He felt a rush of pride for his brother. Niall was making a name for himself in Scotland's capital. He'd a growing clientele and he and his wife were accepted by Scottish society. He had already bought a grander house in New Town and was talking of renovating the mansion at his wife's country estate. Niall's reputation was one of the reasons Ian was anxious that Logan avoid trouble with the authorities. 'The porter will know where to find him.'

She gave him a kittenish look. 'I can't contact you directly?'

He did not trust that look one little bit. It offered honey and kisses and smelled of a trap. 'I am no' sure where I'll be from one day to the next.'

Her expression didn't change, but he knew she wasn't pleased by his evasion.

He bid her farewell and left, before he did something stupid like changing his mind and following her up to her chamber.

To Charity's surprise, Jack was waiting for her in their private parlour, sitting in the chair by the window looking down into the street. He looked over his shoulder at her entry. 'I thought you planned to be gone for a few days?'

'Did you have a fine time with yon sprig of Scottish manhood?'

An innocent enough question, but there was nothing innocent about any word Jack spoke. 'We saw the King land.'

'And?'

'We went for a drive along the shore.'

The expression on his face shifted almost imperceptibly. Imperceptible to anyone else. He had something on his mind. 'You are back earlier than I expected.'

Her heart racing, she untied the ribbons of her bonnet and lifted it carefully from her head so as not to disturb the curls beneath. She tossed it on a side table and stretched her neck, easing the tension. 'He had another engagement.' She sat down on the sofa.

Jack eyed her narrowly for a moment, then pushed to his feet. He drew closer, looming over her. 'You were supposed to keep him busy all day.'

'I cannot force him to remain at my side.'

He glared down at her. 'So what did you do?'

What on earth was going on? 'We talked. We drove. We took tea at an alehouse along the shore.'

'What did you talk about?'

She shrugged. 'Things. Life. The weather.'

'Did he tell you where he stays?'

'No. He made a point of indicating you should contact him through his brother's law office.'

Jack went to the window and glanced down into the street. 'I'll put Growler on it.'

'Jack, be careful. He has friends in high places.

Today, he had a pass for seats reserved for important people.'

'What friends?'

'I didn't ask, but I think it might be Lord Sanford. They were together at the inn that first night.'

Jack's mouth tightened. 'Sanford has the reputation of a rakehell.' He frowned. 'He came to the Rouge, but only once.'

'Perhaps he didn't find it to his noble taste.'

Undisturbed by her jibe, Jack chuckled. 'We offer something to suit all tastes. Ring for tea, would you, girl?'

Girl. Was she now his servant? Perhaps he was punishing her for not falling into bed with Logan and keeping him busy all afternoon. It would be like him. Gritting her teeth, she crossed the room and tugged at the bell.

He gestured for her to sit on the sofa. 'It is haggard you look. Was he so hard to handle?'

'How charming you can be, Jack.' She was tired. With the strain of being with him. Of keeping her façade tightly wrapped. Until today, she had thought it a second skin. Part of who she was. But there were chinks in her armour. Big ones.

She worked her glove off her fingers, watching her busy hands. 'No difficulty at all.' She glanced up at him. 'I did learn one thing. They employ some sort of trick to make their still appear to be legal.'

His eyes sharpened. 'What sort of trick?'

'He didn't give me details. Likely he thought I wouldn't understand, since I am playing the simpering fool.'

He gave a grunt. Not a pleased grunt, but not an angry one either. 'It seems you made more of an impression than I thought.'

Relief flooded her at his words of faint praise. She hated that he could make her feel that way. 'I told you, I know what I am doing.'

'I want you to find out more.'

'What?'

'You heard me. I want more information. I want to know the route he uses to take the contraband over the border. And where they keep the whisky before it leaves. McKenzie says it is not at the distillery.'

She frowned. Something had changed. 'I am to act as a spy now? Who did you meet today, Jack? What is going on?'

He strolled back to the sofa, leaning over her to give the point of her chin a hard pinch. 'Is that any of your business? Not fallin' for his pretty face, are ye? Growler said ye were mighty close when ye left this morning.'

'Don't be ridiculous.' She jerked her chin out of his grasp, but did not look away from that penetrating gaze. 'I'm just not sure he trusts me that much. Do you expect him to draw me a map?'

Jack's eyes narrowed. 'I expect you to do as you're told.'

She got up and paced in front of the hearth and then looked at him closely. She wasn't the only one hiding things. 'The whole idea of this trip was to make a deal with the Gilvrys.'

A wry smile twisted his lips. 'I haven't said I won't. But from the things I'm hearing I am having second thoughts. I need information. And you are the one who can get it.'

They both knew what he meant. Bile rose in her throat. She paced away from him, pulling hard at her other glove. She dragged it off and balled it in her hand. Then spun around. 'He invited us to dinner on Saturday. Us. Both, Jack. He's no fool. He believes I am your woman. If you never come with me, he will suspect I am after something.'

Jack rubbed at his chin. 'All right. I'll be there. And I will use the chance to test his mettle.'

'Jack, I don't think—'

He grabbed her by the arm and pushed his face into hers. 'You'll do as I say. The lad's too cocky by half. He needs to be taught a bit of respect for his betters.'

She gazed into Jack's pale blue eyes, afraid to blink in case he thought she was hiding something. Afraid he might use his fists to make a point. Logan would have to look after himself, but she dreaded Saturday, knowing the sort of teaching games Jack enjoyed. Smart as he was, Logan Gilvry didn't stand a chance.

She bent and picked up the glove she had dropped, smoothing the pair in her hand before placing them beside her bonnet. 'I'll let him know we accept his invitation.' She suddenly felt weary and not a little fearful.

Chapter Six

Dinner at the Waterloo Hotel had gone well, Logan thought. While he had imbibed ale, and Charity nothing but a couple of glasses of burgundy, O'Banyon had downed glass after glass of whisky. And appeared none the worse for wear. The man had a cast-iron constitution. Or stomach, at any rate.

And the more he drank, the more unpleasant he had become to Charity.

The strain of not hitting the man had become a sharp pain at the base of Logan's skull. The kind that makes your hands curl into weapons.

Right now the Irishman had one arm over her shoulder and his fingers rubbing along the rise of her breast where it disappeared beneath the edge of the blood-red gown. The gown that made her skin look bone-china white and skimmed the peaks of her breasts. One small downward move of that coarse blunt finger and every man in the place would be seeing her nipples.

They were all watching and hoping. Logan didn't have to look about him to know. The atmosphere was charged with male interest. If it had a smell, it would be filling his nostrils. The way anger filled his gullet and made his hands clench with the urge to plunge his fist into the Irishman's leering mouth.

Control. Breathe slow. He kept his gaze fixed on O'Banyon's face and his expression all business. 'Has the money you were expecting arrived from London?'

O'Banyon looked up from inspecting the flesh he was stroking. He shook his head slowly. Rather stupidly. 'Not yet. Takes five days, the banker told me.'

'But you have looked over the document I delivered to you earlier in the week.'

'Sush as…' O'Banyon slurred. He straightened in his chair, removing his hand from around Charity's back and leaning forwards across the table from which all the dishes had been removed except his fifth glass of whisky and Charity and Logan's coffee cups. 'Such as it is.'

A waft of whisky-laden breath hit Logan

in the face. He held his ground, indeed leaned closer. 'You didna' expect all the details before we have an agreement, did ye?'

A shift at the table beside them, caught in the corner of his eye. O'Banyon's man making his presence known. A not-so-subtle display of power. Impatience grabbed Logan by the throat. 'Are ye a man or a mouse? Call off your dog, O'Banyon, or this ends right now. We'll find another partner in London.'

Charity stiffened. A quick glance showed the anxiety in her eyes. Damn. Clearly his words had somehow made her afraid. Would the Irishman take it out on her, if their deal fell apart? Blame her? He wasn't a fool. He knew she was bait. Knew she was O'Banyon's creature, but he hadn't suspected she might be in physical danger. She'd seemed too resilient, from the first, far too cold and calculating to be anyone's victim.

During their outing to watch the King land and later at the inn, she'd seemed much more vulnerable, almost fragile at times, as if she was held together with paper and string. Easily ripped apart. Or not. A cold mask had quickly descended after their kiss. If she was afraid, she hid it well.

Yet during the few days since that afternoon, the worry he sensed within her seemed to have increased. And it made that ache in his skull deepen.

O'Banyon jerked his chin in the direction of his man stationed at the next table. Growler. He had drunk nothing at all. The man rose and left, but Logan had no doubts that he would be waiting outside. He also suspected there was more than one of O'Banyon's men lurking nearby. The rest of them were more discreet. Which didn't mean Logan was happy about their presence. But he had made his point.

O'Banyon pulled out a cigar and Charity took it from him, cutting off the end with an expert snip with the shears she extracted from her reticule. A very personal service that riled Logan more than what had gone before.

'You can't smoke that,' he said coldly.

Her brow went up. Other men were smoking cigars, that little flick said.

'Not in the presence of a lady,' he elaborated.

O'Banyon leered at Charity. 'Lady, is it, colleen?' His soft chuckle insulted the idea.

Logan wanted to hit him. Didn't he know what he had in Charity? All right, so she wasn't good society. Something had happened to her. But she was a lady for all that. 'Well, O'Banyon, do we have a bargain or not?'

The Irishman shook his head slowly as if trying to clear the mist from his mind, but there was a gleam of cunning deep in those bleary eyes. He wasn't as half-seas-over as he appeared. 'Whist, man. Are you always in such a hurry?' He put a hand on that delicate sloping shoulder. 'Char, here, is enjoying her first visit to Scotland.' The grip tightened. And though nothing showed on her face, Logan guessed she would have bruises from the pressure.

He held still, barely. Charity was this man's woman. By her own choice. It was not up to him to object. Not when she accepted his touch without flinching. Perhaps she liked pain. He'd heard that some people did. But one flinch and he'd have the man by the throat.

Did she know what was in his mind? Was that why she held so still? So unmoved? So removed from all around her?

'What is your point?' He could not keep the growl from his voice.

O'Banyon didn't appear to notice, but Charity's eyes widened a fraction.

'The point is, boyo,' O'Banyon said, 'you promised us a ball later in the week. If I seal our bargain today, I'll have no reason to stay.' He emptied his glass in one long swallow and anger flashed in his eyes. 'And besides, I'm thinking I need to consider a counter-offer. You are far too expensive.'

Naturally. They weren't going to start off low.

Now they were talking. He settled more comfortably. 'We take all the risks.'

'I can get my whisky elsewhere.'

'You can get gut rot anywhere.'

Charity's lips twitched as if she wanted to smile. What? Did she think he didn't know how to negotiate? He'd been doing this since he was eighteen. And doing it well. It wasn't just the good whisky that made Dunross successful.

O'Banyon leaned back and looked around. 'Are we done here?'

Logan narrowed his eyes. 'We are just getting started.'

'Aye. But I've a mind to rattle a dice box while we talk.' He grinned at Charity. 'What do you think, my darling?'

'You know I hate listening to you talk business, Jack,' she purred. 'I could use a bit of excitement.' She licked her ruby-red lips.

Logan tried not to notice his blood's hot surge. 'The Reiver, then?'

'Aye, that'll do.' O'Banyon rose and helped Charity to her feet. 'We'll talk more there.'

A waiter rushed forwards with her wrap, much to the disappointment of the male occupants of the room. And Logan's, if he was truthful as he followed them, gritting his teeth at Jack's proprietary arm over her shoulder and his heavy lean.

One chance, one opportunity to pay the man back, without causing her a problem was all he needed.

He headed for the tavern-owner ostensibly to pay the bill. He'd already arranged for the chit to go to Niall's house because he'd half-expected this tactic of O'Banyon's. The Irishman wasn't the first to try to get Logan drunk to gain an advantage and it seemed as if they were in for a long night. He just wished Charity wasn't part of the ploy. Because she was. Of that he had no doubt.

Just as he knew that if he held out long enough, she would give Logan whatever he wanted. To get a deal. The idea sickened him even as his body tightened, his arousal making walking a less-than-pleasant experience.

Sometimes he agreed with his ancestors. A man was better off in a kilt.

He followed the innkeeper into the office, then with a wink and a coin in the other man's palm, he slipped out through the kitchen door where Tammy was waiting to make his report on what he had learned about O'Banyon's dealings with McKenzie.

'Give it up, Jack. He's on to you,' Charity said in a low voice as they walked slowly up hill arm in arm in the warm dark to the Reiver, dallying to give Gilvry time to pay the shot and catch them up. The bonfire on Arthur's Seat lit up the sky and all along the street windows were full of illuminations in praise of King George. A band of boys wove through the crowd with torches held high and on a corner a group of sailors were dancing a reel to the sound of bag-pipes. Never had she seen a place so dazzling and full of celebration.

'Hen-hearted, sweet?' Jack breathed against her ear like a lover whispering tender words. 'With your help it will be like robbing a blind man. Bait and switch, my darling.'

'Has the whisky fogged your brain? If he catches you out, he'll walk away. Is that what you want? Are you trying to drive him off?' And if so, why?

'Is it soft on him you are, giving him so much credit? And me none at all.'

She gritted her teeth. 'He is nothing to me. But how will cheating him out of a bit of gold help our cause?'

'The wee lad needs a lesson in humility, so he does. He thinks he's so damned clever. If at the end of the night he owes me a bit more than he can afford, then he'll be easier to manage.' He gave her a sharp look. 'Not enough to put him in the poor house, mind, just enough for him to feel his obligation. To make him squirm at bit.'

Cold ran through her veins. Power. It was Jack's thing. 'I don't think he cares about money. It's all about family for him.'

Jack made a scoffing sound. 'All men care about money.'

Let him think what he would, but she surely hated cheating. It went against everything she'd learned as a child. She could do it, of course. He'd trained her in the way of it at the club, but she never needed such a crude ploy. Not with the green'uns Jack usually marked for her plucking. 'On your head be it.'

Jack smiled nastily. 'Understand this—if I lose tonight, you will carry the debt in his place.'

Her stomach dropped. When Jack played deep, as he usually did, he risked more in a night than she could earn in five years. Was this his way of ensuring she could never leave him? Surely he hadn't guessed her intention? She glared at him. 'I'll do my part, for half of what you win.'

A smile curled his thin lips and inside she cringed. Slowly, he nodded. 'It is a bargain we have.'

The relief she expected from his capitulation was not forthcoming. Because she hated the idea of cheating Logan out of his money. Yet what choice did she have?

She glanced back over her shoulder and saw Logan approaching with long easy strides. She gave him a brilliant smile and he increased his pace. Behind him, one of Growler's men detached from the shadows of an alley and followed at a distance. 'Where's Growler?' she asked Jack in a low voice, aware of the sudden rapid beat of her heart.

'Gone ahead. Why?'

'No reason.' No reason except that Growler's man should have followed Logan out of that dining room and instead he'd been outside waiting. A laugh caught at her throat. A little gurgle of amusement she had trouble swallowing. He'd given Growler's man the slip.

Oh, he was a rogue, all right. Jack certainly had his hands full. And so did she.

The thought sobered her. If things did not come out as Jack planned and Logan walked away, she would lose the bonus he'd promised her. An amount that would take three years of gulling green youths and drunken old men to achieve.

Not to mention that Jack would be furious.

Cold determination filled her chest, a bitter gall her throat. But Logan had not been forced to accept Jack's challenge. It was all his own doing.

'Just be careful, Jack.' It was all she could

manage before Logan caught them up and walked alongside. All she could bear to say, because in spite of everything, she didn't want Jack deciding Logan was more trouble than he was worth.

Jack removed trouble in the most final of ways.

'Thank you for dinner,' she said, giving Logan a long glance and a slow smile.

A smile hovered at the corner of his mouth as he looked down at her. Femininity swept through her. Weakness.

'My pleasure,' he murmured.

The velvety purr struck a chord low in her belly. And her palm tingled with the memory of the touch of his lips. She gasped at the shock of it and saw the gleam of amusement in his eyes, yes, and the triumph. An emotion that fired her anger and made it easier to do her job. An emotion he would regret.

And yet if she was right and Jack was wrong, after tonight she might never see him again. A sense of loss filled her. Loss tinged with relief, because if he walked away from Jack and his schemes, he'd likely be safe.

Jack barged through the tavern door. Growler stood just inside in the shadows and nodded, signifying all was well before they went down. She led the way downstairs and stepped into the smoke-filled cave. Fifty faces turned in their direction. Fifty pairs of eyes dropped to her flaunted bosom. Fifty heads emptied of thought, as their blood headed south.

She pouted a plaintive smile. 'Oh, our usual table is occupied.'

At a look and a step in their direction from Growler, the men in the corner got up and moved.

'Apparently not,' Logan said drily.

He pulled out a chair for her to sit down.

Such perfect manners. Such a gentleman. She was going to miss him after tonight. 'Thank you, Logan,' she said as if he'd offered her the sun and the stars and the moon.

He cast her a look askance, as if he sensed something of her mood. Her fear that soon enough he would be caught in Jack's web. Surely he wouldn't be stupid enough to let Jack lead him to ruin. She'd said he was clever, now she would see if she was right. Her stomach clenched. She felt like the executioner about to drop the axe. Or perhaps not. Executioners didn't care about their victims. And damn her, she did. About this one. Only this one.

'Red wine for me,' she said lightly as if he'd asked.

He beckoned a waiter.

'I'll have whisky,' Jack said at the waiter's enquiring look.

'Red wine for the lady,' Logan said. 'Ale for me, please.'

'Can't drink your own liquor?' Jack said derisively.

He shrugged. 'Make it whisky. Bring the bottle.'

Another man who couldn't resist a challenge to his manhood. She hadn't thought him such a fool as to match drink for drink with Jack. But she was wrong. Perhaps she was wrong about a lot of things. Perhaps he did deserve this lesson. And if Jack's need for power drove him away, would it not be a good thing? For him at least. Jack wouldn't be happy, which would not be a good thing for her.

The waiter pushed off through the crowds to fetch their order.

Jack pulled a box from his pocket and a pouch containing die. 'Play with these, Gilvry, or call for fresh.' He made it sound so natural. As if it would be an insult to doubt his word.

Charity pouted. 'Jack,' she admonished, picking up the die, knowing they would fall the same way each time if one didn't adjust for the shot inside. She pulled a paper-wrapped set of dice with the maker's seal still intact from her reticule. 'We should start afresh.'

Jack glared at her as if annoyed, just as they had practised, then shrugged. 'I've no objection.'

Logan raised his eyebrows. Gratitude gleamed in his eyes. Her heart squeezed painfully as she wished she wouldn't be the one to engineer his downfall. Though she'd do her best to keep it from being a complete disaster, she realised with a shock.

She gathered up the loaded die and passed the new ones to Logan. 'Check them.'

While he inspected the die, she deftly slipped Jack's inside her glove beneath the table.

For one moment, a fraction of a second as she whisked them away, she thought she saw a flash of green from beneath Logan's lashes. But, no, he was weighing the ivory, inspecting them closely. He tossed them on the green baize twice and nodded. 'Thank you, Mrs West,' he said calmly.

Jack laughed. 'Up to snuff, aren't you, Gilvry?'

He smiled sweetly at Charity. 'I should certainly hope so.'

Somehow Charity thought she saw a devil lurking in that smile. It disappeared too fast to be sure. Wise he might be in the way of business, as he had proved at dinner, he was as innocent as a babe when it came to her dark world.

Pain stopped her breath and she was grateful that the waiter chose that moment to bring their drinks.

Jack tossed his back. Apparently not to be outdone, Logan did the same. Charity sighed and wanted to shake him.

On his own head be it.

The play began. Hazard was the game of fools, yet Logan, it seemed, had the luck on his side. The money went back and forth across the table, but the pile of guineas at his elbow grew. And all the while he matched Jack in glass after glass of whisky.

She wanted to strangle him for being such a fool.

'Another bottle,' Jack called, emptying the one on the table.

Behind Jack, Growler leaned against the wall, his eyes drifting closed in boredom He'd spent too many nights like this to have much concern. But he wasn't asleep by any means. He had the instinct of a dog, one out-of-place move and he'd be alert.

Clearly feeling the effects of the drink, Logan loosened his cravat and leaned back in his chair, all muscle and bone and sleepy-eyed good cheer. The waiter delivered a bottle and two fresh glasses. He looked at her half-full glass in question. She shook her head.

More men gathered around their table. It would be a very public humiliation when it came. But at least it was mostly Jack's money he would be losing.

She steeled herself. Braced. Oh hell, she didn't want to do it.

Jack's turn. He upped the ante. Logan pushed in a pile of his guineas. Most of it he'd won from Jack.

He called a main of eight and nicked with two sixes. Winning the pot.

Now walk away, she willed. Get up and walk away. She didn't want to do this.

She shot a quick look at Jack, but the old lion remained relaxed. Oh, his tail was twitching and his large paws ready to strike, but he had not given her the signal. She wished she could stop it now before the tide turned against him and he became one of Jack's victims. But how? Jack would likely murder her if she tried anything of the sort.

'Another round,' Jack said.

Logan nodded and picked up his glass, looking at her over the rim. There was something in his eyes. Regret. Sadness. He set his glass down off kilter and it fell over and rolled towards her. Luckily it was empty.

Drunk. The idiot. And cup shot enough to show it. It would be all Jack needed.

Jack pushed all of his money into the table with a cheerful grin. 'What do you say? Double or nothing.'

Don't, her mind screamed. Leave. But even as her chest tightened she began working the die from inside her glove. Palming each one carefully.

Logan nodded, his eyes gleaming at the sight of that pile of guineas. 'Double or nothing.'

'I'll need your note,' Jack said, writing his own.

Inside she was shaking. Her throat was dry. Her palms damp. She did not want to do this.

Jack's foot came down hard on hers. His hard smile delivering the instruction. And the reminder of her task.

A small sharp twist of the base of the box and the good die would drop into the cavity below. A flirtatious kiss at the box while holding the mark's gaze, a little fumble and the loaded die would be ready to go. She had practised many times under Jack's eyes, but never been called upon to put it into practise.

Damn Logan. She had not encouraged him to play so deep. Had warned him off. And she was the one faced with a terrible choice. Him or years off her bid to freedom. Her heart raced and her hands trembled.

Inhaling deep, she held the loaded die lightly

in her palm. With her other hand she reached for the box. To her shock and horror his hand was there before her, warm, large, with long elegant fingers. He turned his palm, trapping her fingers within his. She closed her eyes briefly, half-expecting the touch of his lips, everything inside her straining towards the coming storm of sensation.

Heat blazed a trail up her arm. Her breasts tightened. She forced herself to look into his face. His eyes were bright and sharp and clear and knowing.

Frozen, she stared at him. Licked her lips. She pouted a salacious offering of bliss. 'I thought to bring you luck.'

Men around the table stirred and shifted. But not him, his gaze held hers, unblinking green.

And…oh Heaven help her. She felt the fingers of his other hand beneath the table, rolling the die around in her palm, stroking that sensitive place like a lover.

Delicious shivers ran down her spine. Her stomach fell to her feet.

He knew.

And in his eyes she saw…acceptance. And intelligence. No haze of drink. No slack-jawed drunkenness. How could he possibly be sober after all that whisky?

He leaned back with a small smile. Gestured for her to continue.

Beside her, Jack tensed. Waited for the kill.

Inside her something shattered. She didn't have a choice. She glared at Logan. 'Call.'

His smile broadened. 'A main of seven.'

She picked up the box in both hands and shook it wildly. Rattled the die in the box, making a show of blowing them a kiss for luck, and tossed them on the table where they clicked and rolled.

She did not look at them. She could only look into eyes that held misplaced forgiveness.

Jack cursed.

Logan glanced down. Shock filled his face.

She looked down, too, praying for luck, praying that the die had fallen the way she needed so he would lose honestly.

They had not. She'd thrown seven. The first seven of the evening. If she had dared exchange the die, there would have been nothing but a two. Two always lost.

Logan's gaze shot to her face. He shook his head in puzzlement, then grinned. 'I win.' He shot a look at Jack. 'My luck is in tonight.'

Jack was staring at her. 'Well, well,' he said. 'It seems you did bring him luck, colleen. But I'm not complaining.' His grin was wolfish as he looked at Logan. 'You will give me a chance to win my money back?'

That she would not stay for. She pushed to her feet. 'I've had enough for one night, if you gentlemen would excuse me. Growler, will you see me home?' And she'd take the loaded dice with her, too.

Growler pushed away from the wall. It would keep him busy. Away from Logan when he made his way home. But whether drunk, or as she now suspected, sober, luck would not help him against Growler's men should Jack set them on him.

Logan gathered up his winnings. 'I, too, have had enough for one night.'

'Come now,' Jack said in oily tones. 'The night is young. I'll offer you double or nothing on that pot too.'

'Och, no. I'll no' be taking any more of your gold. It wouldna' be fair when we are going to be in business.'

Charity swallowed the urge to laugh at the chagrin on Jack's face.

Logan turned his gaze on her. 'Don't forget your final fitting tomorrow, Mrs West. I will pick you both up at the White Horse at nine on Tuesday morning for the King's Drawing Room.' He flashed a wicked grin at Jack. 'You are required to wear a kilt.' He strolled away.

'Aye, he's got ballocks of steel all right,' Jack muttered. He looked at her. 'As do you.'

She leaned closer. 'He knew, Jack. He knew I had the other die. He felt them in my hand beneath the table.'

His brows shot up. 'Careless wench.'

'I told you, he's no fool,' she hissed. 'You wouldn't listen.'

His lips pursed. 'Aye, you told me. But you made a mull of it. You owe me.'

'Only what you lost, Jack. Not what you didn't win,' she bargained, holding his hard gaze.

He nodded slowly. 'Only what I lost. One hundred guineas.'

It was as if the floor had fallen away. Her head spun. Her stomach rebelled. She kept her smile. 'One hundred it is.'

She got up and walked away, shoulders straight, head held high and her heart bruised and trampled. Stupid. So very stupid. And Jack had played her like a fish on a line. She knew from his expression, he had expected her to fail.

Right at that moment she hated Logan Gilvry.

All she had wanted was the freedom to live a life in peace and now she'd lost it, perhaps for years, perhaps for ever. Because of him.

No. Because of her own weakness. Some

misplaced sense of sympathy she thought the past had driven away.

What game had Charity been playing with that last throw? Logan frowned. Had she planned for him to win, to drive a wedge between him and her keeper? Or had she succumbed to a fit of guilt? Either way, she had done him no favour. O'Banyon had been furious for all he'd hid his temper. And Logan, who had been prepared to lose some money, had been unable to risk a larger sum and so had been forced to leave the table a winner.

They hadn't even begun to talk business.

And he'd not heard a word from O'Banyon since. He had never felt so on edge in his life. Ian had placed a great deal of faith in him being able to negotiate this new outlet for their whisky. And he had to get it done soon, so it could be delivered long before autumn storms closed the passes and the glens.

He inserted the emerald pin Sanford had loaned him into the folds of his cravat and nodded grimly at his reflection. It would have to do. And if O'Banyon failed to come through, he'd have to find another way to reel him in. Or he'd have to tell Ian he'd made a mull of it.

He turned away from the mirror and found Sanford gazing at his kilt with a sly quirk to his lips. 'My, you're as pretty as a girl,' he said. 'I'm tempted to ask you for a dance.'

'Damned *Sassenach*,' Logan muttered, adjusting the lace at his cuffs. 'Get anywhere near me and you'll find my dirk at your throat.' He picked the knife up from the table and slipped it in his sock.

'They won't let you in armed,' Sanford observed this time with genuine laughter in his bright blue eyes.

'It's part of the dress,' Logan said. 'Same as your sword.' He looked pointedly at the young lord's scabbard. 'Clumsy thing. Mind you dinna trip over it.'

They grinned at each other and shook hands.

'Thanks for the loan of the pin,' Logan said.

'Just don't gamble it away.' He yawned languidly. 'It is a family heirloom.'

'No need. I'm verra flush in the pocket thanks to Jack O'Banyon.'

Sanford looked at him intently. 'I thought you too downy a one to play with the like of him.'

'Aye, I am. Unless it suits me.' Let the man ponder on that. The only thing was, the results hadn't been quite what he'd been expecting. It hadn't come as a surprise that O'Banyon planned to fleece him. He just should never have let Charity know he was all right with what she was about to do. He'd touched a nerve.

When he saw the regret lurking in her eyes, he'd had a strangely quixotic need to drive it away. To tell her to do what she had to do and find no blame from him. And then she'd done the opposite.

Mentally he shook his head. Lasses. He'd never understand them. Whatever game she thought she had been playing, there had been murder in Jack's eyes, when he saw the fall of the die on that last throw. And in hers, more than a touch of quickly hidden fear. Damn the man. And damn himself. If not for Tammy's wee spy at the White Horse assuring him she had come to no harm, he'd have had to fetch her away. Take a leaf out of his wild ancestors' book and toss her over his shoulder and carry her off.

And that really would have set the cat among the pigeons. If he had not done so already. Anger roiled in his gut. Anger at himself. He'd barely escaped the last trap a pretty lass had set for him. He was no' about to fall headlong into another. No matter how much he wanted her.

He twitched the lace at his throat and turned from his reflection.

'I will see you at the Palace,' Sanford said. 'It will be a dreadful squeeze. O'Banyon should be thrilled.'

He'd actually be lucky if either of them showed up today. Tammy had been watching the Irishman from afar. The man had spent the last three days inspecting McKenzie's operation while Charity, followed by O'Banyon's ruffian, Growler, had shopped and gaped at the King's assorted doings, along with the rest of the city.

Somehow Logan had to find a way to convince O'Banyon he was betting on the wrong horse if he went with McKenzie. He wasn't sure an introduction to the King passed muster, no matter what Sanford thought.

He bid Sanford farewell and strode out to the waiting coach, not entirely certain he'd find his guests prepared to go with him. But they were. The pair of them. Waiting in the lobby of the White Horse.

A quick glance proved Mrs Donaldson a miracle worker. Charity looked like every other débutante making her bows for the first time. No sign of rouge or artifice. Her luxurious amber hair was dressed in modest fashion and topped by two nodding plumes. Despite her height, and she was now taller than her escort by half a foot, she looked…regal. No duchess could look haughtier or more refined.

Or more lovely.

Yes there was definitely more to Charity West than she liked to admit. And he found himself liking her for a number of reasons. Not just because she was lovely to look at and made him feel very proud to have her on his arm. He admired her courage too. And her resilience. Odd things to admire in a woman.

O'Banyon looked thoroughly uncomfortable in his kilt. His white knees peeked from beneath drab green like shy little daisies seeing the light of day for the first time. Logan kept his face straight. 'I hope I haven't kept you waiting. The traffic is ridiculous. Carriages are already lined up at the Assembly Rooms.'

'We only just came down,' O'Banyon said. He turned to Charity. 'I thought she'd never be ready on time.'

Logan gave her a smile. Charity looked down her nose at him. Not a hint of the softness he'd come to appreciate. No doubt she had not forgiven him for revealing he wasn't fooled by their attempt to cheat. He flashed a smile. 'You look positively radiant, Mrs West. You will eclipse our local ladies.'

'I look like a horse in a circus,' she snapped, her feathers nodding with every word.

Not angry. Terrified, he realised. Why would that be? Perhaps not as resilient as he had thought after all.

'Shall we go and get this over with?' O'Banyon grumbled. 'You are sure I won't be thrown out on my ear?'

'I am sure. You have an invitation. They are

all carefully vetted by one of Scott's men, so no one will question it. Least of all our George.'

Jack took Charity's arm. Logan resisted the temptation to pull her away. If there was one thing he was really good at, it was resisting temptation. He'd had years in which to practise.

Chapter Seven

Logan had been right about it being a terrible squeeze. The drawing room was also as hot as Hades. Flanked by her escorts and waiting in the line to greet the King, Charity plied her fan with vigour and regretted being tempted by such foolishness. For giving in to the longing for the way things might have been.

In their hotel room, she'd proved to Jack she'd learned her girlhood lessons well, telling him the rules, laughingly showing him she could walk backwards despite the ridiculously long train suspended from her shoulders. Things weren't different. She'd thrown that life away

Afraid of calling attention to herself, she resisted the temptation to look about her for people she might know. There wouldn't be any, she assured herself. She'd never been out in society.

Her parents had spent most of the time in London, leaving Charity and her brothers to tutors and nannies. They had never entertained visitors of importance at their country home. Besides, even if there was someone here who had known her as a child, they would never recognise the woman. Not in a million years.

She took a deep breath to ease her rising panic and gazed at her escort.

In the teaming mass of men in kilts and the odd one or two in the court-required dress of velvet knee breeches, Logan looked gorgeous. He certainly seemed as comfortable in his kilt as he did in everyday dress. And for all his good looks, he looked as wild and rugged as the scenery she'd seen around Edinburgh. She felt proud to be at his side. And safe.

Poor Jack had a face as red as a beet. Twice she'd tapped him with her fan for pulling the kilt downwards to hide his knees.

A tall blond man detached himself from a group behind the King and headed towards them with a slightly cynical smile on his lips. Sanford. Logan's friend. He looked perfectly as ease in his court clothes, languid, bored, but there was an intensity in his eyes as his gaze took her in that gave her a sliding sensation in her stomach. A look that said he could see right through her façade. That he knew who she was.

He could not.

And then he was bowing over her hand with courtly grace and a wry twist to his lips. 'Mrs West,' he murmured. 'O'Banyon.'

Jack eyed him suspiciously.

'Lord Sanford was kind enough to have you added to the guest list,' Logan explained.

'Good of you,' Jack said grudgingly.

'Ah,' Sanford said. 'I do my best to please.'

Charity had the feeling he pleased no one but himself, but she smiled her appreciation and watched his eyes widen, but not with lust, with something that looked like recognition. A cold lump landed on her stomach. She swallowed, dreading what he might say next, but he turned to Logan. 'Did you ever see such a sight?'

Logan glanced towards the throne at the end of the room where the King was greeting his subjects, brilliant in a red kilt and glittering orders.

'There's something odd about his legs,' Logan said, frowning.

Sanford leaned closer. 'Pink tights. Whatever you do, try not to look at them. You'll go blind.' He gave a soft laugh and walked off to greet another party in the line behind them.

The torture was almost over. They were five groups from the head of the line.

Four. Three. The King was kissing the ladies' cheeks as if his life depended on it. He certainly wasn't looking at them or talking to their escorts. Thank goodness.

Now it was their turn. Heavy perfume choked the air around the King and hit the back of her throat. Oh heavens, he was indeed wearing flesh-coloured tights under his red kilt and matching plaid stocking. It took all her willpower not to stare at those obscenely large pink knees. The first gentleman of Europe leaned in and bussed her cheek, or just above it. 'So lovely,' he murmured with a kindly smile.

And that was it. She'd been introduced at a Drawing Room. An aching hot lump filled the back of her throat and burned at the back of her eyes. Tears. For the girl who had never had a chance to live the life she'd expected.

Whose fault was that? she scolded angrily. None but her own. For being silly. For believing she was loved. The heat of anger evaporated the tears as she stepped back while the two men made their obeisance.

In what felt like a blur she realised they were backing away. All the lessons of her youth paying off as she managed her train expertly, unlike several of the other ladies who had stumbled.

When she looked at Jack his face was perspiring. 'I need a drink,' he gasped.

Charity met Logan's gaze and they exchanged a look. The antechamber fell away as if they were alone, laughing at some jest only they understood. A feeling of connection she had forgotten. Something to be treasured. Yet it wasn't possible. They could not be friends. If they weren't enemies, they were still on opposite sides of a very high fence.

The expression on his face, a kind of bemusement, said he felt it too. He grinned. 'There are supposed to be refreshments somewhere.' He glanced around. 'That way.'

'Not for me,' Jack said, staring at the soldiers on duty each side of the door in discomfort. 'I'm thinking I've used up a week's worth of luck in the last ten minutes, young Gilvry. It is time I was about my own business, if you don't mind.'

The ruse they had planned that would leave her and Gilvry alone. 'Oh, Jack, must you?' she said.

'I'll have the carriage brought round,' Logan offered.

'No need, lad. I appreciate what you did for Char today. She might as well stay and enjoy it for a bit longer.'

'I'd like that,' she said, smiling at Logan who had no choice but to nod his agreement. Not that he seemed to mind. Indeed, he looked pleased as he shook hands with Jack. 'I will call on you tomorrow,' he said. 'I think it is time we wrapped up our business.'

'Past time,' Jack agreed with a broad grin and strode off.

'Why do I get the feeling he's not being honest with me?' Logan said.

Charity raised a shoulder. If she obtained the necessary information today, perhaps Jack would indeed be finished with him very shortly. She just wished she knew exactly what he was up to.

Logan led her through the archway. 'I heard they have champagne.'

'Logan,' a deep voice said from behind them. 'I didn't expect to see you here.'

Logan turned and his face broke into a smile of real pleasure. 'Mrs West, I'd like to introduce you to my brother and his wife. Lady Jenna and Niall, Lord Aleyne.'

Charity's stomach knotted. He should not be introducing her to his family. She dipped a curtsy and dared a quick look at the couple standing in front of her. The tiny auburn-haired lady with emerald eyes regarded her with lively interest. Her much taller, dark-haired, dark-eyed husband had the trace of a frown between his brows. 'Mrs West,' he said with a brief bow as his wife inclined her head.

Did his brother know with one glance what

she was? Had Logan told him? Her palms started to sweat inside her gloves. A feeling of shame twisted in her stomach. Feeling nauseous, she slanted a glance at Logan, but he seemed as he always did, cheerfully confident that whatever he did, would be all right with everyone else.

'I had no idea you were invited,' Logan was saying to his brother.

'Everyone in Scotland is invited,' Lady Aleyne said with a chuckle. 'As long as they came in their kilts.' She gave Logan a frown. 'And you would have known we were invited, had you bothered to call.'

'Leave the man alone,' Lord Aleyne said. 'He's staying with Sanford. Two scapegraces together, I should think.'

'You wrong me, Niall,' Logan said. 'I'm in Edinburgh on business.'

His sister-in-law's glance flickered to Charity and back to Logan. 'But there is time for enjoyment too, I am sure. Perhaps you would like to bring Mrs West to dinner?'

Her husband's eyes widened a fraction, but his expression remained friendly, if a little strained. After all, she was not the sort of woman he would want hobnobbing with his wife. Clearly Lady Aleyne led a sheltered life, if she hadn't already divined the truth.

Still, even his slight reaction stung. Charity gave her very best imitation of regret, smiling archly through the stab of rejection. 'It is so kind of you,' she cooed, 'but I'm only in Edinburgh for a few days and every moment is spoken for.' She fluttered her lashes at Logan.

Logan recoiled.

Lady Aleyne looked quite disappointed.

'Another time, perhaps,' Lord Aleyne said with a bow, but the look he sent Logan was one of an older brother ready to knock some sense into a younger. Defending his wife, no doubt.

Another time would never come, of course. The man would impart the necessary knowledge to his wife in private.

She smiled a seductive smile at Logan, tucked her arm through his and lowered her voice to a throaty purr. 'If I recall correctly, you offered me something to assuage my hunger.'

Lord Aleyne stiffened. 'Good day, Mrs West.' He took his wife's arm and walked swiftly away.

A faint crease between his brows, Logan's gaze followed his brother, then he turned to her with an easy smile. 'Come on, refreshments this way.'

The earlier glow faded, replace by a chilly draught across her skin. She wondered if at any moment someone would appear at their sides with a request that they leave. She couldn't bear it. For herself or for Logan. 'I would like to go back to my hotel,' she said, keeping her voice low and her face placid.

'Already?' he said. 'You don't have to take any notice of Niall, he's naught but a stuffed shirt.'

So he had also felt his brother's rebuff. Aleyne was right, though, in not wanting his family tainted by her presence. 'We did what we set out to do. I made my bows to the King and now it is time to leave.'

The irritation in his face fled, replaced by another expression. Pity? 'Charity, you are as good as any of these people here.'

'Stop it,' she said through gritted. 'Stop trying to pretend I'm something I'm not. If you don't like me the way I am, then leave me be.' She turned and headed for the way out.

She felt him hard on her heels, let him catch up and take her arm, because people were looking and the last thing she wanted was to create a disturbance and draw more attention.

A footman hurried off to find their carriage.

'I'm sorry,' he said in her ear.

Hearing the sincerity in his voice only made the ache around her heart worse. She fought against the pain and managed a brief smile. 'No apology needed.' He could not help being a man she liked more than she should. A man who had the power to hurt her by treating her like a lady. 'Why don't you stay? I am quite content to return to my hotel alone.'

He frowned at her obvious dismissal. 'If that is your preference.'

It wasn't her preference, but if she stayed she would be forced to find a way to get the answers to Jack's questions. And right now, she just couldn't bear the thought. 'I find I have a headache.'

At once, he was the soul of solicitation. Escorting her from the room, calling for their carriage, finding her a quiet place to sit while they waited.

She felt such a fraud. But the thought of what Jack would say when she returned without answers really did make her head thump unpleasantly.

When he finally aided her into the carriage, she was very aware of his touch, his careful draping of her skirts. The gown that had cost him a fortune for two seconds with her King. He'd made an old dream come true and she had to say something. 'Thank you, Logan. For today.'

She meant it. She really did. Even if she had been terrified out of her skin.

He grinned then, the charming boyish smile that lit his eyes and turned her limbs to molten liquid. 'My pleasure, *leannan*.' He took her hand, turned it over and pressed his lips to the palm of the same hand he'd kissed at the inn. 'Feel better soon.'

He closed the door.

Betrayed by the race of her pulse, her fingers curled inwards. As if she could keep and hold on to the lingering sensation of his touch. And what had he said? Lee—something? And in such seductive tones.

Really, she had to put a stop to this foolish mooning. Right now. Immediately. Yet she could not keep from watching him, as the carriage pulled away.

How would she ever explain her weakness to Jack?

'What's this, then?' Jack's tone was harsh with disapproval.

Reclining on the sofa, Charity lifted one end of the soothing cold cloth covering her eyes and temples and turned her gaze on Jack, hoping he could not see guilt in her expression. 'What is what?'

He waved a disgusted hand. 'You. Lying there. Have you got my information so quickly then?'

'I have the megrims.' She swung her feet to the floor.

'Damn it, Char. What did ye learn?'

'I know he is staying with Sanford,' she snapped. She pressed her fingers to the ache above her eyes. 'I do not yet have the address.'

'You were supposed to discover the route he takes to cross the border. One village, one cross-road was all I asked. It is little enough. Why are you here if you have nothing of value?'

'What has happened?'

He glared at her. 'Nothing has happened. That's the trouble, isn't it? You are no help. Growler lost track of him after that thrice-cursed nonsense you dragged me to and now I hear his men have slipped away.'

'Oh.' No wonder he was angry. Clearly it did not do to underestimate the young Scot. A dark suspicion entered her mind. Perhaps Logan was toying with her, just as he seemed to be toying with Jack. A small pang squeezed her heart. Hurt, when she ought to be glad he had more sense than to trust her.

'Why is the route he takes so important?' she asked 'Isn't it enough to know he can supply what you want?'

He put one hand on the arm of the sofa, the other he wrapped around her throat. He squeezed. Not enough to hurt, but enough to make breathing difficult. Blood rushed loudly in her ears. She clawed at his hand, gasping. 'Stop,' she croaked.

He released her. 'Do you see how easy it would be to part you from your breath when you deliberately defy me?'

She rubbed at her neck. 'I could do nothing when I could scarcely see from the pain behind my eyes. I will get your information.'

'My head aches,' he mimicked. 'And what use are ye to me, if you are going to have a headache.'

People were either of use to Jack, or they were not. Her aching throat dried. A panicked tremble in her hands made her clench them together in her lap. She forced a lazy smile. 'Be reasonable, Jack. If I question him too closely, he'll either lie or he'll avoid me. You know he will. And if you think he was going to discuss his smuggling in Holyrood Palace surrounded by the King's men, you've gone daft.'

'Daft, is it? He raised a fist, looming over her.

Instinctively, she flinched. And cursed her weakness when his lips curled in a grim smile.

'You had your orders,' he said in a low menacing voice. 'You failed. Give me one good reason why I shouldn't take my fist to you.'

His temper was hanging by a thread. She could see it in his bloodshot eyes. Her heart raced uncomfortably fast with fear, but if she showed it, he'd carry out his threat. She lifted her chin and gave him a scornful stare. 'Because each time we meet, he tells me a little bit more. You will ruin my hard work with your impatience.'

He stepped back. 'Get it done, Char. Do it and I'll forgive you the debt from the other night.'

Blankly she stared at him, her blood running colder than ice. If he was prepared to pay so much for this information, then there was more going on here than he had told her. And it boded ill for the Gilvrys. But she knew better than to ask any more questions. It would just make him suspicious. She smiled slowly. 'Now that is an offer I cannot refuse.'

He sank down into a chair, his gaze scanning her face, the fingers of his right hand clenching and flexing. 'I was beginning to think you'd forgotten who keeps the wolf from your door.' He gave her a very wolf-like smile. 'I was thinking of sending you back to Miss Lucy's.'

The brothel. 'I'd sooner starve.'

'I can arrange for you to get your wish.'

He would, too. See her back in the brothel, or starving on the streets. They'd argued before, about small things, little bits of dignity she needed to keep herself sane, and sometimes he'd let her have her way. But she'd never stood against him about something he really wanted.

Something he'd eventually get, with her help or without. 'Will you promise me he'll come to no harm?'

Jack's fingers stilled. 'Bargaining with me, is it? He won't want you when it's over.'

'Kind of you to tell me something I already know.'

He laughed. 'Oh, colleen, sometimes you surprise me. All right. Have it your way, if you're fond of the lad. I've no particular beef with him—besides that, he's as slippery as an eel. I pay you nothing and he gets away with a whole skin. I hope he's worth it.'

She'd just given away a great deal of money. The pain at her temples intensified. She was a fool. And there was no guarantee Jack would keep his word. He might, if it suited him. And right now she didn't see any alternative. 'Agreed.'

'When are ye seeing him again?' Jack asked.

'On Friday. At the ball.'

'Three days hence? He'll scarcely remember your name by then.'

She glared at him. 'That I very much doubt. Besides, it is all arranged.'

He grunted and picked up *The Edinburgh Gazette* from the side table and scanned the headlines. He leaned forwards to shed better light on the words. 'Here. This is it.'

'What is it?'

'The King is to accept the keys to the Castle the day after tomorrow. There's to be a procession. Tell Gilvry you want to see it.'

More processions. She held back a groan. 'I will send him a note, through his brother.'

'Do that, pet.' He stood up, leaning over her, the smell of whisky and smoke filling her nostrils as he gave her a narrow smile. 'Take care of that headache of yours or you'll be losing your looks. And what use will I have for ye then?'

The threat sent spiders crawling down her spine.

'Ah, puss, don't look so worried. Can ye not tell it is jesting, I am? We make a very good team, you and I. Why spoil a good thing?'

Fear tightened her chest at the possessive expression on his face. Thank heavens she'd never indicated by word or deed she was saving her money so she could leave. When she had enough, she would find a way to disappear.

'I won't let you down, Jack.'

'See you don't. And, Char, you will do whatever is required to pry the information loose, understand me. Anything at all. I suggest you bring him back here, once the procession is over. I'll make myself conveniently scarce. A couple of days' shooting on the moors should be more than enough time.'

A chill breeze blew through the room, but not because of what he was asking, but because she wasn't sure who would be the seducer and who the seduced.

Logan put down her note with a sense of relief. He'd half-thought she had decided to be done with him, after Niall had been so rude. He looked at Sanford. 'Can you find me a good place from which to observe this damned parade this afternoon?' He glanced out of the window. 'Somewhere out of the rain.'

Sanford put down his paper, picked up his coffee cup and leaned back in his chair, eyeing him with speculation. Lord, what a dandy the fellow was with red dragons writhing over his blue-silk dressing gown. A man needed blinders to face such a sight first thing in the morning. Logan tried not to blink.

'Got you at her beck and call, has she?' the young nobleman said languidly. 'I didn't think you were in the petticoat line. I thought you were having too much fun breaking the law.'

'It is no' about her.'

'Really?'

Disbelief in a single word. 'O'Banyon keeps foisting her off on me.'

'You can't rescue her if she doesn't want to be saved.'

The sarcasm in the other man's tone stung. 'I'm no' a fool. I'll hold out a hand, but it is up to her whether she takes it or not.'

Sanford shook his head wearily. 'Determined to learn the hard way, are you? Her sort of women like their trade rough. Don't say I didn't warn you, when she stomps her pretty feet all over your ego.'

He couldn't agree. The way she'd responded to his kiss told a different story. If she'd pushed him away afterwards, it was out fear, not lack of interest. He'd seen the hunted look in her gaze. The same look he'd seen on men's faces when cornered by the militia. But he wasn't entirely sure what she feared. If it was Jack, she hid it well.

'So can you help me with this or not?'

'It's your skin. Yes. I'll send word later.' On that he got up and retired to his chamber. It would be four hours before he emerged from his *toilette* and headed out for his duties. In the meantime, Logan had a business to run. And Archie had sent word he was in need of another delivery. The trick would be keeping McKenzie and O'Banyon's men looking the wrong way.

The spot Sanford had found for them had a view of the procession and the ceremony of the keys. Logan stared up at the castle wall where the King had stood in the rain and waved his hat to the people of Edinburgh. He had gone now and the people in the streets were dispersing. Seeking dryness and warmth. 'Have you seen enough?' he asked Charity.

'It was quite a pageant,' she said from beneath her umbrella. 'I must thank you for changing your plans to bring me at such short notice.'

'I had no plans, apart from wanting to see you again.'

A startled look crossed her face. Almost dumbfounded. Good. He had decided that there was only one way to deal with Mrs Charity West. Absolute honesty. And while she was digesting that he would impart the rest. 'I want to kiss you again and see if what I think happened at the inn was real, or merely a figment of my imagination.'

'That is all you want?' she asked, her eyes dark and full of heat.

Anger or desire. He tossed a coin. 'No,' he said baldly. 'I want more. A great deal more. But I am prepared to take it one step at a time. For a while at least.'

The look she gave him was far from conciliatory. The shield wall was up and the spears were out. But he came from a long line of warriors and would not back away from a protest of a wee bit of a lass. Not until he knew for sure that she meant what she said.

'You are a fool, Mr Gilvry.'

A warning. But there was also a glimmer of laughter in her eyes, he thought. A good sign surely.

'I am no' asking anything of you, Mrs West. Except to invite you to accompany me to my brother Niall's house for dinner.'

Another look of surprise. Good. Many a battle was won by surprise. And he intended to scale the battlements and win the war.

'You can't be serious,' she said. 'Lord Aleyne made it quite clear he heartily disapproves of me.'

'He does this for my sake. Because I asked him. And besides, Jenna is looking forward to meeting you again.'

A look he could not read passed across her face. 'I don't know,' she said with a tremor in her voice. She turned to head into the drawing room behind them. He had never seen her quite so flustered. He wanted to take her in his arms, soothe her ruffled feathers, but she would not thank him. Not yet. She was as skittish as the deer that roamed the hills. It would take time to convince her to trust that he meant her no harm. O'Banyon had done his job well. And if she ever did, he would keep his wits sharp. Because he certainly wasn't about to trust her. He could still remember how Maggie had smiled at him as she sat on his knee and giggled as if he was someone special. Pretending to be shy and modest, while all the time she was swiving his best friend.

He'd almost paid for that piece of stupidity with a lifetime of misery with a woman for whom he had lost all respect. He certainly wasn't going to make the same mistake again.

He led her down the stairs and into their carriage. Once safely ensconced inside, she sat twisting the strings of her reticule around her fingers. He took her hand and she looked into his face. Her eyes were dark, clouded.

'Will you accept the invitation, then?'

She took a deep breath and straightened her shoulders. Clearly a decision made. 'All right.'

Now why did he have the feeling that was too easy? 'You may say what you wish to me, but you will have a care with my sister-in-law, aye?'

Her eyes widened. 'Why, Mr Gilvry, having second thoughts already?'

'I am letting you know I am trusting you to behave like the lady I know you to be.'

The surprise returned to her face and then

she chuckled a little, her eyes full of genuine amusement. 'You do like to live dangerously.'

She certainly knew how to make him worry. Even so, he was looking forward to it.

Chapter Eight

The streets of New Town had a completely different atmosphere to its ancient neighbour, Charity noticed. Neat squares. Broad streets laid out in formal patterns, like the houses themselves. They pulled up at one such town house and Logan opened the door and leaped down.

She took his hand and stepped down, looking about her. A prickling sensation stirred at the back of her neck and travelled down her shoulders. The sense of eyes watching. Eyes that would report back to Jack on her movements. Making sure she kept to her side of the bargain.

Jack was leaving nothing to chance.

The thought stopped her breath. Never before had she felt his distrust so strongly. Did she fear she'd betray him? What other instructions had Jack given her watchers? A cold dread solidified in the pit of her stomach. A knowledge that if she didn't obtain the information he wanted tonight, Jack would take matters into his own hands and her bargain with him would no longer stand. He might decide to serve Logan some mischief as part of his price for her failure.

He was probably wise. She really wished she had never set foot in Scotland. And hated the idea of getting close to Logan for such an underhanded purpose. But it was only information. Nothing dangerous.

She swallowed and smiled at her escort. 'Your brother must be very successful.'

He glanced up at the house with pride in his face. 'Aye, he is.'

The door opened before they could knock. They were obviously expected. The footman who bowed them in took their outer raiment. She smoothed her skirts, hoping Logan would approve of her gown. The fichu in the neck provided a degree of modesty, as did the shawl over her shoulders.

'Don't worry to see us up, Morrison,' Logan said. 'I can find my way.' He took her arm and they mounted the stairs to the first floor. A drawing-room door stood open in welcome.

'Here we are,' Logan sang out as they entered the elegant space.

Blue walls, white paint, furniture upholstered

in stripes and chintz. A place designed to impress, but also to welcome, Charity decided as the tall lean Baron Aleyne moved from his wife's side to greet them.

'Welcome to my home, Mrs West.' His bow was formal and his expression cool, but not hostile.

Relief allowed her to breathe again. 'My lord.' She dipped her curtsy.

Aleyne stood aside and gestured to his wife seated on the sofa. 'You know my wife, Lady Aleyne.'

The Baroness held out a hand and Charity moved forwards to shake it. 'How nice to meet you again, Lady Aleyne.'

The small red-haired lady dimpled. 'Why dear Mrs West, I am delighted Logan was able to persuade you to join us for a family dinner. We see so little of him when he is in Edinburgh. Please…' she patted the sofa beside her '…do be seated.'

Charity settled herself beside her hostess, the welcome warming her from the inside out. The warmth of family. Something she had not experienced in a very long time. Warmth to which she was not entitled. Something churned in her stomach: guilt. She should not have agreed to this, but, oh, how she had wanted to feel accepted. To be treated as if she belonged to this world again.

Logan bowed over the small lady's hand. On his face there was genuine affection. 'I come as often as I can, Jenna,' he said as he straightened. 'You know full well the Laird keeps me busy with business.'

'It is Rabbie who pines for you the most,' his sister-in-law said with a smile. She turned to Jenna. 'Rabbie is our son. Named for my father. He's just passed his first birthday and is a very adventurous young man. Like his uncle.' She gave Logan a roguish smile.

'Now, Jenna,' her husband said with obvious fondness in his smile, 'there is nothing more dull than tales of other people's children. You'll have Mrs West yawning with fatigue before she has been here half an hour.'

'No, indeed, Lady Aleyne,' Charity said, amused by their banter. 'I like children, I assure you, although they are very much a novelty in my life.' She hesitated, realising how much of the truth she had spoken and how much of herself she had unconsciously revealed. She glanced at Logan, testing his reaction to such a revelation, but he did not seem to notice as he had picked up a book lying open on a table and was leafing through it with a crease between his brows. '*Parliamentary Process?* It sounds exciting.'

'It is,' his brother said, 'if you are interested in creating laws and no' breaking them. Can I offer you a glass of ratafia, Mrs West? Or perhaps you would prefer sherry.'

'I'll take a dram,' Lady Aleyne said swiftly and smiled at Charity. 'It is traditional in Scotland to welcome old friends and new with whisky. Do you like our national drink, Mrs West?'

'It is certainly popular in London, my lady,' Charity said, non-committally.

Lady Aleyne laughed. 'You are nearly as political as my husband. No need to haver, Mrs West. Please. I grew up on the stuff, but it is not to everyone's taste. Feel free to state your preference.'

Lady Aleyne was a breath of fresh air. Despite Charity's desire not to encroach on their kindness, she felt drawn to the young woman. Had things been different, they might have been friends. But they were not. And really Logan had been wrong to bring her here. Lord Aleyne knew it, even if his wife did not.

But she was here now and she could not very well throw their hospitality in their faces. If she walked out, she would no doubt burn her bridges with Logan. Not something that would serve her purpose. 'Then I would love a dram,' she said with a smile at the way the unfamiliar word felt on her tongue. 'If it is from Dunross.'

'Aye, it is,' Lord Aleyne said. 'No finer whisky in all of Scotland, even if I do say so myself.'

She took her glass and, when they were all served, Aleyne offered a toast. 'Family before all.'

At her puzzled look, Lady Jenna explained. 'It is our family motto.'

Would that her family had a similar one. A sadness she had not felt for a long time dampened her spirits. Ridiculous. She had no room for regret, or patience for it either. It did not one scrap of good.

They downed their drinks in one swallow. She did the same. The whisky was as smooth as hot silk sliding down her throat. Jack would be a fool to buy from McKenzie.

'How long will you be in Edinburgh, Mrs West?' Lord Aleyne asked, putting his glass down on the table beside the book. He sat down on the chair opposite, his gaze direct and thoughtful. Was he wondering how soon she would be gone from his brother's life?

'I'm not sure, my lord.'

'Did you come because of the King's visit?' Lady Aleyne enquired.

She glanced up at Logan still standing, his body seeming too large, too full of energy for the cool quiet room, yet he did not look in the least uncomfortable. She turned back to Lady Aleyne. 'The King's visit was part of the reason.'

'Your husband does not accompany you?' Lady Aleyne asked.

Charity suppressed a wince. 'My husband passed away a long time ago.'

'Oh, you poor thing,' the baroness said. 'I am so sorry. Do you have children?'

An interview for the position of wife? A quake of shock shuddered in her bones. 'No,' she said weakly. 'No children.' From the look on the Baron's face, he was not at all happy about this turn of the conversation, but was too polite to put a stop to it. As for Logan, he was watching her with interest, judging her reactions like a panther watching his prey.

'Mrs West is here with a business associate looking into the purchase of Dunross whisky for a gentleman's club in London,' Logan said.

Surprised by his intervention, she gave him a quick smile. 'Le Chien Rouge,' she said. 'Perhaps you have heard of it, Lord Aleyne?'

'It has been pointed out to me, Mrs West,' the baron said in a tone that said he wished it had not.

'How very interesting,' Lady Aleyne said, her eyes bright. 'I find a woman in business fascinating.' She must have seen something in Charity's expression, because she made a slight gesture with one hand. 'No, truly. I have always held that a woman's intellect is equal to a man's.'

Her husband gave her a rueful look. 'It is a fact I would have trouble disputing, my love.' He raised his glass in a small toast and there was deep affection in the couple's exchange of glances.

'And what role do you play in the business, Mrs West?' Lady Aleyn asked.

'Mrs West is what one might call a sleeping partner,' Logan said quickly.

Aleyne choked on his whisky and his brother shot him a warning stare.

'Her interest is financial,' Logan explained.

'An investor, then,' Lady Aleyne said, appearing not to notice her husband's struggle to gain his breath.

It was as good an explanation as any other. Charity had certainly invested a good deal of her time on Jack's behalf. She nodded and smiled, not wishing to cause her host an apoplexy by going into the detail of what she did for a living even if it wasn't as bad as what Lord Aleyne imagined.

The gentleman in question set down his

glass. 'And what is your opinion of our country now you have been here for a few days?' A neat change of topic. One Charity gratefully accepted.

'I am struck how different it is to the countryside of England with which I am most familiar,' she said. 'Quite starkly beautiful, but somewhat overwhelming. I can only imagine how it must be in wintertime.'

'Oh, aye,' Logan said. 'It is a harsh land then, to be sure. But if you want stark beauty you should go further north.'

'Do you plan a visit to Dunross, Mrs West?' Lady Aleyne asked.

Charity gave a regretful shake of her head. 'There will not be time. We must return to London very soon. It took long enough to get to Edinburgh. The roads in this part of the country make travel very slow. I am assuming they are no better to the north.'

'Worse,' Aleyne said with a grimace. 'It is no wonder the King came by sea. You should have done the same, I am thinking.'

'My associate does not care for sea travel.' After his experience of the Irish Sea, Jack always swore he would never again set foot on a ship. But this talk of roads and travel played very nicely into her reason for spending this time with Logan. It seemed almost too good to be true and she would have to step very carefully if she was to make the most of it.

'Is that how you plan to transport your whisky to London?' she asked. 'By sea, since the roads are so bad?'

Lord Aleyne chuckled. 'Not roads. Road. There is only one. But although it is dreadful, I doubt ships are an option.'

Logan lifted a shoulder. 'It might have done in the past, but these days there are too many excise officers roaming the seas. Without a war to fight, sailors need to do something. No, it is safer to go overland.'

'But how would that work in winter? In such rugged countryside as you describe? Are there secret paths through the hills?'

She held her breath, wondering how much he would say.

His expression shuttered. 'Any Scot can travel anywhere in his own country, at any time of year, Mrs West. It is how we have survived.'

And that was as much as he was going to say. For now. But it was an opening she would make good use of later. When he took her home and she invited him up to her chamber.

The footman who had let them in scratched at the door. 'Dinner is served, my lord.'

Aleyne rose and brought his wife to her feet. 'Let us eat. And you will give us impressions of

Edinburgh and its displays of loyalty over dinner, Mrs West.'

Logan helped her to rise and placed her hand on her sleeve. 'I don't know about you,' he murmured in her ear, 'but I am famished after all that fresh air this afternoon.'

Charity nodded, but didn't think she could eat a bite. This family had admitted her into their midst, made her feel more welcome than she would ever have expected and she had nothing on her mind but betrayal.

Guilt was a heavy weight on her shoulders and a hard lump in her stomach. But she had done all she could to ameliorate her intentions by convincing Jack not to harm Logan. At least not physically. It would certainly teach Logan not to be so trusting in future. A lesson everyone needed to learn, surely?

So now she was trying to make herself feel good about what she was doing? She wasn't. From the roiling sensation in her stomach, it wasn't working.

As dinner progressed, Logan could not help watching the beautiful woman on the opposite side of the table. The barriers were higher than ever, tonight. The cool smiles. Manners so polite he could have cut them with his dirk. The adroit turning of questions of her into questions of her own. Those questions about whisky delivery had been quite pointed, he thought. But not necessarily unexpected.

None of it troubled him in the least. Nor did the attraction he felt. He had it well under control. No. It was what he saw behind the mask she presented to the world that gave him pause. It wasn't fear, precisely. It was the sort of vulnerability he'd only seen when approaching an animal caught in a trap. Anger. And the knowledge there was no escape.

He glanced at his sister-in-law. Jenna might be willing to help. She'd shown herself to be a woman who was prepared to forgive the past transgressions of others. At least, as long as no harm came to those she cared about. Perhaps an offer of decent work, if Niall would allow it, would get Charity away from O'Banyon. Of all of his brothers, Niall was the one least likely to bend. And who could blame him? Jenna was a treasure well worth protecting.

Besides, no matter how he tried, he couldn't envisage Charity accepting a position as anything so lowly as a maid.

He would have to think of something else. But what?

Mistress?

The thought sent a hot jolt low in his belly.

He had money enough from his winnings

the other night to keep her for a while. But he found the idea of keeping a mistress distasteful. It seemed to him that if you liked a woman well enough to keep her in style, you liked a woman well enough to offer her marriage. And finding and marrying the right woman was a good thing. He saw that from watching his brothers and their wives. When he found the right woman, a woman of worth that he could respect, he wouldn't hesitate.

A man would have to be blind to think Charity West would make a good wife. In her case, a man would have to be thinking with a part of him unconnected to his brain.

Although the thought of leaving her to return to London with O'Banyon was not sitting well anywhere inside him. It was something he would discuss with her later. When they left here. But whatever they agreed upon, he did not want it ruining the bargain with O'Banyon. That would be the sort of mistake Ian would not tolerate.

The servants removed the cloth and brought the decanter and glasses.

'We will leave you gentlemen to your dram, then,' Jenna said. 'Please don't be too long joining us for tea in the drawing room. We do not keep late hours, Mrs West. Rabbie still wakes me in the night.' Jenna rose to her feet.

Niall and he followed suit. His brother grinned at his wife. 'Experience tells me you will be asleep before the tea tray arrives.' He picked up the decanter. 'Why don't we all adjourn to the drawing room? I'll bring this along for Logan.'

Clearly he did not want to leave Charity alone with his wife. He wondered what Niall would think if he knew Logan was thinking of rescuing her from O'Banyon. 'I'd just as soon have tea.'

They followed the ladies to the drawing room where Jenna seated Charity beside her and poured tea for them all.

'I hope you will not be disappointed by our Assembly Rooms tomorrow,' Jenna said, curiosity rampant in her expression. 'I understand it is nowhere near as fashionable as Almack's in London.'

'I have never been to Almack's,' Charity said calmly. 'It was kind of Mr Gilvry to arrange tickets for me and my business partner. As far as comparisons go, I will not be of much value, I am afraid.'

Jenna waved off the apology. 'It is of no consequence. I was curious, that was all.'

Niall grimaced. 'Once I am a Member of Parliament, my love, you will have your fill of Almack's and any other delights London has to offer, if that is your wish.'

'Have you been elected?' Charity asked. 'Or will you take a seat in the Lords?'

'The Aleyne peerage is one of the few held through the crown,' Jenna explained. 'Niall has not yet taken his seat. He has been too busy heretofore establishing his practice, but we hope to go next Season. Will I like London, do you think?'

'It is not so very different from Edinburgh, as far as I can tell in so short a time.' Charity said.

'London is much bigger,' Logan said.

'You have visited?' Charity asked.

'Several times. The last time I stayed with Sanford.'

An expression of disapproval crossed his sister-in-law's face. She had taken an instant dislike to the languid English lord, calling him a wastrel. A view shared by Ian. Both he and Niall had been surprised by Jenna's unusual lack of generosity.

'He took me about,' Logan continued. 'Showed me some of the sights. Vauxhall. The Tower. Covent Garden. White's.' He shook his head at Mrs West. 'Not the Chien Rouge, I'm afraid.'

'Perhaps next time,' she said with a smile, but something in her voice said she hoped not.

A scratch at the door and a rather harried young woman appeared in the doorway.

'Why, Carrie, what is it?' Jenna said. 'Is something wrong?'

'It's Master Rab, my lady. He's fussin' somethin' awful. You said I should tell you if he woke.'

'Poor little fellow,' Jenna said. 'He's cutting another tooth.' She looked at Charity. 'Would you like to meet him?'

Say yes, Logan silently urged. If anything would strengthen his sister-in-law's liking for someone, it was admiration for her son and heir.

Charity hesitated, then straightened her shoulders, as if preparing to face some unpleasant duty. 'Yes. Yes, of course. I would love to see him.' She looked at Logan and he saw appeal in the depths of her eyes. 'Then we really must go.'

'Aye, we must,' he agreed, concerned. She had said she liked children, and while much of what she had said had been somewhat elusive, he had not thought that was a lie. And yet, he didn't know, did he? Not really.

Dutifully they quietly left the room behind the Aleynes. At the bottom of the stairs, he held her back for a moment, looking down into her face. Seeing the shadows in her expression, he murmured, 'Are you sure you want to do this? I can make our excuses and we can leave now.'

'No. I said I would visit the child, so I will. But then we really should go.'

And he learned something new about her. She kept her word. For once he felt respect. Given the life she led, it was a surprising discovery. What that meant in its entirety, he wasn't quite sure, since he did not know what promises she had given O'Banyon. He would no doubt soon find out. He took her arm and followed silently up the stairs behind his family.

Before they reached the top his nephew's cries were loud and clear. The little chap had a fine pair of lungs as he'd heard more than once. In the nursery, Niall picked up his son, patting his back while his mother stood behind him, peering into her little boy's drooling open mouth. 'Oh, I know, pet. It hurts.'

The nanny handed her an ivory ring on a silver handle. 'He keeps throwing it on the floor, my lady.'

Rab caught sight of him and Charity, blinked and stopped crying.

'Ah, I see you have discovered we have company,' his father said.

Rab had reddish-coloured hair like his mother, but was a solid young lad already showing signs of the square chin from the Gilvry side. Logan held out his hands and the child leaned towards him. He plucked him free of his brother's grip and held him in the crook of his arm so Charity could see him better.

He gazed at her, blinking like an owl, and shoved his thumb in his mouth.

'I should invite you up here more often, Logan,' Jenna said, gently stroking her son's cheek. 'If you can silence him so easily.'

'It is Mrs West who has him enthralled,' Logan said. He held the child out to her and she took him in her arms.

'He's beautiful,' Charity whispered with one of those daft smiles women got around babes. All the hard edges dissolved before his eyes and his breath caught in his throat. He didn't think he'd seen anything in his life that made his heart contract with such a sweet ache.

'He's a lot like my father,' Jenna whispered. 'A true Aleyne.'

'There is a lot of Gilvry in him, too,' Niall objected.

Charity glanced from one parent to the other. 'He seems to have a lot of both of you.'

His mother laughed. 'Very tactful. But at least he is built like his father and not a shrimp like me.'

The little lad rubbed his eyes with his knuckles. Jenna touched his forehead with the flat of her hand. 'He feels a little warm, but I do not think he's feverish.' The boy reached for her. 'I think he wants a wee bit of comfort. I'll feed him for a while and see if I can persuade him to sleep a while longer.' She took Rabbie from Charity's arms.

'We will leave you to it,' Logan said with a half-horrified look at his brother.

Niall was too busy gazing fondly at his wife to notice. He came to himself and gave them an apologetic smile and ushered them out of the nursery. 'I'm sorry to cut our evening short. Nanny or no, that young man seems to take up a great deal of our time.'

'He's a lovely child,' Charity said. 'You are fortunate. I thank you for your hospitality, this evening.'

'Don't bother to show us out,' Logan said. 'I know the way.'

Their hats and gloves were produced by the footman when they arrived in the downstairs hall. Logan helped her into her wrap and donned his hat and gloves. The footman went to open the front door.

'Wait,' Logan said. 'We are leaving through the back.'

'What?' Charity said. 'Why?'

'I arranged for the carriage to meet us behind the mews.'

It sounded reasonable and plausible. So why did she have this odd feeling of danger? A prickling in her scalp. It didn't make any sense. Not once in Logan's company had she felt a morsel of fear. He certainly wasn't anything like Jack or the men he employed. Those men did make her skin crawl from time to time. If she let them.

With a quick breath, she pulled herself together. He ushered her down the passageway to a back room. A sitting room with French doors that led out into a small walled garden at the back of the house.

Logan turned the key and opened the doors. He turned to the footman standing ready behind them. 'Lock the doors behind us.'

The young man touched his forelock as if it was all in a day's work. An everyday occurrence. 'Do you usually leave this way?' she asked as he held her hand and walked her down the path to a gate at the back.

'I stable my horse back here when I visit.'

She relaxed. Of course. That would explain it. The coachman would naturally bring the horses back here. They passed through the gate. The mews were on the other side of the narrow alley. It was not the dirty alleyways of London's St Giles, but a spotless lane for the town houses' private use. To her surprise, instead of entering the stable block, Logan ushered her along the alley into the next street, turning away from the Aleynes's property and into another laneway.

'Where are we going?'

'To my lodgings. With Sanford.' he said. 'It is but a few steps from here.'

Her heart raced. A strange heartrending feeling of excitement mixed with fear. He was taking her home with him. They were to be alone together. As he must have planned all along. The visit to his family had dulled her wits. Made her complacent. Still, the outcome was exactly what she had wanted. What Jack had demanded. Apart from the fact that they were not supposed to go to his rooms. It would hardly make a difference whose rooms they went to, she supposed. And this way she would be able to tell Jack exactly where he was staying.

She looked about her. There were no eyes watching them, she was sure of it. They were likely at the front of the town house, expecting his carriage to collect them at the front door.

'Where is your carriage?' she asked breathless as he hurried her along, keeping close to the wall, making use of the shadows cast by the lanterns at each gate they passed.

'In front of my brother's house. He will stay

there until around one in the morning, then return to the livery.'

And Growler would have no idea where she was. The sense of freedom was almost heady. Until reality brought her back to earth. Jack would be furious at her disappearance. And she would have to tell him and Growler where she had gone. Freedom would be very short-lived.

And whatever happened, she must come back with the information Jack needed.

Her heart sank.

She'd enjoyed this evening more than she cared to admit. The Aleynes were nice people and listening to Logan talk with his brother, and watching him as he teased and joked, had been like entering another world. It would be wonderful if she could forget all about Jack and his instructions. But she didn't dare. Not if she wanted to be sure he wouldn't do something terrible to Logan.

The food she had eaten at dinner suddenly felt like a cold hard lump in her stomach. 'Is it much further?'

'Just a few steps more, lass.' He slowed his steps to allow her to catch her breath.

A few yards further along the alley, he stopped. 'This is it.' He opened a gate. and pulled her through to the back of another house. A larger version of the one they had just left from the size of the walled garden and what she could see of the structure ahead of her.

At least this would be a feather in her cap. Growler had been unable to discover Sanford's lodgings after days of watching both men. The nauseous feeling got worse, but there was nothing she could do. She had to have something to tell Jack. And not even that would be enough.

He unlocked a side door to the house and they crept into a dimly lit narrow passageway running alongside a set of stairs leading up. 'I see I'm one of the first home tonight,' he murmured softly, picking up an unlit candlestick from a collection set out on a table and lighting it from the wall sconce above. 'This way.'

Half-turning as he walked up, he guided her up the stairs and along another hallway with an array of closed doors, each one with a polished brass knob and a number. He stopped at number four, pulled out a key and let her in.

She stepped into what was obviously a single man's domain. Heavy comfortable furniture in front of a hearth equipped with a crane for boiling a pot, a griddle and an array of toasting forks.

'Let me take your wrap.' He relieved her of her coat and bonnet and gloves and hung them on a stand near the door.

She looked around. There was a small table

by the window with two chairs facing across it. Idly crossing the room, she pulled back the closed curtain a fraction and glanced out. The dying sun threw dark shadows into the street. She could see nothing but the houses opposite and the dusky sky. The street itself looked much like the one where his brother lived.

'Where are we?' she asked.

'At my chambers.' He was kneeling at the hearth making a fire.

'No, I mean where in the city are we?'

He looked up then, his eyes hooded. 'Thinking of running off, are you?' He cast her a roguish smile to soften his words and she realised he was teasing. Did he have any idea how close he was to the truth of what was in her mind? 'We are a few minutes from the palace, aye?' he said. 'And not far from your hotel.'

Was he being deliberately mysterious? Somehow she must get the address out of him before she left. She looked around. There were two other doors leading out of the room, in addition to the one through which they had entered. 'What is through there?' she asked, pointing, although she could guess.

'Sanford sleeps in there and me there,' he said, pointing to each door in turn. 'He invited me to stay wi' him the while.'

Sanford was a smiling nobleman with world-weary eyes. She'd run across his sort before in Jack's hell. A shiver passed across her shoulders. 'Is he likely to return soon?'

'Not him.' He turned back to the fire where he had got a flame among the kindling and began blowing gently. The flame caught and soon the fire was burning merrily. He added coal one lump at a time. 'Poor chap,' he continued. 'Old Georgie keeps all his gentleman dancing in attendance until the wee hours. I wouldna be in his shoes for all the whisky in Scotland.' He stood up. 'Talking of which, would you like a dram? Or would you prefer tea?' He pointed to the fire. 'It won't take long to make.'

Now the shock of their mad dash had worn off, she was aware of the unsteady beat of her heart. It resonated through her body. Drummed in her bones. The knowledge of why she was here and how far she would go making her nervous. 'Whisky.'

But it was excitement, not fear, making her tremble. She was nervous because she liked him and wanted him to like her. The fact that she was attracted to him on so many levels would mean that tonight could be something special.

He went to a cupboard tucked neatly against the side of the chimney breast and pulled out a decanter and two glasses. There were cups in there, too, and a tea canister.

'You have no servant to help you?'

'Not me. Sanford does. His man has a room on the top floor. A bell lets him know when he's needed.'

'He lives in London, you said.'

'He has chambers at the Albany. I stayed with him when I was there last time. Sir Walter arranged these lodgings. Tossed some poor chap out, I'm understanding. There are other members of the household residing here and elsewhere around the city. Sanford insisted I take the extra bedroom. There was another chap who wanted it, but he's no' so keen on his company.'

Carrying his hoard to the table, he carefully measured out the whisky. She could not help watching his broad back. The easy confident way he moved within his skin. The litheness, the grace of him. It was like watching a large and magnificent, though dangerous, cat.

The trembles inside her changed to something else. A low sensual hum in her blood. Her skin felt warm, her senses alive. It was years since she'd felt this way.

Resolutely she turned her face away from the intriguing sight of his body and was gazing into the glow of the coals when he sat beside her, handed her the whisky and clinked her glass with his. *'Slàinte.'*

'Good health.'

He swallowed his drink in one gulp. Perhaps he was as nervous as she was. The idea made her want to smile. She sipped at the golden liquid. It burned her throat going down, but settled warm in her belly. She leaned back against the cushions and took another warming sip. 'You've led Jack a merry dance these past few days,' she observed.

She cast a sideways glance at his face and was pleased to see by his expression she had caught him off guard. He looked at his glass. 'I'm for another. Do ye want one?'

'Not yet.' She knew better than to drink too much around a man. She just had to hope he would not drink too much either. He was a big man. Far beyond her in strength despite her height. The fear she should have felt at such a thought was not present. Not once had he acted anything but the gentleman. Not even when she had kissed him at the inn had he been anything but controlled. Unlike herself.

Her heart gave a heavy thump in her chest. A warning to be careful. To guard herself from reading too much into his gentle manners. She forced herself to remember that men changed when they drank too much. Some fell asleep, like Jack. Others became violent. Hopefully, he wouldn't do either.

His glass refilled, he came back to the sofa,

sat down beside her and stretched out his long legs towards the fire with a sigh. 'What was it you asked me?'

'I didn't ask you anything. I said you had led Jack a merry dance.'

'Jack's men,' he said briefly. 'Aye, I played wi' them a wee bit.' He was clearly trying not to sound pleased with himself. And failing.

'Why?'

His eyes narrowed to slits, the green of them catching the glow of the fire and reminding her of the panther again. A rather angry panther. If he had a tail, she was sure it would be twitching right about now.

The urge to stroke him, to smooth away the crease between his eyes, curled her fingers in her lap. Her breathing shortened. Her mouth dried. As it should. One did not pet a wild creature with impunity.

'I dinna like to be treated like an idiot. I ken he's talking with McKenzie.' He shrugged. 'That's business. But where I go and what I do is no one's concern but my own.' He flashed her a smile as if to soften the words.

'Shall we forget about business concerns for a while?'

He gave her a long look, before half-turning towards her and laying one arm along the back of the sofa, his fingers close enough to touch her shoulder, should he wish. The skin at the point of her shoulder tingled in anticipation. Heat spread outwards, rippling along her veins. Her heartbeat raced. The dangerous surge of warmth in her blood was a terrifying loss of control.

Shocked, she drew in a quick breath. Years had passed since she'd wanted a man's touch. Usually, she felt as if she was enfolded in a blanket of ice. Men generally sensed that coldness. It was why the abbess, Miss Lucy, had been happy to let Jack buy her out of the brothel.

She tried to find that coolness. To reach for distance. This was her seducing him, not the other way around.

Chapter Nine

His eyes grew heated, his expression becoming beguilingly gentle. 'What a comely lass you are.'

The sincerity in his voice was a deep thrum in her blood and her bones.

'And it seems meeting the King has turned you into a courtier,' she quipped lightly. She let her gaze roam his face, the hard delineation of bones in his cheek beneath intense green eyes, the light golden fuzz on his jaw, the sculpted lips.

Slowly, she rose to her feet and he followed, as she had known he would.

Standing so close, he was a good few inches taller. It was a pleasant change to look up to meet a man's gaze, even when those eyes searched her face so intently.

He smiled.

Such an attractive man. The epitome of virility. And she no longer cared about why she was here. He made her feel like a desirable woman, but, more importantly, he made her feel special. As if she was a real person. Why not have these next few hours for herself, and forget about the world and its petty cruelties? She could make him happy and feel good doing it.

It wouldn't last. It couldn't. Their paths were too different. But right now they intersected and she wanted to make the most of it.

She dropped her gaze to his beautiful broad shoulders encased in dark-blue superfine and placed her hands flat on his chest, feeling the energy. The life of him. The steady beat of his heart. The rise and fall of his chest with each indrawn breath. The heat of him crashed against her, making her own breathing jerky, and the scent, bergamot and bay, filled her every breath. Delicious. Her heart picked up speed.

He swallowed, the strong column of his throat rippling beneath the golden tan of his skin. Yet he remained still, waiting to be sure of her purpose.

She stroked his lapels, feeling the smooth weave of the fabric against her skin. She slid her hands up to his nape, combing the tendrils of hair there through her fingers, lifting her chin with a smile she hoped looked confident, before touching her lips to his.

Their mouths melded easily, familiarity remembered. He tasted of whisky and smelled of cologne and smoke from the fire. And something unique to him. A dark note of musky male that curled around her senses and set her adrift on a languorous current of desire. Her insides tightened and fluttered and heat pulsed through her veins. Hot little surges of heat in time to her heartbeat.

His hand, the fingers trembling faintly, curled around her nape while his thumb stroked her cheekbone. Large hands. Strong hands that could crush her on a whim. Yet as gentle as butterfly's wings against her skin. Great strength leashed. It promised physical fulfilment without fear of harm.

Something she had not known for years. If ever. Her passion with Mark had always been edged with the danger of discovery. With Logan, it seemed different. Safer.

Only it wasn't. They were both at risk. And for him, she was the danger.

Slowly she broke the kiss. He let her go, with many small kisses on her lips, kisses that lingered as sweet as honey. His chest rose and fell with his ragged breathing, his eyes were hazy with desire, and as foolish as it was to let emotion enter into it, she felt the ache of her heart. A twinge of regret, that this could not be more than it was.

'Are you sure you want this?' he asked softly. 'You dinna have to do it.'

A pang twisted her heart, because something told her that she should trust him. But if he realised she had followed him here on Jack's command, to seek out the information he wanted, he might turn her away. She did not dare take the risk.

'I want to.' Heaven help her, it was the truth.

He smiled then and clasped her hand in his, rhythmically stroking her palm with his thumb. 'Let down your hair for me, *a ghra?*'

The way he said it sounded more like a breath in the back of his throat than a word. It was also incredibly sensual. 'Agra?'

'Ach, not Agra. *A ghra.* It means my dearest.'

What would it be like to be someone's dearest? She would never know. Nor did she want to. Not really. It would only lead to disappointment in the end. She began removing the pins, until the heavy mass fell to her shoulders.

He combed his fingers through the waves. 'So thick it is,' he murmured. 'And of such a colour. Like toffee threaded with gold.'

The gentle stroke of his fingers sent shivers of desire down her back and she wanted to purr like a cat and revel in his gentle, almost reverent touch.

She offered him her mouth up for a kiss.

A long slow exhalation of surrender warmed her lips and somehow touched a tender place in her heart. A gentle soothing touch.

While their lips melded in perfect harmony, she stroked one hand down over his chest and then slid upwards inside his waistcoat, boldly exploring the wide muscled back beneath the superfine of his coat, the narrowing waist beneath his ribs that rose and fell with each breath, the firm swell of his buttocks. Then moved on to find the bumps of his ribs and his nipple tight and hard beneath his linen shirt. She rolled it between thumb and forefinger. He arched into her with a hiss of indrawn breath and an arrow of pleasure darted straight to her core.

He gasped and raised his head, his eyes dazed with the onset of intense desire. Nothing angelic about his expression now. Pure seduction in the smile he gave her. Her knees felt weak.

And she wasn't the only one losing the strength to stand upright—she could feel his thighs shake with effort. She turned within his arms, presenting him with her back. 'The laces,' she gasped.

He seemed to struggle a bit with the ties of

her gown and her stays, while she waited, her heart thumping in her chest.

'Done,' he said finally.

The straps fell from her shoulders, and as she turned to face him she let the garments slide to the floor.

A breath of admiration left his lips and he gazed as if in awe at her breasts, covered only by the sheer fabric of her shift. An odd feeling stirred in her mind. A faint recognition of something elusive that was gone like a wisp of mist at his hot gaze.

She steeled herself for what would come next. The passion. The loss of control. The wanton desire that was already arising, making her pulse race and her body warm. It was a long time since she'd felt so abandoned.

There was something in the purity in his face that left her defenceless.

His large warm hands went to her shoulders and smoothed down her arms in a spine-tingling caress. He threaded his fingers with hers, bending his head to look into her eyes. 'So lovely.'

'Thank you.' Shocked by the husky rasp in her voice, she cleared her throat. 'And am I to have the pleasure of looking at you? Or do you prefer to keep your clothes?'

A rueful smile spread across his face as his

hands went to his stock. 'I am no' as pretty a sight as you.'

Charity leaned against the bedpost to watch him toe off his shoes and shrug out of his coats. Such a pleasure. Like unwrapping a gift. He was as broad beneath the fine linen of his shirt as he had been beneath his coats. No padding or corsets gave him his manly shape. It was all his own. And the shirt, while it hung to mid-thigh, did not disguise his jutting arousal.

Slowly he approached her, and pulled her close and kissed her. At first hard and then more softly, as if in a struggle with himself. A struggle to maintain control. A struggle she intended him to lose.

She twined her arms around his neck, leaning into him, feeling the blunt thrust of him against her belly and the quick rise and fall of his ribs against her breasts. 'Take me to bed, Logan,' she said. 'Now.'

He half-laughed, half-groaned, but lifted her easily and pulled back the sheets while he balanced her effortlessly on his other arm. Strong as an ox, this man. Yet as gentle as a lamb. He laid her on the sheet, looking down at her, lust etched deep in his expression. Her body answered with a flush of heat.

'Take off your shirt,' she said, the need to see him naked a pressing urge.

With a roguish smile he drew the billowing fabric off over his head.

He was lovely. Golden skinned from head to waist. Pale from there on down from lack of sunlight. His male member, dark-veined and engorged, thrust up from a nest of crisp dark-gold curls, standing as straight and rigid as any of the soldiers they had seen on parade.

He climbed up on the bed to kneel beside her, gazing down into her face, the desire and heat between them a tangible thing.

She reached up and pulled down on his shoulders, lifting her own from the bed when he remained as solid as a rock above her. She nipped his lower lip, licked the corner of his mouth.

Shivers rippled through him as their lips connected. It was a hard kiss, full of passion and demand that went on and on until they were breathless.

His lips explored her face with small little kisses, her cheekbones, her temple, the tip of her nose, her chin and drifted to her ear. He breathed softly into its depths. Prickles raced across her body.

'Like that, do you?' he asked running a finger over the little bumps on her arm, his face alive with interest.

'As do you,' she said, her voice little more than a sigh.

He didn't answer. His tongue was already exploring the little ridges and delving deep inside. More shivers. Accompanied by little clenches low in her abdomen.

A moan broke free of her lips.

With a smile, he moved from her ear to her neck, tasting and licking his way down to her collarbone, where he traced her clavicle with his mouth and tongue, while his hand cupped her breast.

Tingling awareness tightened her nipples. Her breasts felt full and heavy. With a swift glance up at her face, he licked the beaded tip through the fabric of her shift, then blew lightly.

Torment indeed, from such a light gentle touch. And even that film of fabric seemed too much of a barrier between them. 'Take it off,' she said.

Hazy eyed, he stared at her.

'The shift,' she said, plucking at the neck. 'It's in the way.'

It didn't take him long to dispose of the garment over her head. She lay back down, naked as the day she was born, stroking the arm supporting his weight. The muscles bulged and rippled beneath the smooth skin of his upper arm. Not very hairy, she noticed. A light golden fuzz on his arm, small triangle in the centre that was coarser on his chest.

His nipples were pale and tightly beaded. She raised herself up on her elbows and teased them with her tongue and teeth. He hissed in a breath of pleasure and an expression of pain crossed his face.

Then his hand came to her breast, cupping first one, then the other, lifting each one in turn as if to measure the swell, then sweeping his palm across the sensitive tips, bringing them to little nubs of hardened flesh. So painfully sensitive.

He lowered his head, nuzzling with his mouth into the softest part, kissing and licking and deeply inhaling. A low growl of pleasure issued from deep in his throat.

A growl stirred things up inside her. Flutters and trembles and shivers raced through her in a succession of little thrills.

A delicious sensation. But more was required and soon or she would go mad.

She shifted, moving to bring the hardened peak to his lips, and he took the top of her breast in a hot wet open-mouthed kiss and then suckled.

Her hips arched off the bed. She twined her arms around his neck, pulled herself upwards and swirled her tongue around his ear.

He gave a moan, grabbed a ragged breath as his mouth let go of her breast and his knees nudged her thighs apart. He closed his eyes in a grimace of pain. 'I canna wait any longer. I am going to…' he muttered, his voice hoarse with strain.

He rose up on one hand, looming over her, his broad shoulders obscuring all, his gaze fixed on her face. He took himself in hand and drove home. Large and hard and hot.

His thrusts were steady, pressing into her, each stroke edging her a little higher in the quest for release. His hips and hard buttocks moved beneath her hands, the muscles rippling. Her limbs felt languid, while inside she was as tight as a coiled spring. Bliss beckoned, just out of reach.

'I'm sorry, lass,' he said, his face a picture of agony. 'I canna wait any longer. I—'

The deep groan came from somewhere in the depths of his chest. His neck corded and the tendons stood out. His arms shook with the effort of holding his body up, while he pounded into her, his gaze never leaving her face. With her legs, she clasped him around the waist, crossing her ankles at his back, holding on to his shoulders. He drove into her again and again, each stroke ending with a slight twist of his hips that sent a sharp jolt deep within her, until her vision darkened at the edges and all she could see was the sheen of sweat on his face and the grimace on his lips.

Nothing existed, but the feel of him and the tightening within. And the way he looked at her.

And then it was happening. The violent falling apart. A shattering explosion. Small cries filled the air. Cries of gasping pleasure. Hers.

Dimly, she heard him breathe her name. Never had it sounded so sweet. And then he was shuddering. Filling her with his hot seed. The life that would never come to fruition.

A sadness filled her and mingled with the aftermath of pleasure and joy. Never had she been so shaken to the depths of her being by any man. Not even her first. More astonishing was the expression in his eyes as he took them both over the edge. The awe along with the lust.

It was as if it was all very new to him, what they had done together. It somehow felt fresh and wholesome.

Rather than tainted.

A swelling softness filled her heart. Beneath the adventurous rogue was a good man. A man she could have loved if things were different. She could almost see them in a small house, here in the Highlands, roses at the door, children running wild in the hills and dales. Glens, they called them. A farm, perhaps. Sheep. Almost.

Yes, he wanted her, of course, but not that

way. What decent man would? This was lust. No, those old dreams of hers were just that. Dreams. She had her life mapped out. This was a small diversion, that was all.

Vaguely she felt him collapse beside her and pull her close within the circle of his arms. Such a warm comforting feeling.

The questions would wait. For a while.

Chapter Ten

He wanted to do it again. Logan came to full consciousness as hard as rock. Right now. With her.

Charity lying lax at his side, sleeping so sweetly, he could not bear to wake her. Ignoring his baser urges wasn't so easy when he could feel her soft curves pressed into his groin and one of her breasts filling his palm. Her hair lay over his chest like a silken veil and he let his free hand wander through her tresses. Long and silky and wavy like a field of oats in a breeze.

Ah, what would she think of him, when she awoke? At the end he'd been out of his head with lust. He, who prided himself on his control. He wasn't even sure she had also…. He'd make sure next time.

She stirred. Her shoulders tightened as she

became aware of her surroundings. Of him, of his state of arousal. He should have moved while he had the chance, but he had been enjoying the feel of her against him too much.

He could not hold back his soft groan as she shifted, inching away from him. She stilled, as if waiting for something to happen. Did she think he would ravish her without her consent? He loosened his grasp around her shoulders. She twisted to look up at him, her smoky eyes searching his face.

Boldly and with a feeling of great tenderness, he kissed her forehead. 'It is awake, you are?'

To his surprise, she smiled back, shyly and blushing. And it made him feel as proud as a stag. He grinned at her.

She raised up on one elbow, her hair surrounding them like a curtain, looking down into his face. The expression on her face was one of puzzlement. He tensed.

'That was your first time, wasn't it? Your first time with a woman.'

His gut pitched like a ship in a storm. He almost groaned out loud. He raised his gaze to the canopy above his head and closed his eyes. 'It was that clumsy, then?'

Silence. He opened one eye to look at her. She wasna' laughing, thank goodness, but she had a puzzled expression. 'It wasn't bad. Quite the opposite. It was just that…' She hesitated and he tried not to wince in anticipation of what she would say. 'It was wonderful. Truly. But…a woman knows these things.'

'Wonderful, was it?' He wanted to crow like a rooster. As it was he couldn't keep the smile from his face.

She struck his upper arm with her fist as if she thought she could hurt him. 'I am right, am I not?'

He combed his fingers through her beautiful hair, sweeping it away from that hard-angled face and met her gaze full on. She thought what they'd done was wonderful. And so did he. He let out a short breath. 'You are right.'

Shock filled her gaze. Perhaps even horror. 'How can that be? A man of your age…'

'I had some thought of keeping myself for the woman I would marry, ye ken.'

She placed a hand flat on his bare chest. Her fingers were cold. Her eyes narrowed. 'And you chose to break your vow with me? I hope it was worth it.'

The bitterness in her voice with the underlying hint of pain shook him out of his feeling of satisfaction. Why did she sound so insulted?

He tilted her face up to see her expression. She kept her lashes lowered, her gaze fixed on the hand stroking the hair on his chest, grooming it with her fingers. Tugging at it a little harder than seemed necessary. He covered her hand with his.

'It wasna so much a vow. Ours is a small village. All of the girls eager to wed. I made the mistake of kissing one of them once and the knot was almost tied. She needed a father for her unborn child.'

'You didn't marry her?'

She sounded shocked. Judgemental. Like the rest of the people at Dunross. He felt the sting of their black looks all over again. 'It wasna mine. Not that anyone believed me until her father discovered that I was not the only boy she'd been kissing. My best friend was bolder than me. It was his child and he married her.'

'A lucky escape, then.' Her tone was dry.

'I suppose you could say that. I wasna so popular with the people in the village after that. The mothers who had daughters, at least. I suppose they thought there was no smoke without a fire.' He'd been pretty well ostracised for a time, the folk thinking that Ian had paid Craig to marry Maggie in Logan's place. Maggie hadn't exactly helped matters in that regard.

He remembered his feeling of utter panic when he thought Ian would force him to the altar and shuddered.

Both Maggie's treachery and the clan's suspicion had been a bitter pill to swallow. So he'd decided then and there that the lasses were not for him. That he would seek his excitement elsewhere. Until now.

Not that he was considering marrying Charity. Was he? Just because… But he could remember his brother's words to Drew all those years ago. A Gilvry does not debauch a lady and not marry her. Not and keep his honour.

Most would not consider Charity a lady. Not by a mile. Yet… Yet he wasn't so sure he was ready to let her go back to her crude Irishman. The very thought of it made his stomach curdle.

As if she sensed the churning of his thoughts, she pulled her hand out from beneath his and ran her finger down his jawline. 'You are in no danger from me,' she said softly. 'I am not the marrying sort.'

'And if we made a child?'

She patted his chest. 'Not a chance.'

A feeling of relief shot through him. He curled his hand around her fingers and brought them to his lips, pressing a soft kiss into her palm. 'How can you be so sure?'

'I took precautions, of course.' There was an edge to her voice.

'You expected this?'

She rose on her elbow, looking down at him. There was amusement in her face, but in her eyes there was a darker emotion. Regret? Sadness. 'Of course. A woman of my sort—'

'Do not say it.' The spurt of anger came as a surprise. Was that not just what he had been thinking? He shook his head, at himself. At her. 'You are a lady. You should be treated as such.'

She laughed softly. 'What a good man you are, to be sure.' She snuggled back against him. 'I had no idea that Highlanders were so sweet.'

'No doubt you thought we were savages.' He was feeling a bit of a savage at that moment. He wanted her again. He wanted to make it better this time. Better for her. Surely it was too soon?

'Is it very wild, where you live?' she asked. 'Your brother and sister-in-law seemed to say as much.'

'About as wild as it gets, I would say. For Britain. What you see around Edinburgh are only the foothills compared to the mountains to the north.'

'I'd like to see them one day. It must be difficult, bringing whisky through the mountains.' She tilted her head, her breath falling on his throat in a pleasurable little tickle as she spoke. 'I suppose you are only able to do so when the weather is good. I imagine there is quite a bit of snow in winter?'

'Is that what O'Banyon is worried about? Our ability to deliver?'

'Can you blame him?'

It wouldn't be the first time their customers had wondered. 'It is not so easy in winter, but it can be done if you know the passes.'

'There must be a great many routes through the mountains to the border. And you know them all?'

'Not so many as I would wish. The Great Glen forces me to come a whole lot closer to Inverness than I would like, no matter what time of year it is. All the trade must come close to the road there and the revenue men know it.'

'Is there no other way to go?'

He'd probably said more than he should have, but no more than was common knowledge. That part of the way south was always touch and go. But his men knew their work. 'There are a few. But they are not easy ways in winter with a string of loaded mules.'

'And you sleep under the stars and travel the empty wilds as free as a bird.' Her voice sounded dreamy. 'Like a character in Sir Walter Scott's novels.'

He chuckled. 'Not near as romantic, I'm afraid. It's mostly cold and wet and dirty, with a bunch of men sleeping around the fire or packed like sardines in a friendly crofter's barn. I dinna think you would like it.'

'And once you cross the border? There can't be many friendly crofters then.'

While her questions sounded innocent enough, a sort of idle interest, he knew the answers were not only for her benefit. He didn't like the idea of lying, so he had skated around the truth. Given her enough, but nothing that McKenzie wouldn't already know or guess. And his routes to the border were no one else's business but his own.

This last question, though, pushed a little harder than he liked. And yet it was important. O'Banyon had to know they had a plan. A good one. 'There's a man Ian knows, just over the border into England. He will keep wagons ready for us. When we travel through from there to London we will look like any other merchant on the road. We'll be making good time, then.'

'You would trust an Englishman?'

'Ian trusts him and that is good enough for me. Besides, the man used to be a pirate of sorts.' Not to mention that he was a lord and his wife was Lady Selina's best friend. That information was not for anyone to know.

'Why do you do it? Why live a life of crime? Why not just farm your land?'

That's what they all thought, these *Sassenachs,* that the Scots liked being outlaws and criminals. 'The English Parliament forces us to it.'

She made a sound of surprise. 'Why would they do that?'

'Their law is unjust, Charity. What is legal for an Englishman is illegal for a Highlander. Should we not all be equal under the law? We have the same King. The same Parliament. Should we not have the same rights? And if we do not, should we be bound by such injustice?'

'Should you not work to change the law?'

'Now you sound like Niall.'

Once more she raised up to look at his face, a crease between her brows. 'You do not agree with your brother, then? Or is it the danger you enjoy?'

He rubbed a strand of her hair between finger and thumb, feeling its silky softness with a kind of wonder. 'I will admit there is some satisfaction in outwitting your enemies.' A smile tugged at his lips at the thought. 'But I would not be unhappy if the law was changed.' He wouldn't know what to do with himself. But that was another matter. It would be safer for his brothers and their families and what man wouldn't want that for those he held near and dear. 'In the meantime…'

'In the meantime you will risk your life.'

Ah, there it was. The worry of a woman.

Hadn't Maggie nagged at Craig until he stopped coming on the road with Logan? And wasn't that when he'd started acting all grim and sour? No fun any more. Why should a woman change a man to suit herself? Happy as his brothers were with their wives, they had also changed. Why could a woman not just accept a man as he was? 'I do what my family needs me to do. But I do not take unnecessary risks. My men rely on me to bring them home safe.'

Och, now he sounded defensive.

'So what would you do, if the law changed?'

It was something he'd asked himself more than once. He sighed and rubbed at his stubble. 'I'll decide when it happens.' He looked up at her lovely face, at the high elegant cheekbones, the small nose, the full lush lips. Such a lovely face, but with a hardness born of life's hard knocks. 'What about you? Is this the life you want?'

Her eyes widened with surprise, as if no one had ever cared enough to ask. Her expression softened and those purple eyes turned inward as if seeing something else. She blinked and the softness was gone. He wondered if he had imagined it. 'What else would I want?'

He frowned, sweeping her hair back from her face, the better to see into those mysterious eyes of hers. 'A home. A husband. Children.'

Wasn't that what most women wanted? Wasn't that why he avoided the tricky little things, because they'd have you married with or without your consent, if they could?

'Men, decent men that is, don't marry women like me,' she scoffed. 'And why would I want one man when I can have my pick any day of the week?'

He didn't like the sound of that at all. 'And Jack?' he asked, wishing he hadn't. But the idea of her and Jack made him feel ill.

'Jack is business,' she said.

'And this?' He waved an arm around the room. 'Is this business?' The idea that it might be was a solid lump in his gut.

A pouting smile curved her lips. 'This is sex. What else could it be?' She kissed his mouth. Pressing her lips to his, sweeping the seam of it with her tongue until he let her in.

His heart thundered and she rolled on top of him, pressing her thigh between his, his shaft trapped deliciously between them and her woman's flesh hot and damp against his upper thigh. She raked at him with her nails, tweaked his nipple, first one, then the other, making him buck beneath her and grind his hips against her belly.

Yet there was nothing loving in this. She was

colder than ice. It was, as she had said, just sex. But that was not how it had felt earlier.

He clasped her shoulders and held her away from him. 'Charity,' he growled. 'What are you doing?'

She glanced down at his groin. 'Evidence suggested you wanted more.' She pulled out of his grasp and slipped off the bed, standing naked beside it. She curled her lip and glanced down at his swollen shaft.

He could not stop himself from looking at her bounteous breasts, the dip of her waist, and the flair of her hips, and the dark-gold curls between her long elegant thighs. She was the most beautiful thing he had ever seen in his life.

But when he looked up at her face, her eyes were as cold as winter. She gave a hard little laugh and went to the table. 'I gather once is all a boy like you can manage,' she tossed over her shoulder as she poured herself a glass of wine.

Anger blazed inside him at her taunt. Furious, intent on proving her wrong, he leaped from the bed and was beside her before she could take more than a mouthful.

To the sound of her gasp, he took the glass from her hand and set it down. She looked up at him with a taunting smile. Goading him to do his worst. To prove himself unworthy. And right now he had a very strong urge to do just that.

To take her and toss her down on that bed and show her that he was more than man enough to take what he wanted. And wanted badly.

A barely perceptible flinch halted him in his tracks. A look at her face told him how close she was to breaking. How vulnerable. His brain jolted to life, horrified by where his anger, his loss of control, had been leading.

With some difficulty, he pulled back from the brink, picked her up and carried her to the chair by the hearth. Sinking down into it, he settled her on his lap and enclosed her gently in his arms, praying she would not insist he release her. Because if she did, he would have no choice but to do it. And he did not want her to leave with such anger between them.

'What fantasy is this, then?' she said harshly, looking up at him. 'Shall I straddle you? Maybe suck you?'

The words twisted like knives in his chest, because of the rage they revealed. And the pain. He clasped her against his chest and stroked her hair back from her face and was shocked to see how his fingers shook as he tried gentle her. Tears stood out in her eyes, but she blinked them away.

'Hush,' he whispered. 'Hush. Strike me if you must. Cry if you must. But dinna hurt your-self so.'

The tears spilled over. Running down her cheeks. Silent sobs shook her body.

'Shhh. It's all right.'

'It is not all right,' she gasped. 'Let me go.'

Hating to do so, yet knowing he must, he opened his arms.

And she lay against his chest, gasping for breath as if trying to stem the tide of tears. He remained utterly still beneath her, letting her cry, though it killed him not to hold her. Not to offer comfort. Because he did not know how to mend what was wrong.

Finally, she put her arms around his neck and wept softly against his shoulder. And then his arms came around her, hands stroking her back until she gradually found peace.

'You must think me such a fool,' she said finally, sitting up, blotting her eyes with the heel of her hand.

'No. I think you walk on a knife-edge. You are verra brave, lass.'

Her grimace said she did not believe him. 'You should not have taken me to your brother's house,' she said stiffly. 'I am not at all a suitable woman for decent company. Don't you know that?'

He sighed. 'If you are good enough for me, you are good enough for my brother.'

'But we crept out of the back door. What must they think?'

'Niall wasna' best pleased, I must say, but he knows the kind of people I have to deal with. And O'Banyon's men know we left. I made sure they saw us in the alley before we gave them the slip.'

Her eyes widened. 'Is that your plan? To drive a wedge between me and Jack?'

Startled by her accusation, he swallowed and tried not to look at her breasts inches from his face, a hairsbreadth from his lips. 'I wasna' thinking much beyond what might happen here, this evening, but now you mention it, do you think it would work?' He raised his brows in question and tried a charming smile.

'Men,' she said. She pushed away from him and stood up.

And he was done for. His shaft was as hard as granite, his body chilled by her sudden departure, and her so beautiful standing naked before him. She gave his erection a glare, as if his reaction was all his fault, and stomped to the bed, her luscious breasts bouncing as she walked, her soft round bottom and long legs a symphony of motion. She wrapped herself in the red-and-white counterpane from the bed. It covered her from her shoulders to her heels.

Disappointed, he cursed softly and moved behind her to snatch up a sheet and wrap it around his waist. It seemed there wasn't going to be any more loving. He returned to his seat and she perched on the wooden chair at the table, looking worried.

'Jack likes to keep an eye on me.'

'Dinna fash yourself. He knows I have you safe. And now he knows I'll not let his men follow me around.'

She stared down her nose. 'You think this is some sort of game. Well, it is not. Take me back to my hotel.'

'It is no game, lass. My family's livelihood depends on it.'

She stared at the carpet, hiding her thoughts from him, then lifted her head and met his gaze square on. 'You are using me to get to O'Banyon.'

'Perhaps,' he admitted. 'But you came at O'Banyon's bidding, did you not?' he asked, trying to lighten the mood, yet knowing he sounded just a little bitter. 'You were using me, too.'

'That is different.'

'How is it?'

She spun around. 'You know I work for Jack. What did you expect?'

The walls were back up. Women. A man never knew where he stood from one minute to the next. From tears to anger in a matter of moments. And this one, while she always gave the appearance of being as strong and bright and hard as a steel blade was far more vulnerable than he had suspected.

He could kill O'Banyon for putting her in such a position. There was no fondness between her and Jack. He would have sensed it if there was. If she would just let him help her. He stilled at the implication. There were several ways he could do that and only one way was certain. Marriage.

His chest tightened. His heart gave an odd sort of jolt that wasn't all that unpleasant. Still, there was no reason to think she would accept. And to say anything right now would jeopardise his negotiations with O'Banyon. If it made her more comfortable to keep him at a distance, to pretend nothing significant had happened between them, he would play along. For now.

He shook his head at her with an rueful look. 'I expected nothing and got far more.' He went over to her, bringing her to her feet, 'Let us not argue. The evening has been a pleasant one for us both, has it not?'

'Yes,' she said, smiling, though her eyes were still misty. 'It has. Thank you,' she said and rose up on her toes and kissed him on the mouth.

A sweet kiss. Lips to lips. Their heads tipping

to just the right angle as if they had been kissing all their lives. Her arms snaked up around his neck and the coverlet fell to the floor. The soft swell of her breasts pressed against his chest and blood headed south. Again he was hard. Never had he experienced one arousal after another as if it was she who had command over his body.

He growled low in his throat and backed her up towards the bed. He lifted his head for a second looking down into her face, her lips rosy from his kiss, her eyes closed, her expression slumberous. Not the sensual pout with which she faced the world, but a soft, almost innocent, expression.

'You had better tell me now if you dinna want this again,' he managed to say, while cursing himself.

Her eyes opened. And he could see the longing within them. She gave her head a small shake as if she did not quite believe it, but she also smiled. There was regret in that smile. Something he had not expected to see. 'I want this,' she whispered. 'Before I go.'

He did not like the word go, but he pushed the feeling aside. He would deal with it later. 'What do you want?'

She blinked, looking puzzled even as her hands stroked his face and her fingers slid through his hair, and her gaze fixed on his mouth, encouraging him to kiss her again.

'What do you like?' he asked, feeling just a little self-conscious. 'You gave me great pleasure, you deserve the same.'

Her gaze shot to his face, her lips parted in surprise. 'Not all men like what I like,' she said, half in laughter, half in warning.

He swallowed. Nothing he had heard about had seemed like something he wouldn't want to experience for himself. 'How will I know if I don't try?'

A pleased and secretive smile crossed her lips. 'Indeed. Lie down on the bed on your back.'

He did as bid, aware of his shaft pulsing and standing stiff and straight from his balls. Getting harder by the moment as she looked him over. Her tongue flicked over her lips. And he wondered if she was going to taste him.

But, no, when she climbed up on the bed she threw one leg over his body and sat facing him, her damp quim resting on his chest. Shudders rippled through his body. Anticipation. Need. His hips lifted of their own accord.

'You must not move. Not a muscle.'

He frowned. If he did not move, then…

She reached around behind her and cupped his ballocks in her hand, watching his face as she rolled them in her palm. They grew heavy and hard and ached like the very devil. Unendurable pleasurable pain. When she released him, he squeezed his eyes shut with the strain of not tossing her on her back and thrusting his aching shaft inside her heat.

'Yes,' she murmured softly. 'That's my brave lad. Hold very still.' She rose up on her knees and shifted backwards. He took a deep breath and opened his eyes, reaching for the control that had kept him secure from women's wiles all these years as he lifted his head to watch her hover over him.

She stopped, looking at him with raised brows. He let his head fall back on the pillow with a groan. 'It is not so easy, lass.'

'If it was easy, it wouldn't be worth it,' she said with a sly grin. But there was something else on her face. A considering expression, as if this was a test. Of his manhood? If he failed, would she use it as an excuse to push him away? Then he would not fail.

Her fingers circled the base of his shaft. Unlike his own hand, her fingers arrived unexpectedly, firm and cool. Oh, this was not going to be the least bit easy.

Vigorously, she stroked him from head to base, over and over. Light flashed behind his eyes and his ballocks tightened. He could not contain his gasp of surprise or the groan as he tried to remain still. Every muscle in his body became rigid with the effort. Even so he found his hands clenching the bed sheets either side of him.

But when he looked up into her face and saw the smile on her lips, the torture was worth every moment of agony of maintaining control.

And then she guided him inside her. Her hand was nothing compared to this encompassing heat and tightness. Slowly she slid down his length and rose again. He shuddered at the pleasure she gave him and the urge to rise up to meet her, but somehow he held himself utterly still, his body a bundle of shivering nerves.

Inner muscles clenched tight around him, pulled at him. He lost his grip.

'Mercy,' he yelled. He'd lost the battle. He beat at the bed like a wrestler admitting defeat. 'Charity, please.'

She leaned over him, raising him by the shoulders to bring his mouth to her breast. He suckled at first one, then the other, and she made those sweet cries he'd heard earlier, little sounds of pleasure while she continued to ride his shaft, moving her hips to her own rhythm, angling him deep into her body, deeper and deeper, tighter and so damned hot, his mind spinning out of control. And then she was upright again, circling her hips in a wild rhythm, and he wanted, he wanted to join her in the dance, but he had given his word he would not.

He had granted her control of this wild joining. Control. That was what she sought. He must not take it back… Must not move…

And then…her high keening cry of pleasure ripped through the sound of their gasps and moans. The pull and pulse of silken wet heat around his shaft finished him off. His ballocks pulled up tight and he was spilling and spilling and falling into a void of hot sweet pleasure.

She collapsed against his chest. And she was still voicing those cries, softly now, but still as if it was too great a pleasure to bear. And there was nothing he could do but hold her close to his thundering heart and breathe as if every breath would be his last.

Banging.

Someone knocking. 'Logan,' a male Scottish voice shouted.

Charity rolled off the warm body beneath her and hunted around for the sheet, while prodding Logan in one massive shoulder. 'Someone is at the door,' she hissed in a whisper.

Logan cracked an eye and sat up.

'Logan,' the voice shouted again.

'Tammy,' Logan muttered. 'Whist, man,

you'll wake the whole house.' He slid out of bed and walked to the door and Charity could not help watching him cross the room. Long legs, muscled thighs, slender flanks and tight buttocks. The male grace of him stopped her breath. He didn't open the door. 'Is it done?' he asked in a murmur.

'Aye,' the lowered voice came back. 'All safely away.'

'Go then and take your ease, man. You made sure you were not seen?'

'Aye. I came over the roof.'

Charity felt her eyes widen. And a sneaking cold suspicion spread up from her belly. When Logan turned from the door and saw her watching him, his grin was a little shamefaced.

'What did you do?' she asked.

'What could I have done? I was with you.'

The question, along with the roguish smile, gave him away. 'You used me as a decoy.'

He strode back to the bed and kissed her on the nose. 'All's fair in love and war.'

Didn't he realise how dangerous Jack was? 'What did you do, Logan?'

'I delivered some whisky to a customer who doesn't like dealing with McKenzie.'

The effrontery of the man. He didn't have a fearful bone in his body. Unlike her. She almost laughed out loud despite knowing how angry

Jack would be when he realised what had happened. As long as he didn't think she was part of it. 'I think it is time I went back to my hotel.'

His face tightened. 'Are you sure you want to?'

She stilled. Then chuckled and patted his cheek. 'Nice as it has been, Logan, I have to go.'

With somewhat bad grace, he helped her tie her stays and her gown, and while she put her hair into some sort of order, he dressed. He was still pulling on his boots when she lifted one edge of the curtains to look out into the street. 'Where exactly are we?'

He didn't hesitate. 'Ten York Place.'

She spun around to face him. 'Jack will have to know.' Blast it, now why did she sound as if she was sorry? She was, but to let him see even that much was folly.

His expression remained calm, if a little resigned. 'Tell him what you must.'

She felt like a traitor. The grime of it clung to her skin. But hadn't she given him something in return? Something small, to be sure. But something. But she couldn't help feeling as if the scales all tipped her way. The inner cold that usually kept guilt at bay seemed out of reach. She took a breath. 'Thank you for a pleasant evening. May I give you some advice before you entertain another woman in your bed?'

'There isn't going to be another woman,' he said with irritatingly quiet assurance.

A small ache tugged at her heart. Relief. Happiness. She pushed the emotions away. It did not matter to her what he did. Could not matter. Her future was tied to Jack O'Banyon. 'Then it is back to living like a monk for you.'

He bowed. 'I will see you on Friday, for the ball. But tell O'Banyon he has until Saturday to make up his mind, or the Gilvrys will be taking their business elsewhere.'

'You still intend on taking me to the ball?' She could not keep the surprise out of her voice, or the welling joy out of her heart at knowing she would see him again.

'We had a bargain.'

Of course. His bargain with Jack. But even with that thought the joy remained. A joy that she must quell or it might eat her alive. 'I'm not sure Jack will care to let the bargain stand after tonight.'

She had the dubious satisfaction of seeing anger flare in his eyes. And she couldn't quite help wondering what he would do if Jack said they would not go.

Dressed in all her finery, Charity waited in her parlour for word that Logan had arrived to carry her off to her very first ball.

Jack had laughed when she had told him how Logan had fooled his men to get her alone. He had twitted Growler about it in front of her, making her most uncomfortable. Growler had remained stoically silent under Jack's mockery, but since then his eyes had been harder than usual when they rested on her. As if he would love the chance to pay her back. Or Logan.

She'd relayed every last detail Logan had told her, even the part about the mysterious pirate. Jack's eyes had narrowed at that, but he denied knowing who the man might be. Not every last detail, she thought with a twinge. Some things Jack didn't need to know. Such as being Logan's first woman. And how he had touched her heart.

Nor had she told him that Logan knew she was acting as his spy.

For years, her dream of earning enough to set her free had kept her from sinking into the midden of her life. She would not throw it away because of her own wanton desires. Her longings for a man who would throw her away like so much rubbish when he was done with her. She would not let it happen again.

Once free of his allure, she had come to her senses. Or tried to, at least. She had tried to convince Jack that they were done with the Gilvrys. Then he announced there was something new he needed to discover. He needed to know where they stored their whisky in barrels. She had tried to refuse and made him furious, but in the end he'd promised her that after tonight, she would never have to see Logan again. And that made her feel sad. And more alone than usual.

Jack hadn't said why he needed this additional information. And she hadn't dared ask. He'd been too close to the edge of his temper.

A knock at the door heralded her maid. 'The gentlemen are waiting for you, miss,' the girl said.

Mentally, Charity braced herself. It would have been so much easier if she could have met Logan alone. Used her wiles to elicit the final piece of information, but Jack thought Logan would suspect something if they did not attend the ball. And afterwards, when she took him to her bed, she was to ply him with drink to loosen his tongue. And if that didn't work, at a signal from her, Jack would send Growler.

Her heart felt like a heavy weight in her chest as she picked up her reticule and the girl placed a shawl around her shoulders.

A quick glance in the mirror told her she looked her best. As fine as any other of the ladies who would be in attendance. Peach silk. Spangles. And waving feathers. Mrs Donaldson had provided ostrich plumes dyed to match.

She kept wondering if he meant what he had

said about not wanting another woman. The ache in her heart wanted it to be true. And it was the stupidest thing she'd ever wanted in her life. Hopefully he had come to his senses. If so, she would see it in his face and it would hurt.

Head held proudly, she strode out of the room and down the stairs with her maid trailing behind.

In the hotel lobby, she saw that Jack had forgone his kilt this evening, but Logan wore full Highland regalia. Her breath caught. The black and green of his kilt and the green-velvet coat sat on him easily. A born Scottish warrior. The froth of lace at throat and wrist intensified his masculinity.

The way his face lit up when he caught sight of her made her insides hop around. Nothing had changed. The warmth in his eyes kindled a flame in her chest and she found herself pressing her hand flat on her breast to keep her racing heart from leaping out from behind her ribs.

'I hope I haven't kept you waiting,' she said with a smile that said she didn't care one way or the other. A smile she could call on at will. Yet it felt terrible on her face. Stiff and awkward.

Jack picked up his hat and set it on his head at a jaunty angle and took Charity's arm. Logan tensed. She pretended not to notice. She and

Jack swept ahead of him, out into the dusk and the waiting carriage.

Jack settled in his seat. He stretched his neck as if he found his neckcloth too tight. A movement she'd seen him make hundreds of times when the stakes were high and the outcome uncertain. What was he up to?

He gazed straight at Logan. 'How long have you known Sanford?'

He wanted Logan to know she had told him. Wanted Logan to know she was his creature.

Logan, to his credit, looked surprised. As if he did not know she would have told Jack where he was staying. 'He's a family friend,' he replied coolly and shot an annoyed glance at Charity. Playing the game.

She hated it.

She kept her face calm. A slight smile on her lips while inside she squirmed. Had he, after all, hoped she would not betray his whereabouts? Even after her warning?

'Good to have friends at Court,' Jack said.

Logan raised a brow as if he sensed something behind the words. 'That is how I got the tickets for tonight.'

'Does he know who your guests are?'

Charity frowned. What was the purpose of these questions? There was something almost gloating in Jack's voice.

Apparently noticing nothing, Logan flashed him a grin 'He does. It wouldn't do to surprise him now, would it?'

Admiration flashed in Jack's eyes and a shade of regret. 'That it would not.'

Regret? A shiver ran down her spine. As if a ghost had walked over her grave. A feeling that something bad was about to happen. Something terrible. She glanced at Jack and garnered no clues from his bland expression.

Surely he wasn't planning to steal something. Not in front of the King and all his soldiers on guard at every doorway.

The noise outside on the street permeated the carriage. People shouting. She leaned forward to glance out of the window and was astonished by the crowds lining the street, held back by a line of soldiers as they had been on the day of his arrival. Once more the people of Edinburgh were waiting to see their King. George must be enjoying this attention. He certainly did not receive this sort of adulation in London.

The coachman opened the hatch in the roof. 'There will be quite a wait, I'm afraid, Mr Gilvry. There are a good few coaches ahead of us waiting to drop their passengers.'

'Perhaps we should walk,' Jack said.

'You will be safer in the carriage, if I might say so, sir. You will never make it through these crowds.' He grimaced. 'The chairmen are having a hard enough time forcing their way through. I've already seen one gentleman take a tumble at their hands.'

'Do your best.' Logan smiled at her. 'It is a good thing Sanford advised an early arrival.'

The carriage lurched along inch by inch. Logan relaxed in the seat opposite Charity, but his gaze was fixed on Jack. 'Well, O'Banyon, since we have time on our hands, we might as well get down to business. I have kept my side of the bargain. You've met the King and mixed with the high society and you've tasted our whisky and seen our terms. Now it is time to decide. Will ye do business with Gilvrys or do we find another distributor in London?'

Charity barely held back her gasp. No one threatened Jack. Ever. Not if they didn't want to end up dead in an alley. Beside her she felt Jack shift. Had he sensed her reaction? Sensed her fear for Logan? If he had, he would use it to his advantage. She pouted. 'Money talk. How sordid.'

Logan quirked a brow. 'I apologise if my frankness offends you, Mrs West, but I have been dancing to this particular tune for too many days now.'

If he wanted to get himself killed, who was she to prevent it? A heavy weight pressed on her chest. There was nothing she could do. She gazed at him coldly for a moment, then turned to look out of the window at the crowds. To pretend to admire the illuminations in each house's window. A crown above the royal arms here, stars framing G IV R there, the flags and the bunting gaily fluttering while she pretended not to listen to their talk.

'I'll give you my answer tomorrow, Gilvry,' Jack said. 'As I promised.'

'What difference will twelve hours make? You money has arrived from London along with whatever answer you expected from your partner. Why the delay?'

Charity resisted the temptation to turn to see Jack's reaction.

'I see you have had your spies out,' Jack said sharply.

'As you have had yours.'

Logan's calm admission made her want to scream. The feeling that something was going terribly wrong intensified.

'All right,' Jack said, leaning forwards. 'Here is my dilemma. McKenzie has made it clear that if you try to go around him, he'll destroy you. If he succeeds, that leaves me with a problem.'

'He has been trying for years and hasn't managed it yet.' The confidence in Logan's voice startled Charity into looking his way.

'And you want me to risk that he won't in the future.'

Logan shrugged. 'There is no risk.'

'I think there is. Deliver the whisky to London, then you'll get your money. And not before.'

Logan inhaled. 'Deliver without any money up front, you mean?'

'Prove you can do it.'

Logan was silent for a moment. 'I don't have the authority to change the terms.'

Jack leaned back. 'That's what I am talking about. Your brother sent a boy to do a man's job.'

If Logan was angry at the jibe, he didn't show it. He body remained relaxed, his expression nonchalant. 'I'll have your answer for you tomorrow,' he said after a brief pause.

'Ah, yes. The other brother. Lord Aleyne, isn't it? The respectable lawyer. McKenzie said he was in the thick of it. Perhaps I should have been dealing with him right from the beginning.'

At that Logan's shoulders did stiffen. 'I'll let you have my answer tomorrow.'

Jack smiled. It was more like a baring of teeth. The wolf who had a lamb in its jaws. Inside Charity trembled. For Logan. 'Then we will discuss it tomorrow,' Jack said.

The tension inside the carriage was palpable. Would they come to blows?

Thankfully the coachman's voice floated down from above. 'Here we are, sir.' A harried-looking footman hurried over to open the door and let down the steps.

Jack stepped down first and turned to help Charity out. Logan followed. Here, too, a magnificent illumination stood in front of the imposing portico of pale stone. It depicted the Crown and the King's initials arched by large thistle and two stars. The whole was surmounted by elegant festoons. They entered the building through a side door into a pale-cream marble entrance halls whose columns were twined around with flowers.

They mounted the opulently carpeted marble stairs to the first floor, entering an antechamber, already full of men in Highland dress, military uniforms, or black evening suits. Almost all the ladies were in white, with the odd touch of gold and silver here and there. Charity wondered if Mrs Donaldson had offered her the peach colour on purpose. Well, it was too late now. She smiled as she looked around at the waving white plumes. They reminded her of sea foam on stormy beach.

'No wonder they call this Crush Hall,' Logan

said cheerfully, his mood apparently unaffected by the confrontation with Jack.

The ante-room was situated between two ballrooms, one larger than the other. 'It is lovely.'

Jack grimaced. She had never seen him look quite so uncomfortable. Perhaps it was the sight of all the dress swords and a claymore or two.

Logan handed their cards to a footman, and after some considerable time, they heard their names announced and moved into the main ball-room where everyone was gathering to greet the King. A gilt-domed throne, lit by tall candela-bra, had been set on a dais at one end. Sofas upholstered to match the rich blue drapery at the windows occupied two of the other walls. Seats for those tired from dancing, or too el-derly to stand, so they could watch those on the dance floor.

She strolled the length of the ballroom on Jack's arm, admiring the soaring pilasters and the three huge crystal chandeliers and tried not to think about the past, not to recall that, if not for one youthful mistake, this would have been her life.

A roar came from outside in the street and jolted her out of her reverie. 'The King has ar-rived, I gather,' Logan said.

Charity found herself holding her breath

like a child promised a treat. She laughed. Jack grumbled something under his breath about Ireland and boot licking.

Not many minutes later, the King's retinue entered and the band struck up 'God Save the King' while everyone made their obeisance. When Charity finally glimpsed King George he was bowing affably to everyone around him. Not from his throne, but to one side of the ballroom. Tonight, he had squeezed into a military uniform with orders glittering on his chest. He waved affably to the company and the band struck up a spirited reel to start the ball.

Logan held out his hand. 'Will you join me for this set?'

She glanced at Jack. He waved a dismissive hand. 'Run along. I'm going to see if I can find some refreshments and a little less racket. Perhaps there is a room with cards.' He scanned the room as if looking for acquaintances, and not in the way of a man who would rather not meet anyone he knew. Which meant he was looking for someone in particular. Likely someone from London. Jack had many business irons in the fire.

It should mean nothing, but that odd feeling of dread returned.

She and Logan joined one of the lines. Some of the women wore tartan sashes over their white gowns. They made for a nice splash of colour. And her peach didn't seem quite so obtrusive.

The room sparkled as the ladies' gowns and jewels glittered beneath the magnificent chandeliers. The whole effect dazzled.

The King's chubby face beamed and his fingers snapped in time to the music as they passed him and his hovering gentlemen attendants, including Lord Sanford, his expression as bored and cynical as always. He raised a brow as they passed him. Logan nodded.

Charity prayed that the King would not call them over, as he had another couple. But, no, he took no notice of them and they continued down their set. They danced the next set, too, a country dance, and Charity could not remember when she had enjoyed herself so much.

This time when the music finished, Logan walked her to stand against the wall since all of the sofas were occupied. His smile was enchantingly solicitous. 'Can I fetch you some refreshment?'

While no one here would recognise her, any more than they had at the King's Drawing Room, the sense of impending doom lingered like a sour taste in her mouth. 'I will come with you.'

'Verra well.' He held out his arm and she

placed her hand on his forearm. As they passed out of the doors she glanced up at the ceiling decorated with intricately carved sweeping circles and roses. 'I have never seen such magnificence.'

'I gather it rivals the rooms in Bath,' Logan said, following her gaze. 'The Scots are nothing, if not combative.'

She laughed at his dry tone and tried to relax as he expertly guided her through the crowds to a smaller room where footmen in livery guarded enormous glass punch bowls.

And then she saw him. Growler. Dressed in livery, standing against a wall, like so many of the other servants. Her heart stopped. How? Why? She caught his eye. He stared back impassively.

Breathless, she turned to tell Logan, but before she could speak she saw a look of shock on his face. But when she followed the direction of his gaze, she realised he was not looking at Growler. He was staring at Jack, glass in hand, in deep conversation with an older gentleman garbed in kilt and bonnet.

'What is it?' she asked.

His look of shock smoothed out. 'Nothing.'

At that moment, the Highland gentleman saw Logan and, bowing farewell to Jack, he strolled towards them. When his gaze met Charity's he bowed and stuck his hand out to Logan. 'Gilvry,' he said. 'I had not thought to see you here. Is your brother here?'

Logan shook his hand. 'Neither of them, my lord. Mrs West, may I introduce you to Lord Carrick. My clan's chieftain.'

'My very great pleasure, Mrs West.'

His chieftain talking to Jack. No wonder he looked shocked. Charity dipped a curtsy. 'And mine, Lord Carrick.'

'Ah, an Englishwoman from your accent.'

'I hope you won't hold that against me, my lord?' Charity said, smiling into those assessing eyes.

Carrick gave her a vague smile. 'Not at all. That fellow I was just talking to was Irish. It seems that all the world has come to Scotland to see the King.'

'Aye, so it would seem,' Logan said. 'An Irishman, you say?'

Charity blinked at Logan's pretence.

'I bumped into him at the refreshment table. We had a few words about whisky. I am surprised not to find Ian here. Or Niall.'

Logan seemed to take his chieftain's disappointment in his stride. 'As far as I know, neither Ian nor Niall received an invitation.'

Aha. That sounded like a dig. Charity was getting a sense of an undercurrent between the two men. And not a good one. Perhaps it was Carrick who should have seen that the Gilvry brothers were invited.

But why had he been talking to Jack? Their heads had been awfully close together for casual conversation. Their expressions too intent. Yet…it was noisy in here. She had to lean in close to hear what either man was saying. It was probably nothing.

Right. Nothing. Jack never did anything without purpose. And why was Growler here? Likely to make sure she didn't disappear again. That would be very much like Jack. She would let Logan know of his presence the moment she had a chance. Thank goodness she hadn't said anything within Jack's line of sight. She shivered inwardly.

Carrick's face brightened. 'Ah, there is my wife. I promised her a dance. You will excuse me, I believe, Gilvry, Mrs West.' Without waiting for an answer he bustled away, leaving Logan looking thoughtful and his gaze scanning the room.

Charity glanced over her shoulder. Growler was gone. She looked this way and that, but he was not where she had seen him last. Nor could she see Jack in the press of people. Perhaps there was no point in getting Logan upset. He clearly didn't like to be spied on by Jack's men and she did not want to spoil their last evening together. At least not now. Later would be a different story, no doubt.

Her heart sank at the thought of what she must do and how he was going to despise her.

And then the opportunity to tell him about Growler was lost. Sanford was strolling towards them, a gentleman with a slight limp in tow. He was undoubtedly making for her and Logan. For a moment, Charity didn't quite believe her eyes, but a glance at Logan's dancing eyes and slight smile let her know this was something he had planned.

Sanford made an elegant bow. 'Sir Walter, may I introduce you to Mrs West, and my good friend, Logan Gilvry.'

Round faced, his fair hair thinning, the gentleman smiled and bowed benignly.

Logan returned the bow and Charity dipped a curtsy. 'Sir Walter,' she said breathlessly, 'I am a great admirer of your writing.' His penning of the novels *Waverly* and *Ivanhoe* among others was an open, if not acknowledged, secret.

'You are too kind, my dear lady. And have you enjoyed our little spectacle these past few days?'

'I have been truly amazed,' Charity said.

'The whole of Scotland has been pleased,'

Logan said. 'And they are all in Edinburgh, I am thinking.'

Scott looked pleased. 'The King has been most gracious with regard to my efforts. It has been a pleasure to meet you.' He bowed again and strolled away.

'Have you been to the supper room?' Sanford asked. 'It is a thing of beauty. Well worth a visit.'

'Would you like something to eat, Mrs West?' Logan asked

Perhaps Growler would be there and Logan would spot him for himself. But if he wasn't, and he didn't, then she would say something. 'If Lord Sanford says it is worth a visit, then I wouldn't miss it for the world.'

Sanford smiled and moved away.

'Thank you,' Charity said, looking up at Logan, her heart still beating a little to fast.

'For supper? You haven't had it yet.'

She tapped his arm with her fan. 'For Scott. It was your doing, wasn't it?'

'I wasn't sure Sanford would pull it off. But, aye, I did ask him to see if he might.'

An urge to kiss his cheek took her by surprise. To do so here would invite scandal, but she tried to put her feelings in the look she gave him. 'It means a great deal to me, Logan. I will remember it always.'

A faint colour touched his cheekbones. 'I am very glad you are pleased,' he murmured. 'Now, how about supper?'

Once more she took his arm. The strength of him seemed to curl around as if she was wearing a suit of armour. And people seemed to move out of the way. Perhaps his height gave him the advantage. Many of the women they passed watched him with parted lips. As if they wanted to eat him up. Disappointment filled their eyes when they realised he was not alone. She wanted to stick her tongue out at them. Instead, she moved closer to him and staked her claim. Even if it was only for tonight.

As if he sensed her thoughts, his gaze met hers and his sweet smile stole her breath.

After passing around the outside edge of the smaller ballroom where a quadrille was in progress, they moved into the room decorated like a sumptuous tent which looked over a view of the Scottish Highland. But how could that be? 'Oh, how clever,' she said. 'It is a painting. It looks so real.'

He chuckled softly. 'It does. Still, it is better in real life.'

She would never see it in real life, though, so this was almost as good. She would always be able to think of him in the midst of this dramatic scenery. If she dared let herself think of him at all.

Beneath a semi-circular arrangement of columns, tables were tastefully arranged to allow the servants access to serve, as well as providing a view of the painted scenery in one direction and the ballrooms in the other.

With Logan at her side, she could almost believe she had discovered a place where she belonged. She found herself walking taller, looking around her with confident ease. It was his strength that gave her courage. The feeling that he believed in her.

Her heart gave a funny little lurch. A warm little sensation of something tender.

And she knew she would have to tell him about Jack's plans as far as she knew them. Warn him away. But not yet. Not until the ball was over.

She smiled at him with her heart in her eyes. She just couldn't help it. 'Sanford was right,' she said, sitting in the chair he pulled out for her at an empty table. 'It is a sight to behold.'

'I'm glad you approve.' The warmth of his smile in response made her heart stumble. 'Wait here and I'll will get us a drink. Wine for you, or ratafia?'

'Ratafia.' Only fast women drank wine in

public. She did not want to put him to shame. Not when he had been so good to her. So kind.

He strolled away.

'Charlotte,' an incredulous male voice said from behind her. 'Lady Charlotte,' he amended swiftly.

Chill filled her veins as the blood drained from her head. Her stomach fell away in a sickening rush. Viscount Rawley. The man who had beguiled her with sensual pleasures and left her in ruins. Cold as ice, she turned to face him. 'Charity West now, Rawley. Mrs Charity West.'

He looked surprised. As well he might. 'Congratulations. I had no idea you had married.'

'I am a widow,' she said baldly and comprehension filled his eyes. And a predator's heat.

'What a pleasure it is to see you again after so many years.' He gestured to the chair. 'May I sit down?'

She kept her expression cool despite the roiling in her stomach. She had to be rid of him, and quickly. 'I would prefer it if you did not. My escort will return at any moment.'

'I thought I was imagining things when I saw you in the ballroom.'

Why couldn't he take a hint? 'Perhaps it would be better if you pretended you had.' Now, if he would just go.

It was too late. At that moment Logan brought

their drinks and set them on the table, all the while eyeing Mark with suspicion. Mark grimaced as he took in Logan's Highland garb.

Blast it all. 'Mr Logan Gilvry, this is Rawley.'

The two men eyed each other like dogs over a bone. How could this be happening? What was wrong with Mark? Approaching her as if he expected her to be glad to see him.

Mark's top lip curled as his gaze returned to Charity. 'How on earth did you manage an invitation to this affair? I was told it was to be pretty exclusive.'

Logan's rigid expression pierced right through her chest to her heart. The blood in her veins went from icy to boiling in what felt like seconds. He had no right to look embarrassed. He knew the kind of woman she was.

'Mr Gilvry is my host.'

Mark grinned the charmingly sly grin that used to make her stupid heart flutter. Made her forget the rules. Not any more though. Not even a little. 'Well if you want to renew our *acquaintance,* I am staying at the Crown.'

Mark knew what had become of her, of course. What she'd made of her life. Everyone who had known her did, though they would pretend they didn't. He made the word 'acquaintance' sound sordid. The flicker of Logan's jaw said he had heard the implication.

She let anger go and drew coldness around her like a wall. She smiled seductively and leaned closer. 'I wouldn't lower myself.'

He flinched, then shook his hand as if he had touched something hot. He glowered at Logan. 'Watch out she doesn't burn you.' He turned and walked away.

Logan's face expressed shock and perhaps even a touch of horror. The reaction felt like a knife in her chest. And she couldn't bear to stay and face it. It didn't matter. Their evening was over.

She rose and headed for Growler, who had drawn closer. 'Take me home.'

He glanced over his shoulder at Logan, who was still staring at Rawley's back.

'Now, Growler,' she said.

He swung around and she followed him out of the room.

They were on the stairs when she heard the sound of a crash, as if someone had dropped a tray full of dishes. She kept walking, ignoring the stares and the whispers. Ignoring the way the ladies drew their skirts back as she passed as if she could infect them with a touch.

She'd been fooling herself, thinking Logan's presence could protect her. Instead, she'd made him look a fool. She had taken his innocence and ground it beneath her heel. The pain delivered by that look on his face was enough to send her to her knees, if she let it.

But one thing was certain. Whatever Jack was up to, her part in his plan was done.

Chapter Eleven

Sanford lounged at the breakfast table in a vivid silk dressing gown, newspaper in hand, long legs stretched out to one side. For once, rather than bored, he looked annoyed. 'You were lucky they did not lock you up on the spot. And me with you for brawling in the King's presence, let alone challenging a man to a duel. There are rules about these things.'

Logan, seated opposite him, had been up and dressed for hours. He had barely slept. He'd been too restless, too full of energy. Anger remained like a red haze at the edge of his vision. Never had he felt such fury searing his brain. 'It has nothing to do with you.'

'You were there at my invitation.'

Logan stared at his hand on the pristine white tablecloth, stretching and bunching his fingers against the stiffening ache in his bruised and bloody knuckles. 'If you won't serve as my second, I'll find someone else.' Niall was the obvious answer. Damn it. He didn't want to involve his older brother. Duels were illegal and he'd be in for a bear-garden jaw. And besides, if they were caught by the authorities, it would ruin Niall's career.

'You are determined to get me hung,' Sanford said wearily, the cynicism returning to his face and voice. 'I'll go after breakfast.' He quirked a brow. 'I don't suppose you would consider apologising?'

A growl filled Logan's throat. He swallowed it. 'You didna' hear the way he spoke to her. I had no choice but to shove the words down his throat.'

'Such brutality. The madness of youth. And on behalf of a woman who…'

Logan glared at him.

Sanford sighed. 'Well, if you think she is worth getting killed for, who am I to object?'

'I'll no' be the one to die.'

Sanford lost his air of dissipation and leaned forwards. 'Don't be a fool and underestimate Rawley. He's a crack shot. I've seen him culp wafers in his cups at White's. Sober he's deadly.' He leaned back and assumed his indolent position. 'I don't know why I bother. Get yourself killed, if that is your wish.'

It was as if the man didn't want to care about anything or anyone. Logan shook his head against the stray thought. It wasn't important. 'So are ye saying you will be my second?'

The nobleman picked up his paper. 'Yes. That is what I am saying, for my sins.' He disappeared behind the pages of the *Scotsman*.

A knock at the door and the porter stuck his head inside. He did not look happy. 'I beg your pardon, my lord, but there's a woman at the door, asking for admittance.'

A woman? It had to be— 'Let her up, man.'

The porter continued to look at Sanford, who had lowered his paper just enough for a raised eyebrow above one blue eye to be visible. 'What name did she give?'

At Logan's stare, Sanford shrugged. 'You aren't the only one with females clamouring at your door. And I don't want any of mine let in.'

'She didna give a name, my lord,' the porter said. 'Rules say no women allowed.'

'What does she look like?' Logan asked.

'As to that, I couldn't say, sir. She's veiled. I'd say she was young. And English.'

'I'll go down,' Logan said. If it was Charity, he was not going to have her turned away.

'Show her up, Balfour,' Sanford said. 'Whoever she is, she is not going away before one of us sees her.'

The teasing note in his voice made Logan want to punch him in his cynical mouth. He knew it had to be Charity.

The porter retreated. Logan got to his feet, preparing to go down, but he hadn't reached the door when the veiled woman stepped inside. She must have followed the porter up the stairs. Her cloak hid her figure from view and the veil shrouded her face, but he had no doubt about her identity. 'Charity.' He reached out to take her hands.

She whipped them behind her back and looked over at Sanford. 'If you would excuse us, my lord, I would like a few moments alone with Mr Gilvry.'

Sanford's eyes narrowed, but he folded his paper, rose, gave her a sharp bow and strolled to his chamber.

'You won't forget our little piece of business,' Logan said before he closed the door.

'I'll go the moment I am dressed, as I promised.' He disappeared inside his room, where his man would be waiting to dress him. The sound of their muffled voices came through the heavy wood door.

Logan eyed Charity warily. She looked rigid, as if here was the last place she wanted to be. If that was so, why had she come? Had she heard about the duel? It seemed unlikely. She'd fled with O'Banyon's ruffian. By the time he was finished with Rawley there had been no sign of her or the carriage. 'May I take your cloak?'

She shook her head, but sat down on the chair he offered, her gloved hands clenched in her lap.

His gut tightened. 'What is it? What has happened?'

'Listen, you fool,' she said, her voice low and fierce. 'You toyed with Jack and now he is going to finish the game.'

Not here about the duel, then. Or to tell him what Rawley had implied wasn't true. The fact that she said nothing about it made his stomach clench. 'Then let O'Banyon speak to me.'

She shook her head. 'I am as much Jack's creature as Growler. You knew that. And now you will listen. Either you give Jack what he wants or Rabbie will not survive the day.'

'What?' He leaped to his feet and pulled her up to face him.

A bitter laugh disturbed the folds of fabric covering her face as she tilted her head up to meet his gaze. Infuriatingly, he could not see her expression. 'Did you think I would not tell him how fond you are of the child?' she said. 'Or how your brother dotes on him. You took me home to your family. You gave me the weapon. Did you think I would not use it?'

His hands were shaking. Yes, he had been a fool. Trusting her not to involve his family. And damn it, it hurt. But that didn't matter right now. He had to get to Niall. Warn him.

He let her go and went for his coat.

'You'll be too late,' she said.

He spun around, coat in hand.

'There is a woman with the child, waiting for a signal from one of Jack's men. If I do not walk out of here with you prepared to give Jack the information he wants, she will leave with Rabbie and it will be your brother who will give us what we need.' She shook her head. 'If that happens, I can't guarantee the child will be safe. No matter what Jack promises.'

'I can be there as fast as any message from you.' He'd go over the roof to avoid Jack's men.

She shook her head. 'There is no way into that house without being seen. And Jack expects me to bring you to him.'

Logan cursed. 'You thought of everything, didn't you?'

'You gave me everything I needed to do so.' Her voice was like a cold wind across a glacier.

He thought of little Rabbie and what his loss would do to Jenna and Niall and the breath left his body. He let his coat fall to the floor. 'What is it Jack wants to know?'

She glanced at Sanford's chamber door and moved closer, lowering her voice. 'He wants the location of your brother's store of whisky.'

'Why?'

'It's not my business to know why.'

The hands clasped at her chest were shaking. Her voice was calm, almost too calm, but no matter how hard she tried to hide it, her hands were trembling. She was terrified. Of what? Him? Hardly. Her partner in crime, then. But why?

'Charity—'

She turned away from him. 'Come. Now. If you and I do not leave your door together within a minute or two, a runner will go to Jack with the news that you have decided not to help us.' She headed for the door.

And he had no choice but to follow her down the stairs.

But he didn't understand. Why did Jack need to know the whisky's location when Ian had been more than willing to sell him all they had? At a fair price, too. There was certainly no way to steal it. Not from a keep that had withstood centuries of armies at its gates. Which meant there was something else going on.

If he could just figure out what it was. And Charity's part in it.

Outside, a carriage waited at the kerb. Charity got in. Logan joined her, risking a glance up at the window of his apartments as he ducked inside. He was sure he saw the curtain move a fraction. Had Sanford overhead their conversation? It was possible. The trouble was, any interference from that quarter was likely to make things worse.

Sanford wasn't a fool. If he had heard, he wouldn't risk the child's life. Would he?

He sat back against the squabs, trying to maintain an outer appearance of calm. He flexed his hand in his lap, feeling the sting of broken skin.

'What happened to your hand?' she asked from the other side of the carriage.

'Why would you care?'

She shrugged and caused the fabric of her veil to flutter. 'I don't.'

'And I'm not in the mood for idle conversation.'

He stared at her. At the shadowy outline of her face, the cloak wrapped so tight about her as to hide her delectable shape. She was no different to Maggie. Another woman who had proved she would do anything to get what she wanted. Not that he regretted their time together. He would not have missed making love to her, not even if he had known how things would end. Which showed just how much of an idiot he was.

He really had been a fool to think of her as anything but Jack's willing tool. If she hadn't been willing, she would have come to him and asked for help. Wouldn't she?

The pity of it was, he likely would have done anything at all to set her free. Except betray his family.

Clearly she had not seen it. Or had not cared. The realisation was a bitter taste in his mouth.

'Charity, you don't want to do this. If we—'

She turned her face away to look out of the window. 'Do not say another word.'

A trick of the light outlined her profile beneath the white muslin. And there were shadows that— He dived across the carriage and lifted the filmy fabric. A red mark already turning the purple of a bruise ran from cheekbone to jaw. 'Who did this? Growler?'

She shoved at him with her hands. 'Get away from me.'

'Who was it, Charity?'

Her heather-coloured eyes flashed defiance. 'Jack. If not for Growler, it would have been a lot worse, I can assure you.'

'Why?'

'Because I was not supposed to leave last night without the information he wanted.'

'I would never have told you.'

Her mouth twisted in a bitter line. 'That was what I told him.'

He traced the line of the bruise, the marks of Jack's knuckles on her beautiful fragile skin. 'I'm sorry.'

She looked at him steadily. 'I'm not.' She touched her cheek. 'Or I wasn't. I was glad you wouldn't betray your family.' Her eyes shimmered and she blinked the moisture away. 'But I was stupid enough to say so.'

'You told him about Rabbie.'

'No. Growler watched the house after we left. Talked to the servants.' She gave a small shake of her head. 'But my words sparked the idea. I'm sorry.'

The apology meant more to him than it should. 'He never intended to do business with us, did he?'

'I don't know. He doesn't tell me everything. But I knew whatever he was doing was important.' She straightened her shoulders. 'He offered me a lot of money to…to lure you into my bed.'

He flinched at the hard edge in her voice.

She shrugged.

Absently, he rubbed at his knuckles through

his gloves as he stared at the livid mark on her face. What he'd give to have Jack in front of him right at that moment.

She glanced down at his hands. 'You hit him, didn't you? Rawley. That was the crash I heard.'

He grimaced. 'He is a cur.'

'But not a liar.' She turned her face away and he saw the movement in her throat as she swallowed.

'He was your lover, then.' Hell. Why ask a question when he knew the answer?

'Yes.'

The pain in her voice seemed to tighten a vice around his chest, squeezing the air from his lungs. Apparently she still cared for the man. He forced his hurt aside. Right now he had more important things on his mind. Like how to keep Rabbie safe.

'Logan...' Her voice was hesitant.

He looked at her and the sight of the ugly bruise on her face hit him anew. It was like a blow to the kidneys. It made him feel sick. 'What?'

'There is something I think you should know. I heard Jack talking to Growler. He said the moment he had the information he wanted we would leave.' She frowned, then winced as the slight tension must have caused her pain.

He wanted to hit something. Preferably Jack.

'He said he had never made so much money for so little effort. That secrets were worth more than their weight in gold.'

'Secrets?'

'The way he spoke…I think he wanted the information for someone else.'

'McKenzie?'

'Maybe.' She sounded unsure.

'I can't think why McKenzie would care. He closed Edinburgh's gates to us. He has more business than he can handle. It is why we went to Jack.'

Her hands twisted in her lap, her eyes were dark pools of compulsion. 'You have to give him what he wants. He never makes idle threats. If you play him false, he'll find a way to carry it out. Years later, if he must. If he didn't, he would soon lose control.'

'Perhaps someone in authority needs to take a look at Jack and his business.'

She gave a short laugh. 'As far as I know, everyone in authority is part of his business.'

She was wrong. Not everyone. Not Sanford, no matter how jaded the man appeared. But she was right. He could not risk Rabbie's life for the sake of a wee drop of whisky. He would have to tell Jack the truth. Then deal with the consequences. And Ian.

The carriage turned a corner and shaft of

sunlight caressed her skin with golden light. And made the bruise seem all the more ugly. While women could be the very devil with their lies and trickery, he did not believe any man had the right to brutalise them. His fists clenched at the thought of what he would like to do to Jack for that bruise. 'You will stay wi' me.'

She gasped. Her eyes widening. 'What are you talking about?'

'You canna go back to him after this.'

The straightening of her spine warned him she was about to argue.

'No, Charity. You have done as required. Your part in this is over.'

A bitter smile curved her lips. 'And you think he will just let me go? I am too valuable. I know too much. He would kill me before he would let me leave.'

Nausea roiled in his belly. Anger was a hot hard bubble in his chest. 'He told you that?'

She glanced out of the window. 'We are almost there. Get back on your side,' she hissed and pulled down her veil. 'Forget about me. I overheard him talking to Growler. If I leave this carriage, he has orders to shoot me in the back.'

The bubble burst in the rush of fury. At Jack. At her acceptance of her fate. 'I can shield you.'

'No,' she said dully, shaking her head slowly. 'Don't be a fool. Think of Rabbie.'

His fists opened and closed convulsively. Helplessly. How could he endanger the life of a child? But Charity? How could he let Jack take her away?

She leaned forwards as the carriage started to slow. 'I heard something else, Logan. Listen,' she snarled as he opened his mouth to speak. 'I don't know what you can do, but...' She glanced at the door that would open at any moment. 'Logan, it is the militia who is to be told where the whisky is hidden.'

Logan gaped at her.

The carriage door swung back.

Logan snapped his mouth shut and stared into Growler's punchbag-of-a-face, then back at Charity.

'Good riddance, smuggler,' she said in a voice devoid of emotion.

'Out,' Growler said.

He stepped down. In the early morning sunlight, the street looked just as it had the last time he was here. Apart from about a score of hard-eyed rough-looking men idling at intervals along the street, standing in groups of two or three. Watching.

McKenzie's men. And those were the ones he could see. A flea couldn't hop off a dog without these men knowing. A familiar figure stood on his brother's front doorstep. O'Banyon.

The carriage moved off and he glanced over his shoulder. There was no last glimpse of her face. But that didn't mean he wouldna be seeing her again. Growler gestured him to cross the road.

O'Banyon came down the steps to meet him.

Logan quelled the urge to punch the smirk off the florid man's face. Instead he held his tongue, waiting and watching, looking for any advantage that would mean he did not have to betray his family.

O'Banyon rubbed his hands together with a raspy sound. 'Well?'

Right down to business, was it? After days of shilly-shallying. He should have guessed there was something up. But the militia. Why the hell the militia? What was the advantage? Money. Money for secrets, Charity had said. And a lot of it. And if so, was it the government paying? Had he been wrong in trusting Sanford after all?

Well, he still had one small card up his sleeve. O'Banyon did not know he knew why the information was wanted.

He almost groaned as the idea took solid logical shape. He really had been an idiot. 'Gilvry whisky is stored in Dunross Keep, where neither you nor McKenzie could ever get your hands on it. The keep is not going to fall to a bunch of cutthroats,' he bluffed.

'Do ye think so, boyo?' O'Banyon said, his smile growing wider. 'Well now, we will see about that, will we not?' He shifted closer until Logan could see every whisker, some grey, some brown, piercing his jaw and smell the odour of stale ale. 'And if you're telling me lies now,' he drew one finger across his throat. 'A promise is a promise.'

Logan glared at him. 'So Charity said. You have the truth. Now get you and your men out of my brother's house and out of my sight. I'll see you next beating your head against Dunross's walls.'

The Irishman jerked his head towards Growler, who gave a piercing whistle. The men in the street walked away. Two came out of the front door at a run, hustling a young woman between then. O'Banyon and Growler backed away from him and crossed the road. A carriage raced around the corner and picked them up. And just like that it was over. The street was quieter than the grave.

Logan ran up the steps and into the house with his heart in his throat, praying he'd not been wrong to trust the Irishman's word. Or Charity's. She had promised they would be safe. He found his brother and sister-in-law bound and gagged and looking furious in the drawing room. He cut them free. Niall raced for the stairs with Jenna behind him.

His mouth was dry as he followed, taking the stairs two at a time. Let the child be all right. Please. Let him be all right.

He was lying in his crib, waving a rattle and chortling at shadows on the ceiling. Unharmed. Happy.

Logan fell to his knees in the doorway in gratitude, all breath gone from his lungs as Jenna picked him up and held him close. Niall enfolded both of them in his arms, his breathing sounding harsh. Finally, he eased his grip and looked over at Logan.

'I'll never forgive you for this, Logan. Bringing them into my house, my home, near my family.'

The words tore into his heart and his soul like the lash of a whip. 'I'll never forgive myself.'

'Get out,' Niall said, turning his back.

'Stop it, Niall,' Jenna said. 'It is not your brother who deserves your anger. He was taken in by… Well, he was just as taken in as I was. Let us leave it at that.'

Niall unclenched his fists, but he didn't look in any way sorry for what he had said. And nor should he, when he was right.

He watched Jenna rock his child in her arms for a moment or two, then looked over at Logan.

'Your Irishman refused to believe me when I told his man that the whisky was held in the old mill.'

Logan heaved a sigh. 'He's not my Irishman. And he wouldna', because it isna'. Ian moved it into the keep the week before I left. McKenzie must have already looked there.'

Niall looked puzzled. 'I suppose it will be safe enough in the keep for a while.'

'Not if the revenue men have a search warrant.'

Niall groaned. 'That's why I always told Ian to keep it elsewhere. No direct tie.' He frowned. 'But what good does it do to any of them to lose the whisky to the revenue?'

'I wish I bloody well knew.'

'Then you best hurry and let Ian know, hadn't you?' He once more gathered his wife and child into his arms as if he couldn't bear to be apart from them for more than a moment.

It would be a long time before Niall forgave him. He had seen that in his brother's eyes and he understood the feeling all too well.

'Aye. I'll let Ian know right away,' he said to his brother's back and ran down the stairs and out into the street. Yes, Ian needed to know. But anyone could take a message. He had an early morning appointment tomorrow. The honour of the Gilvrys depended on his attendance. And so did Charity's. He didn't care what she was, or what she'd done, no man was going to say such things to her and get away with it.

Doing the right thing was always harder than pleasing your own selfish desires, but in the end you had the satisfaction of feeling better about yourself. In the end. It was a lesson Charity wished she had learned as a girl. Hopefully Logan would be able to make it back to Dunross and salvage something before the authorities arrived.

And in the meantime, she would pray that Jack never realised why.

At the sound of a door opening behind her, Charity turned from gazing down at the crowds on Abbey Hill to see Jack walk in, rubbing his hands together, a satisfied smirk on his face. She breathed a sigh of relief. Nothing in his expression said he suspected she'd played him false.

He swaggered to the sideboard and poured a brandy. 'We'll be leaving first thing in the morning. Ye'll be having that wench of yours doing the packing.'

She nodded. 'I will be glad to return to civilisation.' She walked to the bell pull and rang the bell for something to do. Something to stop her pacing the room. The hotel staff had quickly learned that when her bell rang in the afternoons, they were to bring the tea tray. Right now though, Jack's brandy looked tempting. But she needed her wits about her if she was to keep one step ahead.

He tossed back his drink. 'Aye, the pickings in the taverns are too poor to keep us. These Scots like to hang on to their money. For the most part.' She glanced at his face. Oh, yes, he was gloating all right.

'I want my share, Jack.'

He gave her a look of wide-eyed innocence. 'Your share?'

'Of the money you were paid to trap the Gilvrys. Don't think about lying to me. I know you too well.'

He gave a harsh laugh. 'Can't pull the wool over your eyes, colleen, can I?' He pulled a velvet pouch from the tails of his coat. A surprisingly fat velvet pouch. He tossed it on to the sofa. 'That'll keep you in silk gowns for a year or more.'

She fingered the jewels at her throat. Paste. As clever as he thought himself, Jack would never believe that she didn't care about decking herself out in the finest of everything. And she had never disabused him of the notion. It allowed her to squirrel away some of her earnings.

'I suppose it will make up for the hours wasted on a country bumpkin,' she said, her tone bored and her gaze flicking to that velvet pouch. After all, gold was why she did what she did, and did it well.

He gave her a sour look. 'For a time there, I thought you'd gone soft on him.'

So soft, she'd melted into a puddle. And she had no idea if the information she'd given him would be of the slightest help. Not knowing was the worst part. 'Why, Jack,' she purred in her most seductive tone, 'I thought you knew me better?'

He snorted. 'You won't have to worry about him again. With luck he'll be dead by morning.'

'He's been caught smuggling?' Had he not gone back to Dunross to warn his clan?

'Not him.' Jack put down his bumper with a sharp rap of glass against polished wood. 'The young fool knocked some toff down with his fives, Growler tells me. Handily. The man challenged him.'

She struggled to keep an expression of dismay from her face. He was going to duel with Rawley? Over her? Her heart clenched, a sweet little ache at the thought he cared enough to defend her honour. But that was before what had happened today. He wouldn't feel that way now.

'Pistols at dawn on Leith Links, when they should have had it out with their fists and be done with it the way a real man would.'

Not the nobility. It wasn't their way. But a duel? With Rawley. A crack shot. 'Men,' she said derisively.

'Aye. Too clever by half, that young man. Let us hope the other one puts a bullet in his brain.' He made a sound of derision. 'Half the time these bucks challenge each other and then fire in the air. Honour satisfied or some such rot.'

And Jack was watching her like a cat at a mouse hole. Looking for her reaction. 'Why, Jack, I believe you are jealous.' She laughed. 'Jealous of that naïve boy.'

Jack's fists clenched and she measured the distance between them. He wasn't close enough to deliver another of his backhanded blows. Not without taking a step or two. But that didn't mean he wouldn't. She resisted the urge to touch the bruise on her cheek and forced a smile. 'It seems I managed to fool you as I fooled him. And you know I despise all men equally.'

'You don't despise my money.' He glanced pointedly at the sofa.

'My money, Jack. I earned it.' Just looking at it made her feel ill. She gave a long sigh and hoped it didn't sound as false as it felt. 'Truth to tell, I did have a bit of a soft spot for the lad. He reminded me of my brother. He thought it was all such a grand adventure.'

'Well, the adventure is over.'

'Yes,' she said briskly. 'Onward and upward, right, Jack? You are done with him now.'

A gloating smile touched his thin lips. 'And so are you.'

A shiver rippled down her spine. The threat thickened the air between them. A warning that she would have to earn his trust all over again.

A soft rap and the door swung open. A young lad with the tea tray, his head bobbing, as he walked to the table by the window. 'Your tea, ma'am.' Whenever he delivered her tea, his voice reminded her of Logan, with its soft Highland burr. Most of the servants were lowlanders, their northern cousins being too stiff in the neck to serve *Sassenachs,* Jack had said one day when she had mentioned it in passing. It was something she had intended to ask Logan about, but hadn't. And wouldn't now, of course.

A pain slid between her ribs like a knife finding a new home. She hated Jack. But if she could continue to keep her feelings hidden she could soon be rid of him. 'Thank you. You can put it over there.' She nodded at the table near the sofa.

'Anything else, mistress?' he asked, hovering by the tray, bobbing like a duck in mating season.

'No. Thank you.' She pulled a few coins from her reticule and dropped them in his palm. He touched his forehead with a knuckle. She'd talked to him one afternoon for a few moments. He was the only breadwinner in his family and exceedingly grateful for the little bit of coin she gave him when he brought the tray. 'I hope your mother is feeling better,' she said.

The boy's eyes widened in surprise 'Yes, miss. Thank you, miss. Verra kind of you to remember.'

Jack glowered at him. 'Be off with you.'

He grinned, ducked his head again and shot for the door.

'Ye give them too much,' Jack grumbled as he always did when she gave veils to the servants at the club. 'They come to expect it and turn sullen when they are disappointed.'

'What I do with my money is my business, Jack,' she said calmly, while her stomach tied itself in knots of fear for Logan.

She had warned him to be careful. What more could she do?

'I'll leave you to your tea,' Jack said, picking up his hat from the table where he'd laid it when he came in. 'I have business to see to.'

The business of his plans against the Gilvrys, no doubt. Teeth gritted, she nodded. She took a seat on the sofa, beside the black velvet pouch. 'Shall I have your company here for dinner? Or shall we spend one last night on the town? Bring in a little more coin.'

'Not tonight. I have a meeting with McKenzie and others.'

'Then I will see you in the morning. At first light.'

'Don't keep me waiting.' He strode out.

A duel. Over her? Surely after what had occurred today, he would have withdrawn. Even so, the thought that he had been prepared to fight for her honour made her eyes water. She blinked the foolish tears away.

Whatever feelings Logan might have had for her, they would have turned to hatred by now. She needed a plan that would let her slip away from Jack the moment they arrived in London. Disappear. Panting with fear, she hefted the purse in her hand, felt the weight of the gold and heard the chink of metal as she let her fingers play amid the velvet folds. It might just be enough, with what she had already. Judas had nothing on her.

And if she was going to start having regrets, she would end up driving herself mad. Slowly, painfully, she pulled cold emptiness around her. It had served to keep regrets at bay before and it would have to serve this time.

But it didn't. The ache in her chest worsened. If this duel went ahead and he died, she would never be able to live with it. There had to be some way to stop him from getting himself killed.

She rose and put the pouch in the metal box on the writing table and turned the key. She had earned every coin with pieces of her soul. And possibly Logan's life.

Something inside her shattered.

A small sound behind her caused her to whirl around. The maid was standing behind her in the bedroom doorway. How much had she seen? She hid the box with her body.

'What do you want?'

The girl held up the dress she'd worn to the ball. 'It is ripped,' the girl said, pointing to the dirty rent in the skirt. She frowned. 'Perhaps it can be patched with a piece from the hem. Or a wee bit of embroidery.'

Ball gowns. They would be of no use in the quiet country life she hoped to lead.

'Throw it out,' she said flatly. 'I won't be wearing it again.' She didn't want anything that reminded her of the past few days. It was too painful, the way she kept seeing his face in her mind and remembering his kisses. She'd been right about him from the start. He was a charming rogue and the very worst sort of man for her sort of woman.

And she for him.

She raised a brow at the girl standing before her with her jaw practically dropping on her chest. 'You can toss out all the gowns bought here. I will never wear them again.'

'They are much too good to throw away,' the girl spluttered.

'Then you keep them. Wear them. Sell them. I really have no interest.' Jack wouldn't care what happened to them. They weren't purchased with his coin.

'I wouldn't want the gentleman to think I stole them.' the girl said, all breathless and hopeful.

Hope. It was a fine thing to have hope. She envied the girl with all her heart and managed a gentle smile. 'I will give you a note, saying I gave them to you as a gift.'

'Thank you, ma'am. Thank you.'

An idea formed in her mind. A mad idea as she gazed at the girl. Sized her up. 'Finish packing and then lend me your coat.'

The Reiver was more crowded than it had been last time. Charity sank deeper into the hood of her cloak, merging into the shadows around her corner table. Away from the hearth, out of the light of the nearest lantern swinging from the low ceilings, she still stood out like a sore thumb. A woman alone was a moth to a flame for men. More than one had already approached her. A cold look and a mumbled word about waiting for her man had been sufficient to send them on their way. So far.

The wine she cradled within her palms remained untouched. A deep swallow would give her the courage she craved, a glass or two would numb the pain around her heart, but she needed all her wits. The plan she had formulated had little or no chance of success. But she could not live with herself if she didn't try.

How long since she'd despatched her message. Half an hour? Time seemed to crawl. The longer she remained, the greater the chance of discovery. The boy who had lost a large sum to Jack the second night they'd come here was at the tables again. His face reddened by drink. If he saw her...

It had to work. It just had to. Logan would never forgive her for this. Good. That's what she wanted, wasn't it? A clean break. A way to make sure he got her out of his head and his heart.

If indeed she had made a place there.

He had certainly wormed his way into her heart. And what little shred might be left of her soul. And she had to be rid of him, once and for all.

A stir at the door. Slowly, she glanced across

from beneath the folds of her hood. A chill filled her veins. The squat figure with its low-crowned hat was unmistakable. Growler. Chilling black eyes searched the room. Trembling, she drew deeper into the shadows. She'd chosen this table because she could observe the door while remaining unseen. With Growler standing there she felt as if she had a beacon over her head. She wanted to look away, pretend she didn't see him, avoid his eye. But if she moved, he would notice. She sat frozen, like a sparrow in the eye of a snake.

The man moved deeper into the room, not looking her way. Indeed, he had his gaze fixed on another table by the hearth. A breath left her lips. She stared down at her hands, not moving. Pretending to be as small as an ant. He would never notice an ant. If he was here though, was Jack close behind? Her blood ran cold. She should leave now.

Hiding her departure from Growler would not be easy. He had a sixth sense for anything untoward. For sniffing out secrets. More than once he had seen through someone who intended her harm and saved her skin. But he was Jack's man. Her heart thundered in her ears. She would have to leave and wait for her quarry outside in the street.

The shadows across the back of her gloved

hands darkened. She looked up. Her heart stopped. A breath caught in her throat as she stared into eyes as dark as an abyss. Growler.

She swallowed and met his gaze squarely.

'What are you doing here, Miss Charity?'

She gave him her coldest glance. 'If it is any of your business, I was bored. I needed some company.'

His hard gaze swept over her. 'I can keep you company.'

She could scarcely hear him from the loud beat of blood in her ears. 'Not your sort of company. I'm meeting an old friend.' Truth made her sound convincing. 'Promise me you won't tell Jack.'

His expression didn't change, but she thought she saw a flash of sympathy in those dark eyes, where usually she saw nothing at all. 'I won't tell him nothing, but call out if you need me. The gov'ner'd have my guts for a necklace if anything 'appened to you on my watch. I'll give you one hour, then I take you back to the hotel.'

The crowds at the door shifted. Parted. And then there he was. Rawley.

Growler must have felt her stiffen. His eyes narrowed on the blond man clearly scanning the crowds. 'Him?' He sounded disgusted.

Orders. Growler understood orders. And she'd been born to give them. She glared at him. 'Take a seat over there, out of the way.' She flicked dismissive fingers. 'You can stand guard, if that pleases you, but do not interrupt.'

He hesitated.

One brow arched, she stared him down.

And nearly sagged with relief when he shuffled off to lean against a blackened upright supporting the low ceiling. Far enough away not to hear her words. Close enough to grab her should she try to run. Perhaps luck was with her after all. Growler's presence would stop anything untoward. Rawley was not a man to be trusted.

She flung back her cloak. Lifted a hand and waved. She knew the moment Rawley saw her. His eyes widened, his fair skin flushed and his jaw dropped. She was wearing her red velvet tonight. A gown that exposed more flesh than was decent, even for a member of the demi-monde. Her favourite suit of armour.

And judging from the way he was hurrying to her table, he hadn't noticed Growler. His eyes were fixed on her bosom. Men. They were all the same.

Not quite all. Logan, while he definitely appreciated her female form, had the decency to look at her face most of the time. He would make some nice Highland girl a wonderful husband.

An ache tightened her chest and rose in a hot

hard lump in her throat, making her eyes water. Smoke. Coal smoke from the hearth, smoke from pipes. The air was thick with it.

She lounged casually against the seat back and pasted a welcoming smile on her lips. Not too welcoming. Not too eager. The kind of smile that said she knew he wouldn't be able to resist her invitation. As he drew near, she held out her hand for him to kiss and quelled her shudder of revulsion as she felt the warmth of his skin against her palm and the press of hot dry lips on her knuckles.

She could do this. She had to.

'Charlotte,' he breathed.

'Charity, remember,' she said, with a nonchalant little titter, 'or Char, if you find that easier to remember.' It has been his pet name for her years ago.

'Char.' His gaze roved her face, and then slid down to her chest. He licked his lips. 'You look lovelier than ever.'

'You haven't changed a bit,' she lied. Now she looked at him more closely, she could see his fair hair was thinning on top, but he was still a handsome devil. The kind who could turn a foolish young girl's head without trying.

He sat, grinning with pleasure, eyeing her with lust, and tugged at his neckcloth. 'I was astounded to get your message.'

She leaned closer, twirling her wine glass in her fingers, knowing the valley between her breasts would deepen with the movement. He could not keep his eyes from it. 'Were you?'

He swallowed, still looking at her like a starving man. 'I had been drinking the other night, I wasn't very polite.'

'I put it down to surprise,' she said with a dismissive smile.

He glanced up then, and there was anger in his eyes. 'Your escort didn't take it so kindly.'

'He's a bit of a hot head, I'm afraid.'

A waiter raised his brow as he pushed his way through the crowds to stand at their table. 'Brandy,' Rawley said. 'A large one.' The waiter hurried off.

Rawley put his hand over hers where it lay flat on the table. 'Lord, Char. It is good to see you again.'

She gave him an arch look, aware of Growler's grim stare. Thank goodness, he made no move. He was confident he could be at her side in a second, if she needed him.

He stroked the back of her hand, then picked it up, holding it between both of his and gazed limpidly into her eyes. Spiders crawling up her arm would not have felt more unpleasant. She contained a shiver.

'I really missed you,' he murmured.

Anger surged hot and out of control, under-pinned by all the old bitterness. The hurt. 'You owe me for not telling the truth to my father.'

He flinched. After all, he had seduced her, long before the night they were caught in the hayloft. She'd thought he loved her and would come for her, when she went along with his lies to her brothers.

'What do you want?' he said. 'Money? I've little enough.'

'I heard you gambled away a fortune since your father died.' He'd done the round of the hells. With Jack's permission she had stayed out of sight when he came to the Chien Rouge.

His mouth tightened and he let her hand go when the waiter brought his drink. He took a deep swallow. When he looked back at Charity the warmth in his eyes was fading. 'Is that what you want, Char? To ride over old turf?'

If she didn't stop acting like a cornered bad-ger, he would leave. She could see the intention forming on his face.

She let go a long sigh and smiled. 'You are right. Water under the bridge.' She toasted him with her wine. 'But as I said. You owe me some-thing. Withdraw from the duel and I will con-sider the debt paid.'

He wet his lips. 'I can't do that,' he whispered hoarsely. 'He hit me. I'd be a laughing stock.

My honour in the dust. He is the one who must apologise.'

Logan would never do it. He had too much pride.

'I never asked you for anything, Mark. Not even marriage. And I had the right.'

He shook his head and she wanted to scream. 'I can't.'

'What do you want?' she asked, thinking of the velvet pouch in her writing case. 'Money?'

Guilt crossed his face. 'Some Irishman came to me the other night and paid me to make sure he dies on the field.' He swallowed. 'I lost a lot at the tables this week.'

She stiffened. 'What?' Jack. It had to be. No wonder he had looked so pleased with himself. She cast a glance a Growler. He'd sat down at a table with a mug of ale before him. Watching. He would have told Jack about the altercation at the ball. And Jack had seen it as an opportunity.

Rawley took a deep breath. 'I'd have to wound him at the very least.' He lifted his hands. 'It's the best I can do.'

She opened her mouth to argue.

'It is the best I can do, Char. You don't understand, this Irishman is a dangerous man.'

She understood all to well. 'You promise? No more than a flesh wound.' Rawley had always been an excellent shot. That was what her brothers had said.

'I swear it on my honour.' His mouth twisted. 'And I hope to hell this Scot of yours misses his target. This is going to ruin my reputation.' He tossed off his brandy and looked at her. 'Can I hope to meet you in London?'

She smiled sweetly and leaned closer. 'Not a chance.'

He laughed and got up. 'You always were a wild one, Charlotte.' He strolled across the room to a table with a card game in progress.

She glanced at Growler and pushed to her feet. His face held an expression of worry, but he was not looking at her. He was staring at the door. She followed his gaze, thinking Jack must have arrived.

And saw Logan.

Her stomach roiled. This she had not expected. Behind her Growler signalled to a waiter for his reckoning.

Keeping her gaze fixed on Logan, she strolled to the door and started when their gazes met, as if in surprise.

A tug pulled at her heart as she gazed at his beautiful face. How could she have ever thought she could have him? This beautiful pure young man.

It had been a lovely dream. Magical. But

Logan needed a different woman. An honest girl. Not a soiled dove.

She could not, would not, drag him down into the sewers. It would ruin what she loved about him. Love. Had she really fallen in love? If so, it was nothing like what she had felt for Rawley all those years ago. And if she had fallen in love, which she very much doubted, it was a cruel jest on the part of Eros.

She breathed through the tears filling her throat and blinked back those burning her eyes as she pasted a cold smile on her lips and hoped he'd not seen her with Rawley.

Chapter Twelve

In three swift strides, he reached her, but he was looking over her shoulder. 'What are you doing here?' he growled.

'Business for Jack. I thought you had left for Dunross to protect your precious whisky.'

A barmaid passed them and her gaze lingered on Logan's face as if Charity didn't exist. A stab of jealousy twisted sharply in her chest. She had no reason to be jealous.

'I leave tomorrow morning,' he said.

After the duel. 'Well, I am sure you do not wish to spend your last few hours in Edinburgh talking to me, so if you will excuse me…'

The expression on his face didn't change. Indeed, he looked as if it had been carved from marble. By a master sculptor. She steeled herself for what she must do next.

She lifted her hand and placed it flat on his heart. Through the layers of cloth she felt its steady rhythm and his tension. A weapon about to go off half-cocked. 'You have no need for concern, Growler is with me.' Then she gave him a coquettish sidelong glance. 'Surely you were not hoping for another round between the sheets before I go?'

His eyes heated. He glanced at Growler standing a little distance off and turned his shoulder with a charming smile. 'That is exactly how I would like to spend the next few hours.'

The words seared her, made her melt inside when she had intended to be unbending. 'Sadly, it isn't possible.' She hoped her voice didn't show how breathless she felt. 'If you will excuse me.' She made to dodge around him.

'Charity,' he said softly, shifting to block her path.

As well as desire, there was another expression in his eyes. Wariness. As if he had done something he thought she would not like.

'Can't you get it through your thick Scottish head that I have had enough of you?' Firmly, she stepped around him, knowing Growler would be right on her heels.

'I don't believe you,' he said.

She continued on past him and heard a low rumbling rising from his chest like distant thun-

der. The man was about to explode. She ran up
the stairs to the street, leaving Growler to follow
as best he could, and stepped out into the alley
to the sound of a chorus of chirps and whistles,
as if a flock of small birds were flying overhead.
She looked up. It was night. Then—

A pair of strong arms went around her waist.
Rough fabric brushed her face, a sack. Someone
had put her in a sack. In the distance, she heard
Growler yell. And then a thump, like wood hitting wood at the same moment she was tossed
into a vehicle. A lurch, the sound of horses'
hooves and wheels grinding over the cobbles
and the carriage moved off.

Was this Jack's work? Had he guessed she
might try to stop the duel? Or was Logan trying to get back at Jack for what had been done
to his nephew? Whichever one of those two idiots it was, she was going to make them pay. She
gritted her teeth and let her anger burn.

'Ye should hae seen his face,' Tammy chor-
tled to Logan as the carriage whipped around
the corner.

Logan got up from his crouch to sit beside
him and glance back at the two men hanging
on behind. Everyone safely aboard. 'Watch the
road. We have only a minute or two. He would
ha' seen the carriage leaving.'

His men had got between her and her ever-present watchdog and given him the time he needed to get her into the carriage and away. Now they needed to take advantage of every second of their lead.

Tammy grinned at him. 'The things a man will do to win the love of a woman.'

Tonight wasn't going to win him much in the way of love. Not that his original plans would have served him any better. He'd planned to abduct her from her hotel room. Fortunately the boot boy he had set to keep an eye on her movements had a brain in his head and had let him know she'd gone out. And then followed her. His back teeth ground together hard enough to crack them. He had not expected to find her with Rawley.

Not after her reaction to meeting him at the Assembly Rooms. He was looking forward to her explanation. If she'd deign to give him one, that was.

Women were tricky wee things, and he doubted she'd tell him the truth. He'd just have to be very careful she didn't shove a knife in his ribs when he was sleeping. An image of sleeping next to Charity sent his blood heading south. He shook his head at himself. He doubted she'd ever let him get near her again, after tonight. But at least she would be safe from Jack.

The carriage stopped beside the tenements on Niddery Street that ran along the back of the South Bridge. Logan and two of his men jumped down and kept watch while he hauled her out of the carriage and slung her over his shoulder. 'Put me down,' she yelled, struggling like a trout in a net.

Tammy whipped up the horses and took off down the street.

'You know what to do,' he said to his men who were grinning at him like a couple of idiots. One of them unlocked the battered old wooden door and let him in, locking it behind them.

'Logan?' The surprise in her voice was priceless.

'Yes,' he answered and started down the rickety stairs.

'Put me down,' she yelled from inside her sack. 'You have no right—'

He did put her down and nudged her inside the brick-vaulted chamber. He untied the sack and pulled it off, revealing a deliciously flushed and tousled furious woman.

Lord, but she was lovely when she was roused. He slammed the door shut behind him.

He'd been angry himself, watching her fawn all over that…that *Sassenach*. He wanted to know what she was about, but that wasn't where he intended to start. 'My home is your home,' he said, gesturing to the damp and grimy chamber.

She glared at him, her bosom rising and falling in that revealing dress. It was all he could do not to stare.

'How dare you,' she finally managed to say.

'I'm sorry, *mo chridhe*. This was the only way I could think of to get you away from O'Banyon.'

Her mouth gaped. 'What? Are you mad? Growler was right there. Do you think he won't come after you?'

He had never thought this would be easy, but he had a feeling explaining this to Charity was going to be like sticking a hand in a lion's mouth to see if it had teeth. Might as well get to the point of it. 'Gilvry men do not abandon gently bred females to a life of crime.'

Fists clenched, she spun away from him, took a few steps to the back of the dusty room, looking around her at the ratty old chairs and the bed in the corner. It was his usual bolt-hole when he came to Edinburgh. Staying with Sanford had been a treat. He watched the way her body moved inside that revealing dress, the rounded shape of that lovely bottom, and waited for the next salvo.

When she turned to face him, a beguiling smile curved her lips, but her eyes were as hard as granite. He braced for the storm. In time, she would come to see it was the right thing. If she didn't cut his throat first.

'What you mean is, you haven't had enough of me yet,' she said musingly.

The woman he'd first met was back. The female who hid behind a wall of sensuality. But she could not fool him any longer. He'd seen behind those walls. 'I will never have enough of you, *leannan*.'

The sensual sway of her body as she prowled towards him had his mouth drying and his breath catching in his throat. He could walk away. Of course he could. But he didn't want to. Had no reason to. She was his, whether she realised it or not yet.

And he was definitely hers.

With a graceful movement, her hands lay flat on his chest. She must be able to feel the thunder of his heart under his coat. Had to. He could barely hear his own thoughts for the noise of it.

'I suppose there is no reason not to take advantage of being alone together on my last evening in Scotland,' she murmured in a low purr, her now-smokey gaze fixed on his mouth.

He'd done nothing but think about kissing her again since the last time. And other things. 'None at all,' he rasped and took her lips in a savagely hungry kiss.

He walked her backwards, her body melting against him, her heat driving him wild, until she was stopped by the cot. She sank on to it, taking him down into the cradle of her body, one thigh between hers, his hand on her breast, hers winding through his hair.

Rock hard, his shaft begged him to take her. To claim her once and for all. The foolish thing. She was a prize, to be sure, but she'd no' be taken. Not by him. She would have to give.

He broke their kiss, looking down into her lovely face. Not a pretty face. It was too angular, too blade-sharp to be merely pretty. She had the beauty of granite mountains with ice on their peaks. Hard enough to kill a man, should he try to scale them without permission.

'Charity,' he murmured shaking his head. 'I'll no' be doing this unless you tell me you want it too. Want me.'

Her eyes widened. Her expression changed, slowly, almost unwillingly, softening, becoming almost tender and more beautiful. She sighed, a smile touching her lips, without artifice, if somewhat rueful. 'Oh, Logan, this is madness.' She shook her head as if defeated, not by him, but by something inside her. 'I do. God help me, I do want you. Just once more.'

It wasna' exactly what he wanted to hear,

but it was a start. It was up to him to make her want more.

He applied himself to her lips once more, exploring the deep dark depths of her mouth. Inhaling the dark scent of her perfume, tasting the dry fruitiness of wine. Overriding all of that was the essence of what he had come to think of as Charity. A scent and taste that belonged uniquely to her. Strange as it seemed, he had no doubt he would know it anywhere.

No hesitant maiden, she kissed him back with fervent hunger. With almost desperate haste, as if she could not get enough of his taste. Her hips ground into his groin, making him impossibly harder. The little moans in the back of her throat goaded him on. Fed his male urge to pin her beneath him. To dominate.

His hand tugged her skirts upward. He stroked the satiny skin above her stockings, felt the heated dampness of her desire among the soft tight curls between her legs. He wanted to bury himself inside her.

He broke their kiss, took a breath, sought control.

Her eyes flickered open. She reached for him. 'Don't stop now.'

'I'm no' an animal, Charity. I mean to love ye as ye deserve.' He struggled out of his coats, pulled his shirt off over his head and sat down to work at his boots. It would have been far easier if he had been wearing a plaid.

He stripped off his buckskins and felt the hairs on his body stand up against the cold air.

The chill lasted no more than a second as he caught her sensual expression as her gaze ran over him. Her skin flushed to a warm rosy glow.

He leaned over her. 'Now you, sweet Charity.'

Languidly, she sat up and helped him free the gown from beneath her hips. Given the dip at the back of the gown, there were few laces to untie this time, for which he was fervently grateful as he lifted the gown over her head and tossed the stays aside.

His breath caught in her throat at the perfection of her body. 'So beautiful,' he breathed.

She gave him a smile that seemed almost shy.

He stretched out beside her on the bed and kissed her lips briefly before looking down the swells and hollows of her delectable body barely veiled by her transparent shift.

He traced beneath the edge of the little scrap of lace with a fingertip, watching her face. A flicker of something sensual passed across her face. He dipped his head and let his tongue follow in the path of his fingers. Her low moan was music to his ears. Her hand moved to her breast, lifting it, offering it to his mouth with a soft groan of longing.

A gentleman never turned down a lady's request. He nuzzled beneath the delicate fabric, searching for the peak of her breast with his tongue, licking and stroking at the satiny skin, until he held it between his lips, beaded and hard.

With a long slow suck he drew it into his mouth. Her hips rose with a jerk against his thigh.

Delectable didn't begin to describe the full softness in his hands, or the taste and feel on his tongue. He didn't have the words. The sensations they sent firing in every direction in his body were awe-inspiring.

And it wasn't as if he could focus his whole attention there. Charity's fingers danced through his hair and fluttered over his shoulders. Hot tingles sparked across his skin. His flesh jumped and shivered like a nervous stallion unused to touch.

Touch. It had never occurred to him how much pleasure he would feel from such a feathery stroke. Instinct told him only Charity's touch would hold such power.

Ceasing to suckle, he helped her remove her shift, her limbs languid, her slumberous eyes hazy. Her thighs opened, welcoming him into the cradle of her hips. He smiled down at her and turned his attention to her other equally delectable breast. He sucked and licked and teased with his tongue, learning what made her cry out and what made her pant and shift restlessly.

From there he moved to the valley between, licking her sweat-dampened skin, tasting salt and inhaling her scent. He was so very hard. So very much wanting to be inside the heat of her body. But this time he was in control. Slowly he moved his mouth down her body. Covering every inch of her skin with small kisses as he traversed the flat plain of her belly, swirled his tongue within her navel and located several places at the rise of her hip bones that had her gasping and twitching, while the crisp curls on her mound teased at his chin.

Her fingers in his hair raked and tugged, as her hips pressed into him, urging him where she wanted his touch.

Sitting back on his heels, he gazed at the heart of her sex. He knew all the Latin names, but none of them did justice to the hot pouting lips he parted with his thumbs, or the delicate petal-like rosy flesh he devoured with his gaze. His own hard flesh seemed clumsy and ill-formed by comparison.

Wonder filled him as he swept his tongue along her cleft. The unique flavour on his tongue, the quick gasp, and the lift of her hips, while he sought the tiny bud that would keep her at his mercy, until he had what he wanted.

Her moans were a deep purr in her throat, her hips bucking and flexing. Once more he sat back on his heels, massaging that tiny place with his thumb, watching her head roll on the pillow, her eyes closed. Judging. Waiting. And nearly insane with the need to drive into her body and lose himself. But a man who had remained celibate for years had a certain advantage. Control.

He put his hand on his thighs.

Panting, she opened her eyes and held out her arms. 'Come to me,' she whispered hoarsely. 'Please, Logan. Now.'

'Not until you say you will wed me.'

'What?' She stared at him, consciousness slowly returning to her eyes. 'No.'

He shook his head. 'Then I canna give you what you want.'

Her glance dropped to his erection. 'You can't leave me...' She stopped. She must have realised he could. And he would. She licked her lips. 'It wouldn't be right.'

He drew back.

'Logan...' Her voice was a plea.

'Is that a yes?' He didn't like what he was doing—well, the coercion part of what he was doing. Not at all. But Charity was stubborn as well as tricky and he had to have this settled. Now. Tonight. If he died tomorrow, his family would make sure she was looked after. He'd written a letter that Sanford would make sure was delivered.

Her eyelids slid closed. 'All right,' she said sadly, shaking her head.

It wasn't exactly the enthusiasm he'd hoped for, but it would have to do for the moment. Grimly he nodded and took her mouth in a hard kiss he intended more as punishment than reward. Because he did not believe her.

Her legs came up around his hips. 'Now,' she said, her voice satisfied.

He entered her slowly, feeling her searing heat on his member, feeling his stones pull up tight. He filled her deep, and held still. 'Say it, Charity.'

'Say what?' she gasped.

She still didn't understand. He withdrew again and slid forwards, pressing into her, feeling her hips rising to meet his stroke, sensing her urgency, her closeness to oblivion, and held still.

'Logan,' she groaned, scratching at his back with her nails.

He wanted the legends. He would keep his woman at the edge until he was ready to let her fall. He fought his body's urges and instincts and moved within her slowly, bringing her to the brink three times, then slowing things down until she lost the edge.

She bit his ear, tweaked at his nipples, trying to force him to take her over with him. It took all of his will not to give in. 'What, Charity,' he growled in her ear over and over again. 'What do you want?'

Finally she broke. 'I want you,' she whispered.

'Are you mine?' he gritted out through his tight jaw.

'I am.'

He didn't trust it wasn't a lie. The realisation was a bitter taste on his tongue, but it was the best he could hope for. 'Then you will be my wife.'

He took her with him over the edge and they shattered together.

Rising from the depths of bliss to the sound of someone banging on the door had him groaning and reaching for his clothes.

Charity leaned up on one elbow, looking worried. 'What is it?'

He grinned. 'I have an early appointment.'

'The duel.' Her voice was hard. 'Don't go. For my sake.'

'It is for your sake that I have to go.'

She glared at him. 'How can it be for my sake, when I don't want it?'

His hand stilled on the buttons of his shirt, anger flooding his veins. And jealousy. And he could not stem the tide of his words. 'Was your meeting with him at the Reiver by chance, or did he send for you?'

Her face took on an impenetrable stillness. A little shrug lifted her shoulders. 'You saw us?' She took a deep breath, no doubt trying to decide whether to tell the truth or to lie. 'I asked him to meet me. For old times' sake.' She gestured to the bed. 'A bit like this, I suppose, only he wasn't interested.'

Like this? The claws were out again. 'Not thinking of bribing him not to meet me, I suppose?' he said, his gaze back on his buttons. His fingers were behaving strangely, as if they were frozen stiff as he waited for her answer. If she cared enough to try to keep him safe, it would be something to give him hope.

'He said he might be willing to accept an apology,' she said warily.

She wanted him to back down. His stomach twisted. He stamped into one boot and picked up the other. 'He insulted you.'

A haughty expression passed over her face. 'Promise you won't kill him.'

Standing on one foot, the other boot hanging

in mid air, he felt his chest empty. 'What is he to you?' Damn it all, why did he have to ask? She was his now and that was final.

A sad smile touched her lips. 'You know very well what he was,' she said, slashing at him calmly enough to kill. 'If things had been different, we would have married.'

He had a special place in her heart, then. 'You still care for him.'

She swung around to face him with a bright smile. It seemed almost too bright. 'Yes, I do. Very much.'

He felt as if he'd been struck in the gut with a hammer. 'What do you mean, if things had been different?'

Frost could not have been colder than the look she gave him. 'Another man came between us.' She turned her back. 'Will you please see to my laces?'

Another man. Furious, filled with jealousy, he tugged at the strings. He must have been mad to think last night meant anything. But it didn't make a difference now, they were going to be married. Unless Rawley had offered. He might have offered something. The thought was a dark pain in his chest. He tied off the ribbons and went for his coat.

'Where are you meeting?' she asked, staring into the cracked mirror and repinning her hair.

Such beautiful hair. He wanted to run his fingers through it, but from the stiffness in her shoulders he did not think his touch would be welcome. He kept his hands firmly by his sides, though his fingers did twitch. 'It is not something you need to know. The carriage will take you to Dunross. I will catch up to you on the road.'

'I'm coming with you.'

He almost groaned out loud 'You will not.'

'You take me with you, or I leave for London.'

Some battles just weren't worth fighting. Not when you couldn't win. Nor did he have time. 'Then you will remain with the carriage. No arguments.'

She nodded.

The sky was just beginning to lighten overhead as they stepped outside. The carriage was waiting at the kerb. He helped her inside and closed the door. Lord Sanford rode up with a saddled horse in tow. There were shadows beneath his eyes, but he was dressed immaculately and freshly shaven. By comparison Logan looked positively disreputable. And so very handsome.

The two men shook hands and talked for a moment.

Her heart began to thunder in her chest. Her mind was spinning in circles, trying to remember the rules of this foolish male ritual. She dropped the window and leaned out. 'Logan, it is not too late to stop this. All you have to do is apologise and no one will get hurt.'

His short crack of laughter was harsh. He looked up at the man on the box. 'Follow us to Leith Links. Don't let her out of the carriage.' He swung up on to the spare horse and he and Sanford trotted away.

She sank back on the squabs. If anything the thunder of her heart was worse than ever. She gripped her hands tightly in her lap and prayed Rawley would withdraw. Or not come. The sick feeling in her stomach confirmed her lack of real hope. And her dread.

He'd promised not to kill Logan, but dare she trust his word? He had let her down badly last time. Allowed her to take the blame to save his own skin. And she'd let him. Because she'd thought he loved her. And when her father threw her out and he refused to take her in, then she'd known the truth.

The revellers from the night before were still in their beds. The carriage moved swiftly out of the city and drew up beside another carriage and three saddled horses. Peering out of the window, she could see nothing of the men. They must have gone beyond a stand of trees. They wouldn't want casual passers-by to see what they were up to and call the authorities. She wished she had done that instead of trying to talk sense into a pair of idiot men. She would have, only it might have got Logan transported or worse.

Unable to sit any longer, she stepped down from the carriage. The coachman gave her a look, but said nothing as she paced up and down beside the vehicle. The morning air had a fresh coolness, but it did not account for her shivering. Her blood seemed frozen. She wrapped her arms around her waist, straining to hear the sound of shots, staring into the copse as if she could see through to the other side.

A small movement caught her eye. Some sort of animal flitting among the trees? She had only caught a glimpse from the corner of her eye and now it was gone. She scanned the undergrowth. Too large to be a fox or a dog. Perhaps it was a deer.

Or a man out hunting in the early morning.

Icy fingers travelled up and down her spine, thinking about that damned duel. Not knowing what was happening was driving her mad. The consequences of this for Logan could be disastrous. She should have told him that Jack had paid Rawley to kill him. Warned him. Not relied on Rawley to keep his promise. Mark wasn't a bad man. What had happened to her had been her own fault. And if anything happened to Logan it would be her fault, too.

She ran.

'Hey,' the coachman shouted.

But he was too fat and too slow to run after her and she quickly skirted the perimeter of the little forest, stumbling over rough tussocks and dodging clumps of gorse. When she rounded the turn where the trees ended, the duelists were still a good distance off. In the grey light, she could just make out two hatless men in dark coats and pacing away from each other, pistols at the ready, and three others watching in a group. Waiting for them to try to kill each other as calmly as if they were watching a cricket match. She wanted to ring their necks. All of them. Especially Logan.

And so she would tell him. If he was still alive for her to tell him anything. She ran faster.

A flutter of a white handkerchief stopped her in her tracks.

'Logan!' she screamed. A scream that came out as no more than a croak.

A puff of smoke from Logan's pistol. A loud crack following immediately after. It echoed through the trees.

Rawley sank to the ground. No! Logan had shot Rawley. If he died, Logan would be hung.

She felt sick. 'No!' she whispered and ran faster.

All of the men rushed over to the fallen man. By the time she arrived one of the men, clearly a doctor, had his bag open and was pressing a gore-soaked pad to Rawley's chest while another man supported Rawley's head against his shoulder. She dropped to her knees, and glared up at Logan. 'What have you done?'

He gave her a look full of hurt.

'Is he going to die?' she asked the doctor, choking back the tears that threatened to fill her throat.

'A flesh wound,' the doctor muttered.

She turned to tell Logan he was fortunate, but he had moved away and was talking to Sanford. They were both looking in the direction of the woods. Sanford strolled away. Logan came to stand over her and Rawley. 'I told you to stay with the carriage.'

She got to her feet. 'You said you wouldn't hurt him.'

Logan opened his mouth and then closed it again as he watched the doctor help Rawley to his feet. He gave Charity an inscrutable look. 'He hasna' taken his shot yet.'

'He hasn't?' Her stomach curdled. She spun

to face Rowley. 'You wouldn't. Not now. You couldn't.'

He raised a brow at Logan. 'Not if he apologises.'

'Like hell I will,' Logan said.

'You can't stand there and let him shoot you!' she yelled at him. 'It's ridiculous. Stupid.'

'Take her away from here,' Logan said to the doctor. 'Now.' She had never heard him sound so cold.

'This way, miss.' The doctor grabbed her arm and when she refused to move, he put an arm around her waist and lifted her off her feet.

She kicked out at him. 'Put me down.'

He did and gripped her shoulders and gave her a shake. 'Go, woman. And let me be about my business. I can do no one any good if you make me return to the carriage. Go on back'

He was right. She nodded dumbly.

'Bunch of young fools.' He headed back.

She started walking. Oh, please. Oh, please. The words beat in time to her steps. She looked back once and saw they were stepping out the distance already, even though Sanford was nowhere to be seen.

She made herself keep going until she reached the carriage and the indignant coachman. But she couldn't get inside. All she could think of was what she would say when she had to face his family. She couldn't do it. She couldn't be the one to tell them why he had died.

A shot rang out, and a second one, she thought. No, it must be the echo. Tears stung her eyes and felt hot on her cheeks. She dashed them away with her palm. She would not cry. Would not.

A figure burst from the undergrowth a few yards ahead of her with a long gun over his shoulder and stood bent double, breathing hard.

'Growler?' she cried out, feeling suddenly faint and grabbing at the side of the carriage for support.

He straightened and stood looking at her. 'Jack's dead.' His gravelly voice sent a shiver down her back.

The words slipped out of her mental grasp without leaving meaning. She grabbed them back. 'You mean Logan.' Her legs gave out and she collapsed on her knees in the grass.

He breathed hard a few times. 'Jack.' He looked about him wildly. 'He deserved it, he did. And so I'll tell them what they comes for me.'

Jack dead. Logan probably dying. She wanted to find the nearest bridge and throw herself off.

'I tell you, Miss Charity. I don't mind facing a man toe to toe, but I won't shoot him in the back. Not nohow. I 'ad enough.'

He wasn't making any sense. 'I don't under-stand.'

Confusion filled his eyes. 'I wounded the other'n, to make it look like Gilvry did it, fired at the same moment. They must have figured it out, because he fired into the air. Then Jack told me to kill Gilvry when the other fellow took his shot. I killed Jack instead.' He dropped his weapon and stared down at his hands as if he could see blood on them. 'He shouldn't have threatened my sister Maisie. Said if I didn't kill your lad and make it look like the lord did it, he'd put her to work on her back to pay off my debt. It were my debt,' he said darkly, suddenly glaring at Charity. 'Not 'ers. And now I'll swing fer it. But he won't get 'is 'ands on 'er.'

She swallowed, unsure of this new caring version of Growler. Not that he'd ever actually done anything to hurt her, but he'd always been Jack's weapon. A threat. Clearly even men like Growler had a line they would not cross.

'And Logan?'

'I dunno. I ran before the lord took his shot.'

Fear caught at her throat again. 'Why aren't you running away?'

'Lord Sanford caught me and told me to wait here. I'll not be running.'

Sanford. What was his part in all this? She

didn't care. She only cared about Logan. She stood staring back at where they would walk out from behind the trees. Her breath stuck in her throat. Her mouth dried.

Growler stood beside her, shading his eyes with one hand. 'I always told Maisie you was a proper lady,' he muttered. 'I let him hit you. I should have stopped him, then and there.'

She couldn't think of a thing to say she was so surprised.

The sound of voices made her turn away. Her heart was a wild thing in her chest. But she couldn't bring herself to look.

Growler looked over her shoulder with a grimace. 'Bloody nobs and their duel. Gilvry is fine.'

Her heart leaped and he grinned at her. 'Thought that'd cheer you up.'

Since when did her face show her feelings? Another complaint to lay at Logan's door. Slowly, she turned around and watched the men trailing back across the grass. Logan striding out in front with Sanford. The other men came at a slower pace, helping Rawley.

Logan was fine. Unharmed. Relief froze her limbs, but she could not keep a smile from her face. He was fine. She took a step to run and meet him, to throw herself into his arms and hold him close. But something about his manner, the way he held himself, his stony expression, stopped her in her tracks. She watched him approach with a feeling of dread.

He halted in front of her, his expression carefully blank, looking over her shoulder as if he could not bring himself to look at her face. 'I hope you are happy.'

She gasped. 'Of course I am.'

His glance flickered to meet hers and he gave her a bitter smile. 'You still love him.'

Numb, dumfounded, she could only stare at him, mouth open. He thought it was Mark's life she feared for when she'd knelt beside him. She took a breath, preparing to explain. Felt the pain around her heart at his lack of trust and realised what she must do. This was her chance to make things right. To keep him from alienating his family. To let him find a proper woman. Even if he said he accepted her word, she'd always wonder. And he would always suspect she'd played him false.

There was no basis for a future.

Her heart splintered into a thousand pieces. The pain was shattering. Worth the gift of freedom. His. She smiled. It came easily, the smile, because for once it really was the right thing to do. 'Yes,' she said softly, meeting his gaze head on. Not one tear did she let get past her throat, though the effort made her dizzy.

He closed his eyes and winced as if she had thrust a dagger in his belly. When he opened them again, his expression was bleak. Cold. 'I willna hold you to your promise, then. I should wish you well, but I find that I cannot.'

He strode for his horse, swung up and rode off without looking back.

Sanford, who had been standing a little distance off, looked at her in astonishment. 'He didn't shoot Rawley.'

'I know,' she said in a voice that seemed to come from far away.

'Women.' He gave her a look of disgust and turned his back to talk to Growler. 'I've work for you, my lad, if you've a mind to join the side of law and order, instead of going to prison.'

Charity didn't hear Growler's reply, because Rawley stood before her hesitantly.

'I fired in the air,' he said.

'Thank you,' she said, only vaguely aware that she was speaking.

He glanced to the road where Logan had disappeared. 'He's gone then?'

'Yes. He's gone. Goodbye, Mark.' She turned and climbed into the carriage.

Not until she was safely inside the carriage, and the horses were moving at a smart clip, did she realise she was crying.

It didn't matter how much she told herself

it was the right thing, the tears just kept running down her face. And her sobs scraped her throat raw.

Chapter Thirteen

Charity stared up at the keep from the road, a square stone tower pierced by arrow loops. The only window was an ancient oriel some thirty feet up. And the only way in, through an archway set in the outer wall.

Two weeks it had taken her to get there by ship. They'd run into a storm and had had to put in to a harbour to the south for days. Sanford was wrong about it being the fastest way of travel. But she was here now. And she would deliver her information and be gone as quickly as she could. By mail coach this time. No more ships for her.

Her heart pounded with excitement at the thought of seeing Logan. No matter how much she berated herself for such stupidity. Or how often she assured herself that her visit would be brief. She certainly did not imagine she would be particularly welcome. Braced against what was to come, she strode through the archway.

A large man with a shock of greying red hair appeared from a door in the tower beside the gate. When he spoke she understood not a word.

'I am Mrs Charity West. I am seeking Mr Logan Gilvry.'

He gave her a sharp look. 'Mr Logan isna' here, Mrs West.'

Determination flagged, along with her strength. She straightened her spine against the weariness bearing down on her shoulders. And the worry. 'Do you know when he will return?' She could take a room at the inn in the little village not far from the keep for a day or so.

'Ye will be wanting to talk to Lady Selina.'

That was not what she was wanting at all. 'Is Lord Aleyne here?' He might not be pleased to see her, but at least he would know her name.

'Lord and Lady Aleyne went off to Braemuir a week ago.' He lifted an arm, herding her towards a set of steps on the outside of the tower. 'Best you speak with my lady.'

The man had an expression as impenetrable as the stone tower. Her heart began to thump harder than ever. She did not want to face Logan's family. 'Perhaps I will call another day.'

'Best you come in.' The herding continued,

subtle but irresistible, and she quickly found herself inside climbing the stone steps of the tower. Once inside, the Scot handed her over to a butler who took her cloak and deposited her in a drawing room with the window she had seen from the ground.

Idiot. She should have taken a room at the inn and sent up a note. Now what would she do? Brazen it out. As she always had. She perched on the edge of a chair, setting her face in cool repose.

A petite blonde woman with a lovely face floated in with a puzzled but friendly expression. 'Mrs West?' Her gaze took in Charity's attire and her face froze.

Charity had chosen the most modest of her gowns for this journey and the least flamboyant of those to make this call, but it was still not the sort of gown a lady would wear. She fought the urge to blush. 'I beg your pardon, Lady Selina, I would not have troubled you in Mr Gilvry's absence, but your servants would not take no for an answer and insisted I see you.'

If anything her face became more frosty. 'I see. And why did you wish to see my husband?'

Her husband? The blood rushed from her head to her feet. Logan had married this beauty in the three weeks since he left Edinburgh? She couldn't breathe for the heavy weight on her chest. Her tongue would not work. She could only stare.

The woman's blue eyes flashed fire. 'I don't know what game you are playing, but Ian would never ever have anything to do with a woman like you.'

Heat seared her face even as she was flooded with utter relief. She sagged back against the cushions. 'It is Logan I came to see.'

The woman recoiled, and once more her gaze travelled to Charity's attire, but this time she met her gaze stonily.

Lady Selina nodded. 'I see. You come by way of Edinburgh?'

Thank goodness. At least the woman seemed willing to listen. 'Yes. I have some information I think Logan will wish to hear.'

Again that searching look sweeping her person.

Charity forced her anger below the surface. 'Your servant said Mr Logan Gilvry is not here at present. I can return later.'

'Logan does not live here.'

'Not...' The ground seemed to shift beneath her feet. Sanford had sent her on a wild goose chase. But she was sure Logan had talked of this keep. 'I am sorry to have troubled you, Lady Selina. Perhaps you could give me his direction.'

The woman ignored her hint. 'I assume you

are the reason he returned looking as if he had lost a guinea and found a groat.' She frowned. 'Haven't you done enough damage to the boy?'

Her heart gave an unpleasant lurch. Because it was true. She had done enough damage. Now she wished she had sent a letter instead of making the journey. Except that Sanford had said it might not reach him for weeks. Not that she had got here any faster. She rose to her feet. 'He is hardly a boy. I have important news. If you will not give me his direction, I will leave him a note.' She glanced at the writing desk in one corner. 'If you would allow?'

A troubled look on her face, Lady Selina signalled her assent.

Charity sat down at the desk, which was well supplied with paper, ink and pens.

'I didn't know we were expecting company,' a deep voice said from the doorway.

For a moment, Charity thought it was Logan, but instinctively knew it was not. When she turned, she was not surprised to see another stranger staring at her with suspicion. A big man, dark and tall and rugged. Logan's brother, she assumed. There was something about the jaw that looked familiar.

'This is Mrs West,' Lady Selina said, moving closer to her husband and looking even smaller against his bulk. The Gilvry men seemed to like small woman. All except Logan. Or perhaps she was wrong about that.

'She asked for Logan,' Lady Selina continued. 'Mrs West, this is my husband, the Laird of Dunross.'

Her husband gave his wife a glance that spoke volumes. Lady Selina nodded.

'How did you find your way here?' the Laird asked in that dark dangerous voice, his eyes not at all friendly.

'Lord Sanford gave me directions.' He'd taken some convincing, too.

Lady Selina gave a little start and if anything the Laird's gaze became more intense and more unfriendly. 'I see,' he said.

'I understand I am not welcome here,' Charity said, suddenly tired of it all. Tired of being the object of scorn. Tired of being glared at. 'I will write my letter and leave. If you would be so good as to give me a moment.' She turned back to her letter with no idea what to write.

'Ian,' a new voice said. A voice she knew all too well despite its diffidence. 'Angus said there was someone from Edinburgh looking for me.'

Once more she turned on her chair. This time her heart was so high in her throat she could not breathe. Lord, let her not show how his voice made her quake inside. Let her be cold. Reserved. Practical. But as her gaze rested on his face, her insides weakened unbearably. It was Logan, but he looked different. A shade older. A shade harder. As if the purity she had sensed in him had been worn away, leaving a more cynical, less trusting man. That was her doing.

The pain of it nearly doubled her over. She steeled her face into calm indifference and put down the pen.

'It seems Mrs West has important news.' Lady Selina's gaze dropped to Charity's waist.

Instinctively, Charity covered it with a hand at the same moment she saw the pity on the other woman's face and realised what she must be thinking. Her pity must be all for Logan. 'No,' she gasped. She shook her head, coming to her feet. 'It is nothing like that.'

Logan remained in the doorway. He folded his arms across his chest, his face expressionless, his eyes forest green and hard. 'Perhaps I could have a few words alone with Mrs West,' he said, looking at his brother, 'since she has journeyed such a long way to see me.' The bitter edge to his voice carved a hole in her chest.

'Of course,' the Laird said grimly. Lady Selina looked doubtful, but her husband caught her arm in his and led her out of the door.

Logan didn't move. Nor did he speak. He just waited, standing as cold as a stone statue.

Why, oh why, had she not just sent a letter?

Because he pulled at her the way a lodestone pulled at iron filings. She who for years had been stronger than steel. She forced herself to meet his cold gaze. 'I apologise for arriving unexpectedly,' she said, feeling her way in the face of such grim unfriendliness.

'Why are you here?' He also glanced down at her belly. 'If it is not for the obvious reason.'

The question was a crack in his guard. It provided her with a voice. A very small voice. 'I found something among Jack's effects I thought you should see.'

He shook his head. 'I don't mean that. I mean why did you bring it?'

Hadn't she been asking the same question over and over again? 'Sanford thought I should not risk the mail. If it went astray…' She glanced down at her feet, unable to meet his chilly stare any longer. 'I thought there was some urgency to the matter.' She shook her head. 'I was delayed by a storm.'

Oh, why was she bothering to explain? She opened her reticule and held out the letter. His gaze didn't leave her face. The bleakness was hard to see. Too painful for her heart to feel.

The rogue was gone. In his place stood a hard, cold man.

'Here,' she said, thrusting it towards him. When he didn't move, she tossed it on the writing desk. 'I will leave it then.' Hot tears welled in the back of her throat. She swallowed them down. Surely she had cried enough. She strode for the door. Eased passed him and made her way down the stairs.

He would read it. He would see it was important. Or he wouldn't. There was no more she could do. As Lady Selina had said, she had already done enough damage. She should never have allowed herself to dream of a future with him, even if only for a short while. She'd allowed him into her heart. Seeing him so cold, so distant, hurt worse than she would have imagined.

If she truly had caused this change in him, she was sorry for it. She had intended only the best for him. She could not bear the idea that he hated her so deeply.

But perhaps that was also for the best. The tears welled up all over again. She dashed them away, with a furious sniff. There was no reason to cry.

At the bottom of the stairs the butler handed over her cloak. She marched down the outside steps. Heartsick, she headed for the gate.

To the echo of the light patter of her feet on the stone steps, Logan unfolded his arms and unfurled fists clenched so tight, his knuckles cracked as they opened. If he hadn't gripped them so hard, he would either have shaken her where she stood for risking her life by travelling alone, or dragged her into his arms. Neither of which would have been the right thing to do. If he touched her, he would never be able to let her go.

Why did she have to come now?

He'd settled back into his life. Put her out of his mind. Forgotten he'd ever met the bloody woman. At least when he concentrated, he could forget her beauty and her lies. He glared at the half-started letter, prowled across the room to look at the few words on the paper. *Dear Mr Gilvry.* It seemed she had already forgotten his first name. *I am sorry I missed seeing you...* And there it ended, in mid-sentence. As he suspected, she had planned to leave without speaking to him.

And he'd hared up here like a jackrabbit chased by a hound when Angus had described the Englishwoman who had called. Like a cur called to heel, more like. He wouldn't allow it. He would not play her game any longer.

The hollowness in his chest ached worse than usual. He rubbed at it with his fist, drawing in a breath to ease it and inhaled her lingering perfume, something of flowers and dark spices. Like her, sweet with dark cutting edges. It re-

minded him of her kisses and her nails on his
back— No, he would not think about that. His
brush with Charity, his fool-headedness as Ian
had called it, had nigh on brought his family to
ruin. Only Ian's quick thinking had given the
gaugers nothing to see, but a man's usual barrel
or two in the undercroft. The rest of the stores
had been hidden in the cave near Balnaen Cove.
And Jack's death meant there would be no ret-
ribution. A lucky escape.

He picked up the folded piece of paper she
had brought, tapped it against his thumb. She
had travelled a long way to bring this. She must
have thought it important. He unfolded it and
glanced at the words. It was a note to O'Banyon
dated the day before the duel. *Kill him and ruin
them, I want it finished. Now.* No signature.

A warning that Jack's death had not ended
it. Their enemy was still out there. Waiting. It
was a courageous thing she'd done, braving the
journey to carry it here. She must have guessed
what sort of welcome she would get.

He'd seen it in her face. Resignation. Yes, and
determination, too.

He lifted his head, listening to the wind buf-
feting the walls and her footsteps fading on the
stairs. He had to strain to hear them. Unless he
was just hearing them in his mind. She must be
to the ground by now.

She would go and that would be an end to it.

There had been no carriage waiting in the courtyard. No horse either. Which meant she had no means of transport. His back teeth ground together so hard, he thought they would crack.

He raced down the stairs.

She was already crossing the bailey to the gate when he emerged into bright sunshine. He paused on the top step, watching her feminine walk, the sway of her hips, the proud tilt of her head. If you didna' look at the manner of her clothes, you would know her for a lady. Lady Charlotte Westlake, Rawley had announced, when they left the field of honour.

She'd never said a word about being a noble lady. But from here, from this distance, he could see her pride. The pride that made her fight like a she-cat for what she wanted.

And she didn't want him.

The ache spiked. The way it did every time he recalled her intention to return to Rawley.

So why had she made the journey instead of sending it by mail? And why did he feel this flicker of hope? Was he just too stubborn to believe he had made the wrong choice?

Wasn't Charity just like Maggie? A woman who had lied to his face to get what she wanted.

Hadn't he known it all along? And still he found her irresistible.

He ran down the rest of the steps and caught her up in the cool dark shadows beneath the arch. She must have heard him coming, somehow known it was him, because she kept walking. He could not see her face in the shadows. When they stepped into the sunshine her expression as she glanced up at him could have frozen the water in the moat they were crossing.

'What do you want?' she said. The frost in her voice sent a shiver down his spine.

But there was more than frost in her voice, there was also weariness and sadness. As if he had somehow caused her more pain.

Did she still blame him for Rawley's wound? You would think the damned Englishman would have told her it was Growler who shot him.

Still he could not see her wandering unaccompanied around the countryside. 'Where is your carriage? And your luggage.'

A crease furrowed her brow. 'I do not have a carriage or much luggage. I came by ship and then by carter. It was the only conveyance coming to Dunross before next week. My luggage I left at the inn where the carter put me down.'

'And the return journey?'

She stared straight ahead. 'The carter will

pick me up at the tavern in the morning and take me to the nearest stagecoach stop.'

She'd be gone in the morning. His gut gave a sickening lurch. He should be glad she was going so soon. Knowing she would be in Dunross for even one night was like a blade digging around in an open wound.

They were already passing the first of the peat-roofed small stone houses of the village. They would soon be at the inn. 'I will take you to the ship in the morning, in Ian's carriage.'

She halted and turned to face him, her face unreadable. 'I would prefer it if you did not.'

He lifted his head and stared at the deep blue of the sky. Why? Why had she come to trouble him again? To turn his world upside down? He knew she wasna' as coldly calculating as she appeared, but he wasn't sure she knew it too. And he could not stop the nagging worry in his gut. 'A lady can hardly be travelling in a carter's wagon alone. I refuse to take no for an answer.'

She stiffened. 'You must do as you please.'

Which meant she would likely not be there in the morning. She would probably walk to the coast to avoid him. 'Damn it, Charity.' He winced. 'Now you have me cursing at you. I apologise, but you really have me confused. Why on earth did you come all this way yourself, when you could have sent the note by mail?'

She glared at him. 'I came because I thought the note was important. To make sure it was received.'

'Then I must thank you. I will make sure it gets to my brother.' He hesitated, but there was no way of holding back his question, he had to know. 'Are you done with your Englishman already, then, or did he not want you?'

She recoiled as if slapped in the face.

He wanted to hit something when he saw the hurt in her face. He had not intended to cause her pain. But for some reason that glimpse of hurt made the wee bit of hope burn brighter.

'Well?' he asked a bit more harshly than he intended.

A man in a cart, with two children beside him, drove by them. The man gave a nod. Logan raised a hand in greeting, but he did not take his gaze from Charity's face. If the walls didn't come down now, then they never would. And he would just have to get used to his lonely existence.

'I brought the note. Let us leave it at that, shall we? What is the use of further discussion? It is clear that you don't trust me. I see it in your face.'

Once more her claws ripped him apart and

laid him bare. 'I want to trust you,' he said slowly. Because there would never be anyone else for him. He hadn't be able to so much as look at another woman since he left Edinburgh.

She picked up her pace. 'Very gratifying, I am sure.'

But not good enough.

Something was happening inside him. A growing feeling of dread that he was making a terrible mistake. And that if he got this wrong, she would pay the price. He took a deep breath and caught her arm, bringing her to a halt, turning her to face him. 'I told you about the lass from the village. The one I nearly married.'

She tensed. 'I remember.'

'She tried to pass off another man's child as mine. After that I wasna' very trusting.'

Shock filled her face. 'You think I came to play you such a trick?'

'No! That is not what I was saying. Let me finish.' What was he trying to say? 'When I see what my brothers have—the love, the joy—I knew that was what I wanted. Not some lass using me for convenience.'

The wariness in her eyes deepened. 'Of course. I understand perfectly.' She tugged at her arm to free it.

'Charity, stop. When I saw you on your knees beside Rawley, looking at me as if I had cut out

your heart because you thought I shot him—'
He shook his head to clear the vision from his
eyes. 'I couldn't do it. Not make you wed me.
Not if it was him you really wanted.'

Her eyes glittered with unshed moisture, yet
there was an odd smile on her lips. 'You fool.'

'Aye,' he said around the lump in his throat.
'I was. I am.'

'I thought you'd killed him.'

'It wasna' me who shot him. But from the
look of terror on your face, I knew—'

An odd smile curved her lips. 'I was terrified.
For you. I thought they'd hang you. For defending my honour—' She choked on the word. 'It
was you I feared for.'

The blood drained from his head. He felt
dizzy from a lack of blood. 'You were scared
for me?'

'Of course. I…care for you. To lose you to a
hangman's noose and know it was my fault…
It wasn't to be borne.'

He shook his head. 'That is not what you said,
when I asked you if you loved him.'

'You didn't ask. You told me.' She huffed
out a breath. 'After all the trouble I caused you
and your family, I thought perhaps it was for
the best. I thought you would be better off with
some nice innocent Scottish girl. And I was
right. Your family thinks so, I can tell.' She

averted her face. 'Fool that I am, I just could not stay away.' Her voice sounded husky.

He cupped her jaw and brought her face around. The tears had spilled over and were sliding down her cheeks.

'*Leannan*,' he murmured and opened his arms.

Quietly she moved into them and rested her head against his shoulder and he felt her shoulders shaking. Not wild sobs born of fear, but something infinitely quieter and sadder that caused his heart to squeeze painfully. 'It is all right, *mo cridhe*,' he said softly, manoeuvring around the ridiculous feather in her hat to find her velvety-soft trembling lips.

He put his heart and soul into his kiss and prayed she would know this was their last chance. After this there could be no going back, because if she left him again he likely would not survive.

When they broke apart, she looked up at him, tears clinging to her lashes, her soft pouting mouth rosy red and her eyes soft and misty as a summer morning. 'Oh, Logan, this is so selfish of me. You deserve so much better. You know the kind of life I have led. You came to me pure and good and I corrupted you. You can't know how heavy that guilt lays on my shoulders.'

Corrupted? He tried not to chuckle, though

he wasn't sure he managed to control his face completely when she frowned. 'If you knew the thoughts going through my head, lassie, from the very first time I saw you and still going on, you wouldna' be talking about you corrupting me.' He gazed at her, hard, trying to make sure she understood. 'It goes far deeper than lust. Whether we like it or no', we fit together like two spoons in a drawer. I admire your resourcefulness. I liked you even when we were on opposite sides.' He took a deep breath. He shook his head. 'I should never have let you go. Too much pride.'

'But your family. I couldn't bear it if they cast you off because of me.'

'Why would they do that?'

'It is what my family did. When my brothers caught me with Rawley in the barn. At first it was Mark they blamed. I could see he was terrified that my brothers were going to kill him. So was I. He panicked, saying he was not the first. I didn't deny it. I think I was in shock. My brothers told my father. And when Mark refused to offer marriage, my father threw me out. I went to Mark that night. But he feared his father would cut him off if he took me in and refused to see me.'

'The miserable cur. I wish I had shot him.'

'I don't. I was infatuated, yes, but looking

back I know it wasn't love. If he had married me, you and I never would have met.'

'Aye, there's that about it.' He gave her shoulders a squeeze and looked at her, feeling just a little hesitant. But nothing ventured as they said. 'So if you know you dinna love him, can you know if you love me?'

'Yes,' she whispered. 'I know. But I very much fear your family will not be pleased. Are you sure?'

His shoulders straightened. 'They were free to make their choice. And you are mine.' He took her hands in his and gazed at her lovely face, more beautiful because she was here with him in his beloved Highlands. 'I have never been surer of anything in my life, my own dear one.' He looked into her mysterious heather-coloured eyes and willed her to believe him. 'If you had not come here today, I would have continued going through the motions. Doing my best for my family. But every day I would have been dying inside. I love you, Charity. There will never be anyone else. And if they do not like it, they can go hang.'

She smiled a bit at that. 'Oh, Logan.'

And her expression said she had no more fight left. He gathered her in his arms. 'Marry me, love. Please. And put me out of my misery.'

A small sound like a laugh and a sob came

from her lips. She wound her arms around his neck and leaned into him. 'Yes,' she answered. 'Oh, Logan, yes, please. I do love you, so much.'

The shattered bits of his heart came together, so filled with love it felt too big to fit inside his chest and stole all his words.

So he kissed her instead.

Epilogue

The wedding had gone off very well, with Logan's older brothers serving as groomsman and giver of the bride. Charity couldn't remember ever feeling so happy as she did right now, with the joyous din of the celebration in the Dunross Great Hall echoing off the stone walls. The scent of roasted meat and smoke from the fires filled the air. And servants bustled about filling glasses and plates. The Laird had done them proud indeed.

Charity stretched a hand with its gleaming gold ring across Logan's empty place at her side, to touch her new sister-in-law's arm. She raised her voice to be heard. 'What is going on?' She gave a significant nod at the little knot of men grouped at the end of the long trestle table. 'They all look very serious.'

Three Gilvry brothers and their cousin Gordon, to whom she'd been introduced following her and Logan's marriage, were engaged in deep conversation.

Lady Selina frowned. 'Gordon said he had something to tell Ian when he first arrived. But I hardly think this is the time or the place.' She started to rise, then sat back down as the group broke up.

Charity couldn't help watching Logan as he prowled back to her side. Still cocky. And charming. But his gaze was full of love and his smile was for her only. She smiled a welcome. 'Bad news?'

'Not really. Some vague news of Drew, my brother. A sighting before he disappeared.'

Drew's absence was a sore point at this family celebration, as was the reason why Logan's mother wasn't in attendance. Two empty places had been set for them just in case.

Logan took her hand in his and kissed it. 'It is all right, *leannan*. No reason to spoil the celebration. Gordon is a good man and he wanted us to know, that was all.'

Retaining her hand in his, he sat down and leaned close, looking out across the hall. 'Ah. Now you are in for a treat.'

Four men with two swords apiece ran to stand

in front of the dais, setting them down on the flagstones on the form of a cross.

'A sword dance,' Charity said, covering his hand with hers. She'd requested it as part of the entertainment, having never seen one.

'It doesna seem so very long ago,' said Niall, who had returned to his seat next to his wife a bit further down the table, 'since we were dancing for a purse at Carrick Castle.'

'You never said you knew how to do it!' Charity said, nudging Logan.

'Aye, well, if it is the sword dance you want, Ian is your man.' Logan looked up at his dark-haired older brother at that moment squeezing behind his chair to return to his seat.

'Practise makes perfect,' Ian said and flashed a smile which made him terribly handsome and look years younger. His smile broadened as his gaze met that of his wife.

The piper against the wall puffed a bit and there were a few squeaks and groans, then he was playing a foot-tapping tune. The four men bowed and began their dance.

Charity could not help but watch the swing of their kilts as they jumped neatly over the swords in time to the beat of the music.

'No peeking,' Logan whispered in her ear. 'There'll be plenty enough for you to see when we're alone.'

'I don't know what you mean,' she said primly, then laughed. 'How did you know?'

He grinned. 'There isn't a lass here who isn't looking.'

She glanced around the room. He was right. She gave him a sideways look. 'Will you dance like that for me one day?'

'My feet have no' stopped moving trying to keep up with you since we met.'

She laughed. 'True. But will you?'

A deep sigh gusted past her ear, not impatience, but contentment. 'I'd do anything for you, lass. Anything at all.' He kissed her cheek and some of the folk on the nearby tables cheered and raised their glasses in toast. Logan raised his in return.

The dance ended and the pipes took up a reel.

Logan led his wife out from behind the table to open the country dancing. The floor was crowded with clan members and their wives. He glanced at his brothers who had joined them in the set. He had never seen two happier men. Apart from him, that was. He really did wish Drew could have been with them. As brothers, they'd always stood shoulder to shoulder and they needed him.

They had an enemy. And he had struck more than once in the past. But until recently they had never had any proof of his existence.

'A penny for your thoughts,' Charity said as they twirled around the room.

He jerked out of his reverie. How could he be worrying about such things when he had his beautiful wife in his arms? 'I'm sorry. I was daydreaming. Thinking I couldn't be happier.'

'I will certainly do my best to make sure you stay that way,' she said in the sultry purr that she now kept for him alone.

His body responded instantly. Thank goodness for his sporran. He focused on her, and her beautiful face and their future, and danced until he was out of breath. And all he could think of was them being alone. Together. In their chamber in the keep. The sooner this celebration was over, the better.

'Shall we go?' he whispered as the music wound down.

'Please,' she said, her eyes alight with wickedness.

They moved off the dance floor and were once again surrounded by clan members offering congratulations. They accepted Charity, because Ian did, but they would grow to like her for herself once they knew her. Especially since she would be accompanying him on his smuggling trips. It had been part of her condition of agreeing to marry him. She had bargained hard, and in the end, because he wanted her with him all the time, he had agreed. Not that he would be taking her on the most dangerous runs.

'Leaving already?' Ian asked, coming up behind them with Selina on his arm, both of them looking flushed from the dancing.

'He's been ready these past two hours,' Niall said with a broad grin and a wink and a quick kiss on his wife's cheek.

'Longer than that,' Logan said, pretending to wipe the sweat from his brow.

Charity blushed. She'd been doing a lot of that recently. It suited her.

'We'll have a toast first, though,' Jenna said. 'Then I really must check on Rabbie.'

As a group, they walked up the steps to the dais. The Gilvrys and their wives, side by side. A formidable family.

The room fell silent. 'I know you will all join me in a toast to my brother and his new wife, Charity,' Ian said in a voice that rang through the room. 'May they be as happy as I am and may their house be filled with bairns. To Logan and Charity.'

She had decided to keep the name she'd lived with all these years. It was how Logan thought of her, and she declared no intention of returning to London or getting in touch with her family.

'Logan and Charity,' the people echoed, raising their glasses.

Logan bowed. 'Drink and dance as long as you wish,' he shouted for all to hear. 'The Laird's purse is as deep as the loch.'

The sound of laughter and cheers, whistles and stamping feet rose to the rafters and the pipes wheezed into the opening bars of a strathspay.

Charity tugged on his sleeve and stood on tiptoe to whisper in his ear, 'About that dancing you promised me...'

His body tightened. A grin refused to be quelled, so he let it loose. 'Aye,' he murmured. 'And we'll no' be needing a piper for the kind of dancing I have in mind.'

To more cheers and whistles he picked her up and carried her, a deliciously willing wife, out of the room and up to their chamber high in the keep.

* * * * *

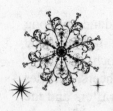

Merry Christmas
& A Happy New Year!

Thank you for a wonderful
2013...

A sneaky peek at next month...

HISTORICAL

IGNITE YOUR IMAGINATION, STEP INTO THE PAST...

My wish list for next month's titles...

In stores from 3rd January 2014:

❑ From Ruin to Riches – Louise Allen

❑ Protected by the Major – Anne Herries

❑ Secrets of a Gentleman Escort – Bronwyn Scott

❑ Unveiling Lady Clare – Carol Townend

❑ A Marriage of Notoriety – Diane Gaston

❑ Rancher Wants a Wife – Kate Bridges

Available at WHSmith, Tesco, Asda, Eason, Amazon and Apple

Just can't wait?

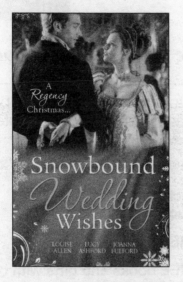

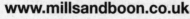

3/MB437

 **MILLS & BOON®** *Book Club*

Join the Mills & Boon Book Club

Want to read more **Historical** books?
We're offering you **2 more** absolutely **FREE!**

We'll also treat you to these fabulous extras:

- Exclusive offers and much more!
- FREE home delivery
- FREE books and gifts with our special rewards scheme

Get your free books now!

visit www.millsandboon.co.uk/bookclub
or call Customer Relations on 020 8288 2888

SUBS/ONLINE/H1